THE SKY IS FALLING

The Sky Is Falling

By Esther Loewen Vogt

HERALD PRESS, SCOTTDALE, PENNSYLVANIA

All names and places in this story are fictitious, and any resemblance to persons, living or dead, is purely coincidental.

DEDICATED
to my parents,
Henry and Agnes Loewen,
whose staunch faith in Christ
and love of our Mennonite heritage
set a living example for their children.

Heaven and earth will pass away, but my words will not pass away.
—Matthew 24:35

PART ONE

1

Hannah Kliewer let the screen door slam behind her as she padded across the back porch and jumped lightly to the ground.

Giant-armed elms, clothed with the dull green of late July, laced the warm earth with a mosaic of shadow and sunlight. The house, big and cool and freshly painted, sat back sedately from the wide circle of weathered farm buildings. *Like a stylish English lady with its dark brown shutters and gingerbread fluting around the porch roof,* Hannah thought as she sauntered down the path.

Could I ever be an English lady? she mused idly.

She laughed softly at the idea as she swung her long, coltish legs over the gate of the picket fence. No, she'd never be a lady of fashion. Mennonites were supposed to be above such worldly things. And anyway, she hated the fuss of pleats and edgings.

8

"Today I can swing on the gate all I want to, and nobody will care," she said to herself. "Mahm isn't home to tell me fourteen-year-old girls are too big to ride a gate!"

Her dark, heavy braids flopped down her gray cotton back like two thick brown ropes. She smoothed the gray skirt carefully over her legs while the gate shuddered under her weight. As it creaked to and fro, she trailed her bare toes over the path which countless feet had trodden into the solid, hard-packed Kansas earth.

"Boo!"

Startled, Hannah whirled around, struggling to maintain her balance on the swaying gate. She saw black, faintly mocking eyes from thin hollow cheeks laughing down at her. A cap of dark curly hair tumbled from under a battered, sweat-stained straw hat. The boy, who seemed about eighteen, was dressed in baggy, dun-colored trousers, and a torn, earthy shirt.

He seemed to enjoy her discomfort as he eyed her covertly. She squirmed under his penetrating gaze, her heart hammering wildly.

"Who—who are you?" she stammered, red color seeping into her cheeks.

He grinned with a flash of white teeth. Doffing his hat he smote his breast with a flourish.

"I'm the son of Czar Maximilian of Russia in disguise, and I go by the homely name of Dan Smith."

For a moment Hannah's gray eyes widened uncomprehendingly and she shook her head wordlessly.

"Dan Smith? My name is Hannah—Hannah Kliewer. My father and mother were once in Russia, too. We"—she lifted her head proudly—"are Mennonites!"

"Not Mennonites!" the boy laughed hoarsely. "Don't tell me I'll have to grow a beard if I want to see you again!"

Something about his brashness infuriated Hannah. She clenched her fists until her knuckles grew white.

"Maybe you'd better leave. You don't understand at all—even if you are a king's son, as you say."

He cocked his dark head defiantly, and again his coarse laughter rang out.

"Smart, huh? Beautiful but clever! No, I don't understand. My name's really Dan Smith. And so here we are, newcomers to the community and already I'm told off. Get this, beautiful Mennonite Hannah, we have as much right to live here as you—or anyone else!"

The dark fury of his face made him almost wistfully handsome and for a moment Hannah felt a rush of pity for him.

"I shouldn't have gotten mad at you. It doesn't matter to me where you live. Where—where are you going to move?"

He broke into a faintly mocking smile. "Now, that's more like it. That's what I came to ask. Just where is the Harnish farm?"

Hannah felt a shiver of excitement slither down her gray cotton back. This brash young man was going to be her neighbor. She pointed southward.

"Till the corner south and then another quarter mile. Then you go that way"—she pointed east—"down the long lane and over the creek. You can see it from here."

The drab, weather-beaten Harnish buildings huddled forlornly like social outcasts in the midst of a blurry green field of sunflowers and cockleburs.

His eyes narrowed as he followed her pointed finger. Then he flashed a derisive smile. "I might've known we'd buy a place like that. It sure fits. We bought it sight unseen, you know. Cheap—dirt cheap."

Her eyes followed him as he swung away and swaggered down the driveway. She began to shake as the excitement of this meeting washed over her.

It was then she saw the decrepit mover wagon, held together with wire and determination. Hitched to a pair of bony, sweat-grimed mules, it clanked ominously down the dusty road. A tousle-haired boy on horseback, trying to ride herd on a few scrawny cows, followed the battered wagon. *And the ill favoured and lean-fleshed kine did eat up the seven well favoured and fat kine.* . . . Hannah thought of the words. Pa had read them from the big black Bible just this morning.

She sighed. So these were the new neighbors who had bought the ramshackle Harnish farm. Just wait until her family came home from the sale. She had lots of news for them!

Abram, Sush, and Liesbet had all gone with Pa and Mahm to the Petker farm sale, and Hannah had the whole afternoon to herself. She had finished baking six loaves of bread, their fresh aroma still lingering over the open windowsill; and the corn was stripped and ready to plunge into the boiling water to cook for supper. She thought guiltily of the quilt patches Mahm had piled up for her to sew. But the thought of going back into the hot, stifling house nauseated her.

"I'll leave that for Sush," she murmured absently. "She likes to sew. And anyhow, I can't now. Not now."

The late afternoon dragged as Hannah watched a bumblebee flirt with a honeysuckle bell in search of nectar on the vines that drooped over the well stoop. Honeysuckles were saving, Pa said. Plain, old-fashioned Mennonite thrift. What more could the good people of Plainfeld Mennonite community expect?

Hannah's gaze shifted to the long, tree-lined lane. This was going to be a good year for walnuts, Pa had said last night. And Hannah breathed a wistful little sigh. She could see the endless bushels of black walnuts she and Hans and Abram would have to pick up from the bare ground next fall. *Not the green ones, children.* . . . Pa was very exacting.

She would beg Pa if she could go to school next winter. At least, until Mahm's new baby would come in January. Fourteen, she was, and in the fourth reader. But Pa seemed to think it was enough if girls learned only to cook and bake and sew.

Still, people were getting to be more educated all the time, her brother Peter often said, and he was eighteen. In five more years—five more years it would be 1900 and then—

Then I will be nineteen. Will I get married and have babies of my own? she thought pensively. What kind of boy would want to marry her, a boyish girl like her? Dark, black-eyed babies like—like—she firmly pushed the thought of Dan Smith away.

Frowning, she slid from the gate and shook her full skirt until it swirled around her ankles. It was wrong to dream wicked dreams of slovenly, handsome people like Dan Smith. People who weren't Mennonites. Wasn't it? Or was it?

She hurried into the coolness of the stone milkhouse, blinking at the opaque darkness until her eyes were accustomed to the light that filtered weakly through the lone window. Mahm's washtubs hung neatly along the north wall, the heavy stone milk crocks sitting like silent sphinxes in the cold water to keep sweet.

The old dishpan hung on a rusty nail. It had sprung a leak the time Abram had banged Pa's new claw hammer against it to see if it made a noise like the drums in the band they'd heard at the county seat last summer. Never would Abram try that again! Pa had an uncanny knowledge where the best peach switches grew.

Humming under her breath, Hannah picked up the pan and strolled toward the row of mulberry trees on the south side of the henhouse. The lazy Rhode Island Reds cackled vociferously as though they had earned a right to advertise their wares. Wisps of straw scattered beneath the trees cooled the soles of her hot dusty feet. Dragging an old wooden barrel under the heavy-laden branches, Hannah climbed up nimbly and began to pull off the fat, purple mulberries and let them plink into the pan.

Every now and then the plumpest, sweetest berries disappeared into her mouth, purpling her full red lips with juice. Moving from place to place, from tree to tree, she had her pan half filled in a short time.

She paused and looked toward the Harnish place. She had seen the worn-out mover wagon creak slowly up the long lane and disappear behind the thickly grown woodlot.

"I think—he liked me," she told herself hesitantly, savoring the happy thought. "Dan—Daniel Smith—"

Her eyes grew dreamy again. But never would she dare tell anyone that.

As she glanced at the sky, she saw the sun like a burnished copper coin suspended above the hedgerows that lined the road, the cloud racks above tinted with glints of orange and bands of red.

She drew her breath sharply and hurried quickly toward the house. Time to get the cows home for milking.

Mahm had ordered her crisply before she left to put the water on to boil for the corn before she went for the cows.

Hannah took the panful of mulberries into the small, lean-to summer kitchen and dipped water from the big wooden bucket on the round stool, and poured it over the mulberries. The water stained purple as she rinsed the berries carefully and drained them, throwing the water out of the back door onto the smiling pink holly-hocks. Mahm would sugar the berries and pour them into bowls, to be eaten with fresh cream for supper.

Taking the gray-enameled kettle, she tripped out to the well. She lowered the rope bucket from the pulley with a screech-screech until the pail splashed into the cold water. Next fall Pa and the boys would erect a windmill. Then they'd have a real pump and the water would come gurgling from the pump spout!

She sprinted across the yard toward the straw barn set southeasterly from the big red horse barn. If Peter would finish plowing the lower forty, he would help her with the milking. The steamy smell of damp straw hung heavily in the air. Pa had made the straw walls snug and tight so that the cows would be warm in winter.

She hated to milk inside when it was hot. Squatting on a three-legged stool out in the open air to milk was much more pleasant.

"I'll throw down the hay to the fodder trough before I get the cows," she told herself as she climbed over the barnyard gate, sniffing the sweet, cloying smell of dried hay from the stack.

Lifting her long skirts carefully, she hopped across the stones that showed clean and white among the dried chips, looking for the pitchfork.

Too late she saw the hayfork, half hidden beside the stack, baring its vicious rusty tines as her right foot plunged headlong toward it. With a crunching sound Hannah felt the prong tear through her big toe and saw it reappear just above the nail.

Agonizing pain shot through her foot and she screamed. Panting with short, sobbing breaths she lowered herself gingerly to the ground and began to tug at the fork.

Each pain-riddled jerk sent chills bounding down her spine, and as she worked the fork this way and that, the tine did not budge.

"O dear Lord," she screamed. "Help me! Help me, somebody—"

But Pa and Mahm were still at the sale and Peter was in the field, and there was no one to hear her cries.

2

The pain was excruciating, and Hannah grew faint. Slow, red blood seeped from her toe and trickled in a thick, ugly stream across her foot.

Her screams fell thin and sick in the evening silence, and then gave way to rasping sobs as she lay helplessly on the ground.

Shadows began to lengthen and gratefully she cowered in the cool shelter of the straw barn. How she wished someone would come! Someone who—

"Say, now, did you hurt yourself?"

Hannah stirred hopefully at the voice behind her. A tangle-haired boy of about ten, with a spatter of freckles across his face, grinned at her.

"Hey, you've sure got yourself in some fix, haven't you?"

He stooped over and gently tugged at the fork in her

foot. She gritted her teeth to keep from crying out, but could not control her whimpering. At last it slipped free, and a great sense of relief surged through her.

The foot throbbed painfully, but in her gratefulness she reached out and touched the boy's ragged pant leg.

"Who are you? I never saw you before, did I?"

"Sure, ya did. I'm Sammy Smith. We just moved lock, stock, and junk to that old farm up yonder," he said, pointing south. *The boy on horseback chasing the scrawny kine.*

"Oh."

Pain shot through her foot again and she winced. She struggled to get up but her leg felt on fire. Quickly the boy drew her up and placed her right arm on his left shoulder. Only vaguely she thought of the boy Dan, with his flashing black eyes, his mocking grin.

"Now you just—hop on yer left foot—like I'm a crutch, see?" he panted, steering her carefully from the rocks to the barnyard gate. "Ye're doin' fine. I'll help you to yer house. Maybe yer ma kin—"

"Mahm—is not home," Hannah said dully as she and Sammy inched slowly across the yard. Never had the distance loomed so great as today.

Already the sky was slate, darkening to black near the eastern horizon. Just as they had reached the picket gate Hannah heard the neigh of horses, and the carriage rolled up the lane.

Moments later she was inside on the old walnut rocker in the long dining room, with Mahm hovering over her while Sush slopped into the room with a tin can of kerosene.

Mahm was dabbing the dried blood from Hannah's

foot with bits of white rag, her gray hair straggling loosely from her tautly pulled knot.

"*Ach*, Hannah!" she said grumpily in Low German, her red florid face creasing with wrinkles. "Why can't you watch where you step? Always you're dreaming and looking toward the world! You'll come to a bad end someday. Did you pick mulberries and sew the quilt pieces the way I told you?"

Hannah felt the sting of kerosene as it dribbled over her stiff, swollen toe, and she clamped her lips at the pain. Oh, how could Mahm think of quilt pieces when her foot hurt so? *No, Mahm. No quilt pieces. Yes, Mahm, mulberries. Corn. And dreams. . . .*

She bit her lip as Mahm wrapped the foot in a giant white flannel bandage.

Sush stood beside her, silently holding the dripping can of kerosene in her plump fingers, her long, butter-yellow braids flopping over her blue-and-white checkered back. Sush—her real name was Sarah, but no one ever remembered that—the obedient, dutiful Sush at nine years, already knew as much about sewing quilt pieces as Hannah.

Mahm hurried Sush out into the summer kitchen and Hannah heard the clatter of pots and pans while they prepared supper.

Later, sitting in the orange lamplight, her foot propped up on a chair, Hannah closed her eyes wearily. Pain still hammered at her as she tried to wipe the horrible experience from her mind. But it persisted. Sammy Smith had heard her cries and had come, his tangled hair and freckles and tattered trousers an alien splash in her strict world. In a way he was like Dan.

"He's an Englisher," Hannah whispered to herself. "Maybe the bulky mover wagon, the thin cows, and the dark, handsome boy—" and she shut her lips tightly. She mustn't say it, but she wondered. *With their coming would life change?*

"But they're not Mennonites. They're Englishers—" Pa said stoutly at the oilcloth-covered supper table much later, "and we cannot be friends. Neighbors, yes. But that's all. Remember that, children."

Peter, sitting tall and solemn beside Pa, crunched the buttered corn ears and nodded. And Abram, his striped shirt buttoned snugly under his twelve-year-old chin, grunted.

Liesbet, dark-braided and five years old, wasn't expected to understand.

"What did you say the boy's name was, Hannah?" she piped, dipping a spoonful of cream over her mulberries. Plump Liesbet liked things to swim in cream.

Hannah, making a pretense of eating, toyed with her own dish of fruit. "Which—which boy? Oh—Smith. Sammy Smith, he said."

Mahm cocked her wispy head. "Schmidt, you say?"

"No, not Schmidt, Mahm! Smith!" Peter exclaimed with worldly wisdom. "There is also Daniel who is as old as I. And a girl named Maggie, Sammy told me."

There is also Daniel . . . Dan. . . . Hannah only half heard the words. Her head ached with weariness and she thumped up the stairs to bed. She couldn't get to sleep. Her foot throbbed sharply and she stared at the darkness, her thoughts whirling in the periphery of the abstract.

Sammy Smith had been kind and helpful. *But they*

are not Mennonites; so we cannot be friends. . . . Pa's
words echoed through her thoughts.

But why? Why couldn't they be friends? She remembered what Pa had told them so many times. *Children, to be a Mennonite means to be separate, . . .*

She knew the story of Mennonites. Pa had told them
how the believers together with Menno Simons, their
chief founder and organizer in Holland, had broken
away from the legalistic formalism in 1536. Because of
persecution his followers fled Holland eastward to Ger-
many, to Prussia, especially Danzig, and later to Russia.
And from there some came to America.

Everywhere they had scattered they organized
churches. They believed in a personal life of faith; in
adult baptism; in separation from the world and separation of church and state. This breaking away from
legalism resulted in separation. Later some went to
extremes and overemphasized separation.

And to love one's enemies! In 1874 many Mennonites
had left Russia because they were forced to take up
arms, and also came to America. Pa and Mahm had
been among them. Trust in Christ for salvation, baptism, to love one's enemies, and be separate.

Her mind grew numb and she could no longer think,
for the swelling of her foot was increasing. Her head
roared with faraway thunder that pulsed like breakers
against surging seas. Dank, reed-grown water, veiled
and murky, reached out to her with its osmosis and she
beat her fists against it. At last she weakened, and the
damp veils wrapped around her, covering her with gray
darkness.

Pain. Pain. Steady, awful, anguished pain held her in

its iron clutches during the few brief glimmers of consciousness that followed, and she slipped gratefully back into oblivion when she could bear it no longer.

Once, when she opened her eyes, she thought she saw Mahm weeping quietly beside her bed, while Sush leaned over, hot tears streaming over her feverish hands. *Am I going to die?* Hannah thought. *But I can't die. I don't know how to die. Oh, dear Lord, don't let me die!*

The darkness pressed around her, over her, under her, and she tried desperately to push it away. She fought its threat to throw her over the abyss.

At last. At last she had forced the blackness behind her. And when she opened her eyes it was light.

Mahm was bending over her, smiling a tear-stained smile.

"Hannah child!" Mahm whispered huskily. "Are you —feeling better?"

She couldn't speak. Her thoughts were formless blobs of nothing.

"Mahm," she attempted weakly. "Mahm?"

Mahm began to cry. "Thank the dear Lord! She's coming to herself!"

Where her right leg should be Hannah felt a thick, tight vacuum pulsing faintly under the bandages.

"My leg?" she asked, trembling.

Sush squeezed her hand tightly. "It's swelling bad, Hannah."

Swelling. Yes, it would. The hayfork had been rusty. The pain was there, always there, hammering dully at her. How long she'd been unconscious she didn't know, but it must have been days.

One day when Dr. Hinz was there Hannah overheard him talking to Mahm.

"If the swelling doesn't go down soon, we'll have to amputate her leg."

Amputate. Mahm didn't understand, until the doctor said in plain words:

"Cut it off."

Cut off her leg? Oh, dear God, no! Never to trail her toes through the dust again; to climb the bluff in the back pasture; to race through the fields knee-high in green wheat. . . .

"Dear God, please—" Hannah prayed weakly, silently. But I don't know God, and He doesn't need to listen.

She cried wordlessly for hours, because she couldn't bear to think of being without her leg. Aching, throbbing misery washed over her in great waves and she drooped listlessly. Would Dan like her with only one leg? She groaned in stricken anguish.

"Hannah, what is it?" Mahm bent over her tenderly. But she only shook her head in stony silence.

One day she saw a Figure seated beside her bed. Gentle-faced, tender, and kind, the Stranger somehow awed her. As though He knew what pain was . . . what frustration meant . . . what separation—

"Jesus—if You really are Jesus—will You—help me? I'm afraid alone. But I'll follow You and do whatever You ask—if You will just make me well!"

Then the Figure was gone. But Hannah knew something had happened to her. The darkness was light, and the night in her soul had vanished.

Looking at the window she saw the sunlight filter

through the slats of the dark brown shutters and dance on her bed. She sat up, crawled out of bed, and hopped painfully on one leg to the window. Throwing open the confining shutters she breathed deeply of the warm August air.

Fromm, the collie, was running around in circles, chasing the old gray tomcat, with Abram clapping his hands in glee. Across the yard Peter ambled toward the barn, the stubborn lock of fair hair falling into his left eye.

Beside Peter was a tall, dark young man, the one who had startled her on the day the bedraggled mover wagon had creaked down the road. Her heart stopped for a moment. It was Dan Smith!

He swung around and glanced casually toward the house, and she caught the sudden flash of his dark eyes, the handsome face with its faintly mocking smile. Then he swaggered with Peter toward the barn.

Hannah's heart pounded. She knew she wanted to see Daniel Smith again!

3

The days slipped by like golden globs of butter. With each passing hour Hannah felt new strength surge into her foot. Sitting propped up by the big south window of the dining room she picked up scraps of dark percale and snipped at another quilt piece.

Sush, seated dutifully beside her, was chattering incessantly in Low German. "Look, Hannah! That's a piece of the material Mahm made my last year's school dress from. Do you think Mahm will make me a new dress this year, or will I have to wear your old gray?"

Hannah paused, her scissors suspended in midair. She smiled at Sush's winsome question.

"My old gray? If Pa will just let me go to school! He thinks maybe I ought to stay home. But—well, I wore out the gray for everyday, remember? I wish Mahm would make our school dresses alike. Maybe something in green-sprigged lawn. . . ."

Sush shook her yellow head pertly. "No, Hannah. That would never work. We could never keep them clean all week!"

"You should always wear your apron," Hannah said flippantly. Trust Sush to be practical.

"Oh, I do," Sush burst out quickly. "But the scraps wouldn't make very nice quilt pieces."

Hannah dropped her scissors with a clatter. "Why not? Why must our quilts be all dark percale anyhow? If Mahm thinks green is too light for a quilt, then we wouldn't need to sit inside and cut pieces."

"You don't like to do it, do you, Hannah?"

For a moment Hannah didn't reply. She looked out across the yard and watched Fromm trailing Abram behind the barns. Boys had all the luck, she thought enviously. Then she laughed a joyous, ringing laugh.

"No, I don't, Sush. If it wasn't for this—" she kicked up her bandaged foot, "I would be outside right now!"

"Well, anyhow," Sush added wryly, "you don't have to hoe."

Hannah cocked her head. Wearing a slat bonnet, the long-sleeved jacket to keep the sun off her arms and neck, was too confining. Still, it was better than sitting inside sewing quilt pieces. One thing she would never do again: get the cows ready for milking. Maybe if she was outside she could catch a glimpse of that handsome Daniel Smith again. Now and then he came on the yard with Peter, but never near the house. *Neighbors, yes. Friends, no.* Pa's voice . . . because they were "Englishers," as he called anyone was wasn't a Mennonite.

One Sunday afternoon in late September, after the Kliewers had arrived home from the Plainfeld Mennonite country church, Hannah changed from her brown sateen full-skirted dress into the more practical "little Sunday" dark straight skirt and blouse. Pa had gone to pay a visit to a sick church member, and Mahm had lain down for a nap with Liesbet. Peter and Hans were outside, and where Sush and Abram were Hannah had no idea.

She sat by the window leafing through the church hymnal. She had been in church for the first time today in weeks, and she tried to hum the tune that the choir had sung. It was new to her, but with Peter's book she could follow it herself. It was *Der Thron Im Herzen*—"The Throne in the Heart." What had gripped her most was the long low notes which had rumbled from the boys in the back row. She couldn't forget how John Penner had lowered his long, narrow chin as each note descended on *"heil'gen thron."* It had looked so comical she'd had to drop her head to keep from bursting into laughter.

That was when she had become aware of John Penner's tall, slender figure and the lean brown sensitive face and the capable hands, and a blush had dyed her cheeks.

She had tried to concentrate on the sermon after that, and today for the first time Elder Harder's message had made sense.

"To follow Jesus Christ," he had said in his clear, clipped German, "means to turn away from the world and let Him have His way in our lives. . . ."

Her life had never been the same since the day the kind, gentle Stranger had sat beside her. But she was still bothered with the Mennonite concept of separation.

What did it mean? Was this what made them different from the Englishers?

Fromm's sudden bark drove her eyes to the window. The tangle-haired, tattered youth pedaling furiously up the lane was followed by the lanky, dark one who slammed to a rasping stop beside the picket gate.

Peter and Hans, lolling on the patch of grass beside the house, jumped up quickly.

"Down, Fromm!" Hans shouted sternly, and the dog slunk away under the porch.

"Hey!" Sammy yelled as he screeched to a stop beside Dan. "Why do you call your dog 'Fromm'?"

Peter laughed. "Don't know, Sammy. To be *fromm* means—well, pious, I guess. And you never saw a more sober-looking dog than Fromm!"

"Pious!" Dan exploded with a mocking smile. "Well, now, did you ever!"

"Fromm has puppies," Hans ventured modestly. "Four of them. By the henhouse."

Hannah slammed her hymnbook and bent forward to watch. Dan wore a blue shirt and baggy gray pants held up by one stretched-out suspender and one piece of twine. His strong, clear-cut features were accented by a crooked smile that made him look as though he were secretly laughing at something. His long, lean figure draped loosely over his two-wheeler as he leaned on the handlebars.

She watched the four boys disappear behind the fringe of mulberry trees near the henhouse where Fromm's pups were housed.

With a happy sigh she got up, smoothed her black cotton skirt over her ankles, and limped across the room. She turned swiftly toward the bedroom door and paused to listen. Yes, Mahm and Liesbet were still sleeping.

Opening the front door she let it close softly behind her as she made her slow way down the steps and toward the picket gate. She lifted the latch gently and pushed the gate forward cautiously so that no betraying squeak would disturb the sleepers.

She limped across the yard toward the henhouse, keeping well behind the building. The lazy cackle of drowsy hens muffled her footsteps. Peering around the henhouse she saw the boys squatting on their haunches, playing with the four bouncy bundles of fur.

The little tan-and-white one playfully nipped Dan's hand when he tried to pick it up. Anger flashed across his dark face and he sprang back.

"Wild beast!" he spat out angrily. "You've got a coyote in this bunch, Pete!"

In her haste to hear Peter's reply, Hannah's long coltish legs stumbled against the lid of Mahm's rendering kettle and it clattered noisily to the ground.

Dan's mocking eyes turned upon her and his look caught hers, fascinated. Hannah felt red color surge over her face as he swaggered toward her.

"Well, well," he said evenly. "So we meet again. I'd wondered who was Sammy's damsel in distress."

She fumbled nervously with her hair, then laughed shyly. "Oh, I am so glad Sammy h-heard me scream. It—it was nice—that your mover wagon—came along. I went this morning to church already—" she stopped. What must he think of her, chattering on like a silly goose?

"I see," he said, looking at her from top to toe. His intense scrutiny made her squirm. She wished he would go back to the dogs. It was time she returned to the house. Mahm would waken and wonder where she was. And under no circumstances must Mahm find her talking to strange boys.

As she turned, he reached over and touched her arm, his eyes lit by his mocking glint. "Look, are you going to go to school next month? Or do you have to stay home and keep the front gate weighted down?"

Hannah blushed and whirled around, fleeing as fast as her tender foot allowed. Oh, her face burned with embarrassment. Why, he had nerve! He—He had a very clever way of speaking. For a minute she felt ashamed of her German accent, her simple, mixed-up words.

Yes, I will go to school! she told herself grimly as she shuffled toward the house. *I will learn to speak English as well as you, Daniel Smith!*

From now on she'd take on her full share of the work. She'd been lazy long enough. She'd prove to Pa that she was well enough to go to school.

"I will even help with the milking," she added darkly. "If I ride Lady, I can get the cows home from the pasture by myself."

Her chance came sooner than she expected. Pa needed both Peter and Hans to help with the haying the following week. Hannah had been busy with baking apple *perishkie* for afternoon lunch, rolling out the circles of pie dough and cutting them into five-inch squares. Then she sliced a few quarters of raw apple into each square with a dot of fresh butter, a sifting of

29

sugar, and just a dash of cinnamon. After folding the four corners toward the center she plopped them into a pan and into the oven. Out they came light brown and crusty, with pale rivers of juice oozing from the corners.

Mahm, setting the coffeepot on to boil, turned to her, "Hannah, we'll let Sush and Abram take lunch to the field. I'll feed the hens and gather the eggs, and you will have to ride Lady to get the cows home. Pa says they're in the back pasture."

Hannah nodded. It had been a long time since she had ridden Lady, although she had always enjoyed horseback riding. More recently Mahm had decided against it. "*Evoh!* It isn't right for big girls of fourteen to ride horses."

But today she was helping the family and it must be all right.

She walked toward the horse barn and opened the half doors. Inside the dimness she heard Lady stomping in her stall, snuffling the fragrant hay.

Throwing the saddle on Lady's back, Hannah tightened the cinches the way Peter had taught her. Then she led the horse out of the barn, near the corral gate, and lifting her skirts apart, climbed on.

She patted Lady's white neck into a slow trot as they left the rutted corral and rode out into the open pasture. The horse, unmindful of its light burden, began to gallop, the feel of the wind on its brown flanks.

Galloping through the lower pasture and around the creek to the edge of the upper, Hannah's spirits soared. The nearby cornfield rustled eerily, beckoning with long brown fingers, whispering in low sibilant voices.

The sun, already slipping down a flame-wreathed sky,

touched with fire the ragged pennons of a blue-black storm cloud hanging sullenly against the western horizon. She could see the cows grazing in the silver-rimmed prairie grass, now gray in deepening twilight.

The horse, rambling along leisurely now, suddenly reared and neighed in terror. And then Hannah saw it—the rattlesnake, writhing on the ground near the mare's dainty feet.

Lady leaped forward and started off at full gallop toward the level west. Hannah hung on to the frightened horse's neck, her long, heavy braids flying in the wind. She caught them both in one hand and drew them over her shoulder as the maddened animal rushed on.

Just when Hannah despaired of stopping her frightened mount the faint staccato of hoofbeats echoed through the pasture and she caught her breath as the lean, dark figure of Dan Smith on a horse raced up beside Lady.

Dan reached out to catch Lady's bridle, when the terrified horse began to rear on its haunches.

Hannah felt herself slide. Dan flung out his arms and caught her, pulling her onto the saddle in front of him. Her fast-beating heart slowed perceptibly.

He caught her face between his hands and looked deeply into her eyes. His dark head was pressed against her swaying figure, and then he touched her full red lips with his fingers, and drew her toward him.

She tensed. Her horse had slowed to a canter. She reached out her hands and tried to push Dan away.

"Let—me go, Dan!" she cried fiercely. "I—must get the cows home. . . ."

He held her at arm's length, his dark, handsome face twisted by his derisive smile.

"You little vixen!" he spat out the words. "All—all right. But someday—someday you'll kiss me!"

He flung her roughly to the ground and rode away without a backward glance.

Trembling, Hannah watched him go. She clenched her hands until the nails bit into her palms.

"I will not!" she fumed. "Never . . . never—"

Then she moved slowly forward and called to Lady.

4

October, with the tang of drying hay and mellow tree-ripened apples, hinted at the coming autumn. Already the giant elms had donned their burnished mantillas and fall had thrown crimson capes over the stately oaks. Summer, shrugging off her green garb, was looking back over her shoulder reluctantly before she made her departure.

Plainfeld school was starting, and in the Kliewer household Peter, Hannah, Abram, Hans, and Sush were tugging at their impatience to be on their way.

Mahm slammed the lid on the last sturdy syrup pail and gave it a swipe with a gray dishrag.

"Now! Hannah, you eat with Sush, and the boys can eat together. I put in corn bread and fried sausage— but just one piece each," she warned, briskly inspecting Abram's ears. "And you, Hans, don't be a pig. You leave some sausage for Peter. And apples. They're not so good this year. I cut out the wormy parts."

Hannah, tall and slender in her dark blue percale, stood with her hand on the doorknob.

"Must we walk, Mahm?"

"Walk?" Mahm's lips pressed together tightly. "*Evoh!* You're strong again, aren't you? And it's only a mile and a half, and besides that, it's not raining. The Martens children walk over two miles to school. Got your slates? Here, you take your buckets and go." And she shooed them out of the house.

The road to school led a quarter of a mile south, then a mile east, right across the road from Plainfeld Mennonite Church. Hannah and Sush tried to keep up with the boys, but soon they were left far behind. Why must boys always be in a hurry to play shinny?

Hedge, prickly osage orange rows, dappled the ground with pale morning sunlight as Hannah trundled down the road, pulling the babbling Sush tightly with one hand and hanging on to the slates and dinner pail with the other.

"We'd better hurry up," Hannah said, after a strained, ten-minute silence, swinging her long legs past the church. "When the bell rings, we are late."

The white clapboard schoolhouse, with its rows of four windows on either side, stood prim and proud in the middle of the large school ground. The schoolyard, circumvented on two sides by the tall, osage orange hedge, and bordered on the other two by the rutted country roads, already swarmed with pupils.

A tall, loosely knit figure with peppery hair, dressed in a drab brown suit, stood waiting on the roofless porch. Harrison Tucker, the new teacher, Hannah thought, is wondering if we are late. She and Sush panted onto the schoolyard a minute later.

Short, stocky Emma Peters rushed up to meet them. "We were afraid you wouldn't come to school because of your bad foot, Hannah!" she cried breathlessly, her dull brown eyes wary. "Bell is going to ring; so you'd better get your bucket on the shelf quick!" With that, she tore the syrup pail from Hannah's grasp and dashed up the steps.

Helene (Lehn) Toews, waiting on the steps, her sallow face wrinkled like an old woman's, hung back.

"Psst! Hannah, are those new Schmidts coming to school?"

"Schmidts?" Hannah paused. "What Schmidts?"

"Your new neighbors," Lehn nodded quickly. "Those Englishers!"

Hannah laughed. "Oh, you mean the Smiths. I guess they will come. But they never hurry up for anybody. They—"

Just as the bell rang, a cloud of dust rolled down the road past the church, and a skinny mare galloped onto the schoolyard. A thin, washed-out-looking girl slid from the horse, followed by the familiar tousle-head Sammy. The tall, dark youth holding the reins searched the milling crowd on the porch until his eyes met Hannah's. Then he flashed her a mocking smile and rode away to tether his horse.

Hannah blushed furiously and pushed her way into the schoolhouse. Oh, if only no one had seen him! She remembered the day her horse had run away and Dan's rescue. And the way he'd held her. . . .

35

"No! No, I will not think of—him," she whispered under her breath as she slipped into the long desk she shared with the other older girls.

Lehn, beside her, stared at her curiously. "What did you say, Hannah?"

She dropped her eyes. "N-nothing, Lehn. I was just talking—to myself."

Roll call followed the hearty singing of "Never, Oh, Never Say Fail." Seventy-two names rolled hesitantly from Teacher's smooth English, for German was foreign to him. Big boys, as tall as Harrison Tucker himself, and shy, buxom girls; medium-sized and little ones— squeezed side by side behind the long desks until not one extra bench was left.

Emma Peters and Lehn Toews sat on either side of Hannah, nudging and whispering cautiously. Slate work she could manage, but when she tried to read, the scraping of one hundred and forty-four restless high-button shoes drowned out her words.

She glanced around nervously. Hen Schroeder's round face split into a wide grin at her roving gaze from across the room. Tall, slender John Penner hid his brown head behind his frameless slate, and winked at her slyly. She didn't dare turn to her right, for she knew she would meet the taunting eyes of Dan Smith if she did. Hannah envied the thin, wishy-washy Maggie Smith who could read with the fifth readers.

Recess came and Emma, her dark red hair falling over her dull brown eyes, fondled Hannah's arm. "Come, Hannah, let's go play shinny."

"Shinny! But girls never—"

"Then blackman?"

Hannah hesitated. She still couldn't run too fast because of her foot.

John Penner sidled awkwardly toward her. "Want to play blackman, Hannah? On the behind side of the schoolhouse!" And like a lean brown weed in the wind he was gone.

Hannah stared after him. John wasn't handsome, the way Dan Smith was. He didn't make her feel shivery inside, either. No, John Penner wasn't exciting like that Englisher. But he was a Mennonite, and she could be friends with him. If she wanted to.

With a wistful sigh she walked slowly out of the schoolhouse door to the north side. If Dan was there—

She looked for his swaggering figure, but it wasn't there. Then John hunkered up beside her, grabbed her hand, and held on tightly as they ran. If one was caught, so was the other. It was too predictable, Hannah thought. She was glad when the bell rang and they marched back into the schoolroom.

School was over at last. In search of Sush and the tin syrup pail, Hannah stopped to watch a race across the schoolyard. Dan, his long legs skimming over the ground, was chasing the lean, fleet-footed John, who kept a fraction of a foot in front of Dan.

"Come on, now, Penner!" Dan was taunting. "Let's see you run like you did at recess—only, this time without a girl!"

Hannah's heart fluttered at Dan's words. Nearly everyone had left by now, and she had the wicked inclination to cheer Dan on. Just because he was an Englisher was no reason to ignore him. And just because he'd tried to kiss her—well, she'd clench her fists and wish him forward so that he could catch that awkward *Hauns Pannah*—John Penner—and—

Wups! John sprawled on the ground flat on his face. Hannah saw Dan pause, then turn away quickly. John got up slowly and wiped his chin with the sleeve of his right hand. It was bloody.

"John!" she cried out. Then she saw the slate with the broken frame. As John had fallen, the slate had cut sharply into his chin. . . .

Hurrying up to him she took his arm gently and led him toward the cistern. She'd wash the blood off and see if Teacher had some salve.

Dan stood at one end of the yard and watched them silently, the cynical half smile twisting his face. Hannah pretended not to see him.

John dropped onto the cistern platform. Hannah took a clean handkerchief from her apron pocket and began to dab at the blood on his chin.

"Emma," she called out sharply. "I need you for help. Will you haul some water up from the cistern?"

Emma's squat figure appeared from nowhere, and immediately she began to pull up the bucket of clear, cool water.

At that moment Sush squealed behind them, and Emma turned quickly. There was a sudden splash.

Sush's big blue eyes widened as she cried out, "Teacher! Teacher, come quick! The *emmer* fell into the cistern! The *emmer* fell into the cistern!"

Harrison Tucker, his thin gray. head cocked like a sparrow's, burst horror-struck out of the schoolhouse door.

5

"What's happened?" he cried, staring at the small group huddled around the cistern platform. "Emma—is she—"

"I'm right here," Emma said mildly, her short, stocky figure leaning itself calmly against the cistern box. "But the bucket fell in and we need water for—"

"The—*bucket*, did you say?" the teacher almost choked in relief. "But Sarah Kliewer said—And what is wrong with John Penner?"

Hannah exploded with laughter until she shook. "Oh, Mister Tucker! It's all in—well, in Sush's—I mean, Sarah's English—I mean, German. We say *amah* for bucket in Low German, and Sarah wanted to talk it the way it sounds in English. *Emmer* for *amah* sounds sort of the same, doesn't it? But—" she sobered quickly, "we need water so John can wash his chin. He—"

"Forget it," John said brusquely, rubbing his shirt sleeve against his bloody chin. "I can go home this way. We don't always have rough people like those Schmidts around!"

Hannah's face flamed. "Smith. The name is Smith, John Penner. And next time you'll have to run faster. Dan will beat you for sure if you don't."

"Dan!" John cried out hotly. "So you stick up for him! Why, he's not even a Mennonite. He's an Englisher!" And he dabbed at his chin violently with his sleeve once more.

"I—" Hannah began, then stopped. How do I feel about Dan? He is handsome and exciting and—I like him. But he is also rough and ruthless. John is right. He is not a Mennonite.

The teacher was looking at the gash in John's chin. "You'd better go home, boy, and have your mother take care of it. It might even be better if you'd go to a doctor. I'll get that pail out of the cistern now."

"Doctor?" John echoed disdainfully. "We never go to a doctor with such a little scratch. It will get better with goose grease!"

He turned around and looked hard at Hannah, then picked himself up from the cistern curb and ambled off the schoolyard.

Hannah watched him go. Such a stupid boy! Why, he'd acted almost as though he was better than Dan Smith. Well, maybe he was. At least, he was a Mennonite. But there was one thing she couldn't decide. Did she like Dan or not? One minute she did; and then she remembered—the kiss—and she almost hated him.

As the winter months wore on and Christmas ap-

40

proached, Harrison Tucker began to plan a school Christmas program.

"Just so he has a religious program!" Pa said stoutly with a shake of his grizzled beard as Sush bubbled over with program plans at home.

"Oh, we have pieces to say," Sush chattered on, "all about shepherds and Wise Men and Bethlehem's stall. We are going to sing *Stille Nacht, Heilige Nacht* in English, too!"

Hannah found herself humming *Silent Night* as she and Sush entered the schoolhouse the next morning. It had grown colder during the night, and the round heater in the center of the schoolroom gave off waves of heat as she peeled off her thick blue scarf, the heavy black coat, and the green mittens.

As she held out her hands to catch the warmth, Emma slipped up beside her.

"Have you baked peppernuts already?"

"Mahm has been baking every day. We put cane molasses in ours and they're awfully good," Hannah said with a gay laugh. "She has already filed a five-gallon crock."

Maggie Smith, her thin mouth wide and hungry, edged closer. "What are peppernuts?"

Hannah and Emma exchanged knowing glances. Emma's dull eyes lit up. "You don't know? They are little balls of—like cookies. We Mennonites always bake them for Christmas."

"It's a real job to roll those little pieces out," Hannah sighed. "We sometimes roll them in long thin rolls and then snip them off with a pair of scissors."

The bell rang and the pupils scrambled into their

seats. After morning exercises were over, the teacher turned to the squirming back rows.

"While the younger ones practice their songs and recitations the rest of you will work on your reading assignments. All right, you children. Up front!"

Hannah tried to keep her mind on her reading lesson, for she did so hope to pass into the fifth reader after Christmas, but the noise of lining up was too distracting.

With the tuning fork Mr. Tucker found the right pitch. After his wavering "hmmm," the clear, flutelike voices began to sing:

> "I love You,
> Little manger Baby;
> I love You,
> Little stranger Baby—"

Hannah's eyes roved restlessly around the room. Dan Smith's mocking eyes caught hers and at each phrase of "I love You," he mouthed them silently, smirking with his twisted lips at every word.

Crimson-faced, Hannah tore her gaze away and looked into her book, trying feebly to keep her mind on what she was trying to read. That Dan Smith—of all the nerve! He made her so—so mad, so furious. . . .

She was glad when the Christmas program had come and gone and she didn't need to worry over Dan's tantalizing teasing anymore. For surely he was only teasing. No decent, well-mannered boy would be as brazen as to mean it. At least, no *Mennonite* boy, she was sure.

One cold, brittle January morning while the stars still

studded the heavens Pa tiptoed upstairs and shook Hannah roughly.

"Hannah, you get up now. Mahm is with pain and I must quick go for the midwife!"

Sleepily she tried to wipe the dreams from her foggy eyes and dragged herself out of bed. As she slid out of her long, flannel nightgown into her gray everyday cotton, her thoughts milled aimlessly. She knew what this meant. No more school for her this winter. Mahm needed her help with the house and the chores. At least, she had satisfactorily finished the fourth reader.

Hannah sighed, half glad and half sad. Now she'd escape the constant embarrassment of Dan's plaguing.

When Mrs. Dyck had arrived and had put Hannah to work heating water, time moved swiftly. Between stirring up corn bread for breakfast and running into Mahm's bedroom to help, Hannah had all she could do until Mrs. Dyck called out,

"*Na*, come here once, Hannah, and see the fat little baby brother you have!"

Hannah was submerged in work after that. What with the washing and ironing, making meals, fixing school lunches, patching endless stacks of clothes, knitting, choring chickens—not to mention caring for Mahm who must stay flat on her back for two weeks—she had little time to think about anything.

One day Mahm was sitting up in the big walnut rocker in the dining room nursing Baby Albert while Hannah folded the clean flour sack diapers to be put into the drawer.

Mahm wreathed her florid face into a gentle smile. "What a nice fat baby! Soon he needs stockings already.

Run to Reimers and see if they brought the mail along from town. I think maybe the yarn I ordered from Jones & Company could be there. Then when I sit here I can knit.''

Welcoming the chance to get out of the house after being confined inside for weeks, Hannah eagerly bundled herself into the old black coat and the blue stocking cap, and trundled down the driveway. The late afternoon was already throwing long, cold shadows across the earth as she tripped lightly along the rutted road.

Past the corner she hurried, and on to the Reimers, who lived in the small white T-house with its narrow lean-to.

Just before she reached the Reimers' yard, a tall, dark figure on horseback galloped toward her. He pulled to a stop and leaned forward in the saddle. Didn't Dan Smith ever do anything but ride horseback? she wondered.

"Why all the haste, Henny? Running away?" he asked with a sardonic smile.

She caught her breath. "I—I want to see if Reimers have brought along our mail from town. It's their turn to get it.''

"Oh.''

He stared down at her silently, his black eyes mocking her, until she squirmed. She almost didn't want him to go; still, she knew she mustn't talk boldly to an Englisher like this.

"Are—you not in school anymore, Dan?" she ventured timidly.

He shrugged his lean shoulders. "I know as much as

the schoolmaster; so why should I waste my time and his? Look, Henny. Since you're not in school either, I figured I might as well stay home, too. You know I like you, don't you?" he said frankly, his eyes intent on her flustered face.

"I—"

"I could go for you in a big way, if you'd let me. You must be all of fifteen by now, aren't you?"

Hannah nodded. "Last month was my birthday. But you are not—you are not—"

"You mean, because I'm not a Mennonite!" he scoffed. "Well, let me tell you something. We live in this community and we deserve to be treated like citizens as well as the rest of you. Just because you and your outlandish Mennonite ways—"

"Stop it!" she cried out. "It—just doesn't fit together. We—we believe in—in separation. . . ." She whirled around and hurried down the Reimers' lane. Well, he could make fun of the Mennonites all day, but she didn't have to listen!

She was glad Mrs. Reimer detained her with asking for news of Baby Albert; and with the wrapping up of a loaf of fresh rye bread for supper, she didn't need to leave immediately. Mahm's order for the yarn had come, and so had Pa's letters.

Two days later when Hannah was in the stone house washing the milk crocks Pa ambled in, his bearded face grim and taciturn.

"Hannah," he said gravely, after he had busied himself with skimming the cream from the crocks with the big ladles. "Mrs. Reimer tells me you were talking the other day to Daniel Schmidt on the road."

45

"Why—why—" she blushed. She hoped Pa wouldn't notice it in the dimness of the stone house. "He just came by and we—talked a little bit. That's all."

"You listen here, Hannah," he said gruffly, "I have said we can be good neighbors with the Schmidts but not friends. For one thing, Daniel is not a Mennonite. He is lazy and good-for-nothing. Why, the Schmidts don't have even their wheat in. And Daniel is not a Christian. He's an Englisher. Just you remember that!" With that, he picked up his ladle and stalked from the room.

Hannah's face fell. So Pa thought she was dreaming of Dan, did he? Well, she did—sometimes. Dan was handsome and exciting and—different. But that didn't make him unfit for her to love, did it—if she wanted to? And why did everyone call him Schmidt, if they didn't want him to be a Mennonite anyhow? There were some Mennonite Schmidts at Goessel, she knew. She was fifteen now. Some girls were married at fifteen, or even sixteen. But she was growing up, and she would make up her own mind. Pa had no right to conspire against her dreams. Or did he?

"How I wish I knew how I really felt about Dan," she told herself again. "Sometimes I like him very much, and other times I hate him. There is no one else for me. Except that—that fat Hen Schroeder—or one of the Leppke boys—or Jake Thiessen—or—"

Of course, there was always John Penner. Since she had begun to sing in the choir after her baptism last fall, John had been trying to capture her attention, the same as he did Emma's. John was quiet and calm and good. But that was all there was to John. Dan was different. Different. That's what intrigued her. She had to see him again.

On Saturday she told Mahm she wanted to see Maggie about a cross-stitch pattern.

Mahm stared at her in disbelief. "But you don't like sewing. You—"

Hannah shook her head doggedly. She had to see Dan again, clear things up in her own mind. Maybe if he started going to church—

After Pa had left for town and she had finished her Saturday's baking, Hannah was off.

The long, winding lane that skirted the woods on the north, straggled across a ravine and meandered toward the ramshackle, decrepit farmyard. She crossed the wooden bridge that spanned the gully and hurried toward the house.

As she stepped onto the flat board porch, she was half afraid it would collapse with her.

Maggie opened the door at her timid knock, her hair hanging in strings down her slightly stooped back.

"Come in, Hannah," Maggie said in her flat, colorless voice, taking Hannah's coat listlessly, "and sit down."

At one end of the kitchen a black range, with soot-encrusted lids, flickered with a dull red flame; the oil-cloth-covered table was heaped with old papers, tattered clothes, and bits of moldy food. In one corner stood the unpainted cupboard with its knobless drawers, one door hanging by a broken hinge. A disarray of manure-covered boots and shoes was scattered over the mud-died, splintered board floor. Wallpaper, once a dark sprigged blue, had been half torn in strips from the walls, exposing the cracked plaster beneath. Of the dirty white chairs only one still possessed a back. The heavy, stale odor of tobacco hung over the house in stifling waves.

Hannah's gray eyes took in everything in one glance, but there was no sign of Dan.

A bitter taste began to fill Hannah's mouth that nauseated her. So this was Dan Smith's home. Its filth and squalor cried out against Hannah's tidy soul, and she choked.

As soon as she could manage it gracefully, she grabbed the proffered sample of cross-stitching and fled.

6

Hannah took Baby Albert out to the yard the first warm day the following spring. He toddled around now, squealing with delight at the creaking windmill and the aimless grunting of the pump below.

The wind, gusting around the corner of the house, composed a symphony of sound in the half-grown pines Pa had planted in front of the house. Frolicking like a young colt put out to pasture, Albert trotted back and forth from porch to pump.

Hannah, poised with an armful of freshly dried clothes, standing on the front porch, watched the little fellow in his childish antics.

A tiny smile touched her lips. "Oh, you little one!" she cried, tossing the pile of boys' shirts on the porch and swooping Albert into her arms. She nuzzled her head against his plump stomach. "Someday I want a baby just like you, Albert!" she whispered tremulously. Dark-haired, black-eyed—

Pain stabbed at her. No—not a dark child, like Dan. Not if Pa and Mahm had their way. A full-grown girl of sixteen had no right to make up her own mind, they argued. Now, take a fine, clean *bengel* like John Penner, who was nineteen already. John—lean, plain of face, and brown-haired, with the scar on his chin like a cleft, from the cut on the school ground last year— John was —well, just plain John. No more. Still, John was everything a good Mennonite boy should be. But—

"Why must Pa and Mahm always say no to Dan?" she flung out bitterly, her fists clenching Albert's soft baby skin. "I could ·change his sloppy ways. . . ."

Albert stared at her, his childish lips shut tight and thin—then he began to cry.

Hannah pressed him close. "No, little brother! I didn't mean to hurt you. I was just—" she set him down carefully. "Now you run around the yard once more while I get the rest of the wash in. Soon it will be time for Sush and Liesbet to come home from school. Abram and Hans—*ach*, those boys! What's the matter with them? Fighting with Sammy Smith, and staying after school for it."

Or did Sammy provoke the quarrels? She shook her head lightly as she carted the load of clean clothes into the house and dumped them onto the dining room table. Sammy had helped her that memorable day when she had stepped on the hayfork. Somehow she would always be grateful for that.

"Hannah?" Mahm's strident voice called from the bedroom.

"Yes, Mahm?"

"Pa and I have been talking," Mahm said, her figureless form a whitish blob in the dimness of the bedroom. She stood in the doorway now, her hands on her full hips. "Pa and I think it is time you and Johann Penner make your intentions known. He—"

Hannah's hand flew to her throat and she swallowed. "But Mahm—John Penner? I don't want to get married to John—"

"You are sixteen and too young to know what you want!" Mahm said tersely. "But Pa and I think it is best if you are promised even if you don't marry yet for two more years. Johann is a good boy. Comes from a good Mennonite family. He is thrifty and hardworking, and he is a Christian. You know how very important these things are!"

Yes, very important. But how I feel doesn't matter. Hannah's shoulders sagged. Why did Pa and Mahm have to interfere? Why did they have to plan for her when they didn't know how she felt?

But I don't know how I feel myself, she admitted grimly. Is it right to tie myself down to someone I don't love?

"It is time we start making quilts already," Mahm continued as though everything was settled. But it wasn't. Not as long as there was—Dan.

She stood silently as Mahm talked, paying no attention to the onrushing words.

"—don't you think, Hannah?"

"Wha—Don't I think what, Mahm?" Hannah flustered.

"Aren't you listening? Where could you find a better boy than Johann Penner?"

51

Hannah's face burned. "I couldn't, I guess. John is—good and fine." *And colorless.* Just plain John.

"So it is all right we invite the Penners over for Sunday dinner and make plans?" Mahm went on, heedless of Hannah's discomfort.

"Oh, Mahm!" Hannah burst out tearfully. "Please wait. I am not sure—I want to think about this longer. I—I'd better run out now and see where Albert is," she flung out over her shoulder as she moved toward the door. She had to stop this ridiculous conversation before Mahm had a chance for more persuasive speeches!

Albert was sitting in the middle of the yard, his red stocking cap pulled almost over his eyes, patting Fromm on her moist brown nose. Hannah ran out and put her arms around him.

"Time you come in, you little one!" she cooed softly. "Soon Liesbet comes home to play with you."

Pa came striding briskly across the yard, his peppery beard a dull splotch of gray on his ruddy face.

"Hannah," he said crisply as he stopped beside her, "you will have to get the cows home. I will go to the school and take Abram and Hans to the store for new boots. Peter is helping Franz Harder with corn planting, but when we come home from town we will do the milking."

Hannah picked up the squirming Albert and deposited him into Mahm's ample lap.

"Pa wants me now to get the cows," she said almost gaily. Lately, it seemed, when she was in the back pasture Dan showed up mysteriously.

She remembered their earlier trysts. Dan, his dark,

intense face—mocking, always unpredictable.

"Henny," he had said the last time they'd met, "why do you shy away from me? You treat me like scum, and I don't like it!"

"No, Dan," she'd protested, "I don't be meaning to. It's only that—"

"Just that I'm not good enough for you—is that it?" he demanded, reaching for her arms.

"No—no!" she'd backed away from him. "I—don't know what I feel about you. I—am—con-confused." It was a big English word she'd just learned and used for the first time.

He had left her alone, although the hungry light that blazed in his dark eyes had troubled her, so that she almost dreaded to see him ride up to meet her when she was alone in the pasture.

She wondered if she'd see him again today. It seemed that all Dan ever did was ride around on his scrawny mare. She wondered how his fieldwork ever got done.

As she pulled a heavy duck coat over her dark blue dress, she grew wistful. Today she almost wished for Dan, because she felt torn between duty and her own heart. Was this love for him she felt stirring in her bosom? Or was it just—fascination?

Lady trotted gallantly today, stepping like a well-bred female. Of course, Lady would. Having a new colt made her proud of her accomplishment, Hannah thought whimsically as she turned in at the back pasture. She craned her neck toward the south to see if the scrawny mare was galloping through the fields, but there was no sign of it.

As she swung Lady around the bluff, Dan swaggered

suddenly into her path, his tall, broad frame blocking the horse's way.

"Dan—" she cried out, startled. "What are you doing here?"

"Whoa, there, Lady!" he called out hoarsely, placing one hand on the mare's shiny flank. "What am I doing here, Henny? Well, when I saw you ride out of your barnyard I thought, 'My love is coming to see me. She thinks she's going after the cows, but she is coming to see me!' " He laughed in amusement, fingering the hem of her blue skirt absently.

Her eyes were grim as she pressed her lips together tightly. Why did Dan persist in thinking she liked him when she really didn't know herself?

"Henny?" he whispered her name softly. "Henny, will you slide down for a minute? I want to talk to you."

She hesitated. Would it be another senseless argument—a worrying encounter? But she had to know how she felt toward Dan before she faced Pa and Mahm and their plans for her future.

"All—right," she said shyly, slipping lightly from the horse's back. "But I must get the cows home for milking pretty soon."

"This won't take long, darling," he said in a low voice, moving forward and touching her face gently with lean brown fingers. Then without a word, his strong arms went around her and he bent her head back across his arm and kissed her softly at first, and then with a swift graduation of intensity that made her cling to him. His insistent mouth parted her shaking lips, sending wild tremors along her nerves, and then she relaxed under the magic spell of his impassioned kisses.

"Oh, Henny—Henny—" he murmured against her lips, against her hair. "I love you! I love you—love you. . . ."

The stale, overpowering tobacco odor and the filthy sweat of his clothes mushroomed into her nostrils and suddenly she felt nauseated. She put out her hands and tried to push him away.

"Please—Dan, I—"

He placed his fingers over her mouth impishly. "Do you love me, darling?" he demanded. "Tell me you do!"

Hannah wanted to respond to his demandings, to know the dark, unknowable of loving him. She shook her head helplessly. "Oh—I don't know—"

"Tell me what's wrong! Why can't you let yourself love me the way I love you?" he said, taking her hands and pressing them against his chest.

"I—Dan, maybe if you'd be—more like us—go to church, and get to be a Mennonite, maybe my folks would—"

He pushed her away from him roughly. "Oh, don't be stuffy!" his black eyes blazed. "Why must you expect me to conform to what you believe? Why can't you accept me for what I am?"

White-faced, she whispered, "Oh, Dan—it's—it's because Mennonites believe different—in certain things—salvation by faith—hard work—sep-separation—" she paused, emptied of excuses.

Dan laughed harshly, his dark face twisted in amusement. "And that's more important than love? Well, just get this. I'm not about to conform to your way of life to please you or your parents. It's *you* I love and want. And if you love me, you'll have to take me just that way. If you don't want me for what I am, you can go!"

With that, he pushed her roughly away from him and turned toward his horse.

Hannah watched him go, her lips still burning from his kisses, and her heart pounding. In a daze, she swung herself on her mount and rode around the bluff for the cows. They lumbered dutifully toward the pasture gates, the fat kine, and at last they were home.

She was still shaking, and more unsure of herself than ever. For she had the feeling that someday the lean kine would devour the fat. And she couldn't think of a way to stop them. Without marrying Daniel Smith.

But her mind was made up. After she let the animals into the straw barn, she stumbled disconsolately toward the house.

Stepping into the kitchen, Hannah found Mahm peeling potatoes for *borscht*, her wispy head bent over the big tin dishpan on the table.

"Mahm—" Hannah said dully, her face burning with the fire of aroused passion as she watched the flip-flip of Mahm's paring knife, "you can tell Pa—that it will be all right. I am going to marry—John Penner. . . ."

7

The days and weeks wore on. Hannah, sitting by the large south window of the dining room one afternoon, busied her hands with sewing. The despised quilt pieces had been stitched together—dark and white, dark and white—and then placed on the frame to be quilted.

For days female friends and neighbors had descended in groups to hunch over the large frame which was set up in Pa and Mahm's huge west bedroom, tongues wagging as needles flew.

Mrs. Harms eyed Hannah shrewdly above her bifocals. "*Na, na,* Hannah!" she spoke tersely in her clipped Low German as her needle poked through the layered coverlet, "I'm very glad you will marry Penners' Johaun. He is a good boy. Did you know he painted the old buggy he bought at Edigers' sale last week?

Shiny, black paint, it is. He is renting ground from us now, and my man says nobody works it as good as your Johaun."

"Ja, ja, M'rie, we know," old Mrs. Toews spoke up sharply, moistening her thread with pursed lips. "I guess it was like with our Lehn and Jake Thiessen. And now Emma Peters has been arranged too already."

"Emma!" Hannah gasped breathlessly. "Who to? She didn't tell me—"

"Ben Hiebert. But Emma does not look like the happy bride to me. She always is so awkward—so schlunsig—anyhow," Mrs. Harms went on, stitching placidly away at the pattern underneath her fat fingers. "She and her fat brown face. Like an Indian, she looks! And her shoulders. She sits hunched over like a swayback mule. . . ."

Hannah felt like sticking quilting cotton into her ears. Mrs. Harms and her analogies anyhow! And Emma—why, Emma was her best friend! If Emma was marrying Ben— But then, she was already seventeen.

Pa and Mahm had been so delighted when Hannah had told them she would marry John. She wouldn't get tied up with that arrogant Dan Smith if he was the last man on earth. Well, almost the last man. Refusing to come to church. Of course, he couldn't understand German preaching, but he could learn. Only, Dan wouldn't, she was sure.

Her lips still burned from her kisses, and unconsciously she rubbed her fingers over her mouth as though she must wipe off the memory. She would be John Penner's wife, the way Pa and Mahm had wanted it. Of course, John liked her, too. He had always liked both Hannah and Emma. But Emma was going to marry Ben. She and John would wait until she was eighteen. Only, that time was rushing along all too fast.

Hannah was glad when the quilt was finally done and placed in the big chest Pa had made for her. She had painstakingly crocheted lace on two pairs of pillow slips—long, wide bands of delicate etching, which would be used only "for company." Hers and John's would do with hand-hemstitched hems. Dutiful Sush had done the work so carefully on them.

"Mine and John's," she said with a catch in her breath. How would it be when she was married to him? *I wish I loved him,* she admitted ruefully to herself. It would be easier that way. . . .

The next Sunday she invited Emma to come over after church. After all, as two new "arranged-for" brides they had so much to talk about!

Emma, her dark red hair piled onto the top of her head giving her short, stocky figure a bit of height, flopped herself on Hannah's walnut bed upstairs until the star quilt wrinkled.

"Are you excited about marrying John Penner, Hannah?" Emma asked pensively, staring at a restless fly that swooped across the ceiling.

Hannah sighed and laced her slim fingers together. "Oh—you know how it is. We've made quilts, comforts, and feather beds. And pillows, with lots of pillowcases. You ought to see Sush. She's as excited as though it were her own wedding. When John comes over, it is to talk to Pa and Peter. I almost never see him myself."

"I know what you mean," Emma said, her brown face tinged with sadness. "Ben Hiebert—Ben is good.

He's a Christian and lives separated. He never smokes nor drinks. He's a good worker too. I ought to be very happy. But I guess I just don't feel like quilt-making and—and pillows. . . ."

"You don't like Ben? You care for someone else?"

"Like Ben?" Emma echoed, her dull brown eyes dropping languidly. "He's all right, like I said. And I'll marry him, like I promised folks I would. But—"

"But you'd rather not?" Hannah asked hesitantly, watching the play of emotions across Emma's sober face.

"I— What about you?" Emma demanded abruptly. "In school Dan Smith always liked you, and I thought maybe you—"

"No," Hannah shook her brown head vigorously. "Dan—he's good-looking. But he is a—a pig. He—he— Don't tell, Emma, promise you won't?"

"Promise what?"

"That—that—well, Dan—Dan k-kissed me once. He—"

Emma sat up suddenly. "Hannah! He kissed you? But Hannah—"

"A long time ago. When I was sixteen. Oh, Emma, I—*I liked it!* And that was sin. Isn't that awful?"

A long-drawn-out sigh escaped Emma. She stared at the fly, now perched on the rim of the dresser.

"Never will I tell, Hannah. But if you liked it, maybe you shouldn't marry J—"

Hannah shook her head staunchly. "No, Emma. Pa has said to me over and over. Dan is not a Mennonite, Dan is lazy, and Dan is not a Christian. So I can't marry him. John likes me, and I—I like him; so I am

60

going to marry John. And that's the way it's going to be!"

"I see," Emma said dully. "Dan will not change?"

"No. Not for me, even. He—told me he would never change to please me—or my folks. He—told me to go. . . . That's when I decided I would marry John."

Thinking about it later, Hannah wondered if liking John was enough. Emma didn't seem to think so. At least, not as crestfallen as she'd seemed when she talked of marrying Ben. But it was a bit exciting. Lehn Toews and Jake Thiessen had been married the month before, and now there'd be three young brides in the church.

The Sunday when the banns were announced for her and John, Elder Harder also spoke them for Emma and Ben.

Hannah felt scared, but Emma seemed almost gay when the service was over and they stood together on the porch of the church, waiting for the men to bring the buggies around.

"Will you have a church wedding?" Emma whispered tremulously.

Hannah smiled wanly. "A big wedding in church. And you?"

The round face fell. "At the house. I just couldn't stand to see all those people—"

Can I? Hannah thought weakly. *But a promise is a promise. . . .*

Emma's wedding would be held at the Peters' farm home just a week before Hannah and John's at church. Ben Hiebert was tall and rugged and jolly, and he would be good to Emma. Hannah found herself wishing that Emma would go into her marriage with the same determination to be happy as she with John.

She tried to be cheerful when the Penners, from parents to Anna and the five boys, dined at the Kliewers for the *Verlobungsfest*—the engagement dinner. A silent fear lurked in her heart and she went about as in a dream.

"Everyone likes it that John and I will get married," she thought to herself. "But if I could just be sure—"

Always, when she thought about marriage, the dark, mocking face of Dan Smith persisted in coming into her mind, and it unnerved her.

Two days before Emma's wedding, the stocky little bride drove furiously onto the Kliewer yard. Tying her mare onto the hitching post, she rushed into the house.

"Hannah—" she cried, her brown face red from weeping. "Oh, Hannah!"

With a pang of fear Hannah embraced her tearful friend. "What's wrong, Emma? Your wedding—day after tomorrow—don't cry like this! Don't—"

"No!" Emma sobbed deliriously, unmindful of Mahm's bulky presence with Albert clinging to her full skirts. "I can't—go through with it. I just—can't!"

"But Emma—"

"I don't love—B-Ben. It's J— I'm—s-scared. . . ."

Without a word Hannah took the corner of her crudely cross-stitched apron and wiped Emma's eyes. Poor Emma! Confused and unwilling to enter into a marriage with someone she didn't love.

Hannah caught her breath sharply, thinking of John . . . of Dan. . . . Her heart hammered. *Oh, if I had the courage to do the same!*

62

8

At the huge south window of the dining room Hannah stitched the last hook and eye onto the creamy white basque of her wedding gown and scanned the dull, wet clouds that hovered low over the bare trees. The bleakness of the afternoon seeped into her spirits as she gave the thread a last snap and let the dress drop effortlessly into her lap.

She stared moodily out the window, trying desperately to cement a smile onto her frozen lips. The fire crackled merrily in the Big Globe heater, and warmth touched her face and hands with pink.

Peter slammed into the kitchen and strode briskly into the dining room.

"It's going to snow, Hannah," he said with a prophet's gleam in his wide gray eyes. "You may have to get married on a bobsled."

A chill swept over Hannah at the thought of disagreeable weather for the momentous occasion.

"And tomorrow we butcher," she said tonelessly, picking off stray bits of broken thread from the voluminous creamy skirt.

Peter looked at her curiously. "What's the matter with you, sister? You don't sound like the happy bride. Is something wrong?"

"Oh—" Hannah shrugged her sturdy shoulders diffidently. "Nothing is the matter, Peter. But everything is so—so comfortable with Pa and Mahm—and —and I'll be moving away. . . ."

Peter laughed. "Only five miles! Now, I tell you, John is going to make a good husband. You'll never be sorry that you married him, I promise you."

Hannah smiled stiffly. She hoped Peter's prophetic powers also held true in this.

"I shan't be sorry," she said resolutely, her eyes pinioned on the drab, colorless landscape. "*Ach*, it looks like it's snowing already."

Gray drizzle, which had begun with the dawn, was giving way to snow—wet, cold blobs which melted at first as they hit the ground; then thickened as the wind rose and began to whip the flakes into fine powder and sifted them against the picket fence.

Pa stomped in purposefully from the lean-to, his bearded face red with cold, shedding his heavy duck coat as he walked.

"You, Peter. Go hitch up the team and get the children from school. This storm's going to be a big one."

"We can't push off the butchering if it storms?" Peter asked gravely.

"No," Pa said stoutly. "The hams for Hannah's wedding must be just right. It's high time we get them ready."

Peter left the room quickly and Hannah picked up the wedding gown which Mahm had sewed and held it up for a final appraising glance. The full, wide skirt fell in a row of tiny pleats around the bottom, with an exquisite design of white braid scalloping above it. The deep, billowy sleeves puffed like giant balloons below the shoulders. The high, banded neckline was edged with shirred lace, while rows of tiny pleats ran down the full length of the bosom to the waistband. Oh, it was a beautiful dress, and Hannah's heart thumped at the thought that in less than two weeks she would be wearing it.

Now she must hang it away in Mahm's big clothes cupboard. All it needed was a careful ironing, and Mahm must do that herself.

Hannah was resigned as she stepped into the large, cold bedroom, and went straight toward the painted wooden doors. She took a board hanger from its nail and hung the dress up with a precision-like gesture.

When she returned to the warmth of the dining room, snow was falling in earnest, light and soft, like noiseless cat feet of winter. It settled on the hen-house and barns and penciled the bare mulberry branches with thin white lines.

Mahm, face red and hands floury from rolling out paper-thin noodle dough, looked up from the table as Hannah entered the kitchen.

"*Na,* all finished with your dress, Hannah?"

"Yes, all done and hung up. You sewed it very

65

nicely, Mahm," Hannah said, trying to keep her mouth curved into a smile she didn't feel.

Mahm was silent as she whacked away with her rolling pin. "I want you to have a nice dress, Hannah. Too bad Peters' Emma won't wear that good blue one her ma made. But I have always said that Emma was a little bit stupid. She could have such a nice man like Ben Hiebert and—*evoh!* what does she do? She says no, and everybody is laughing at Peters!"

"Emma—" Hannah began helplessly, trying desperately to defend her friend's actions—"Emma doesn't love Ben. She—will someday find someone else."

"*Na*, I don't know," Mahm said critically. "I always think she liked your Johaun Penner. It's good that we got him first and that you will marry him."

Hannah shrank back at Mahm's words. What was love that one bandied it around, selling it to the highest bidder? If Emma loved John—but she had never let on if she did. . . . Or had she? Now it was too late. One thing Hannah vowed she would never do. She wouldn't back out of marrying John. No one should ridicule Pa and Mahm the way people were laughing at Emma's parents. She would make sure of that.

By the time Peter rumbled onto the yard with Abram, Liesbet, and Sush, the storm had almost reached blizzard proportions.

The wind howled all night long, piling drifts of snow along the hedgerows, making the roads almost impassable by morning. Temperatures plummeted to the zero mark, and frost encrusted the windowpanes with palm-feathering.

The morning sun flared up in a feeble effort to

frighten back the moaning wind and driving snow. Hannah, up before the laggard hours of dawn, stood at the kitchen window, watching a splinter of sun edge its way through a break in the gray clouds. For Pa had declared the butchering must go on.

"We can't push it off," he said brusquely, scooping thick brown rivers of sorghum molasses over his breakfast corn bread, "even if the Ennses can't come to help. The hams must be smoked so they will be just right for the wedding. I would be ashamed if we couldn't serve the best hams."

No, thought Hannah glumly, carrying the empty platters into the kitchen, above all else the Kliewer reputation for thrift and respect must be maintained!

Washing up the mound of breakfast dishes, Hannah shivered from the cold every time the door opened and the heavy-duck-coated butchers stomped inside with pans and tubs of freshly cut meat, fogging the kitchen with the mixture of steam from the wash boiler and the cold air. She shuddered at the thought of helping Mahm scrape the intestines for the sausage casing.

At Fromm's insistent barking, Hannah paused to listen. The clanking of wagons on the driveway announced the Ennses' arrival. So they would help after all. Mahm and Tante Enns would have a gala time gossiping as they scraped and turned. Hannah could just see them already—a length of casing on a board, scrape, scrape, with a blunt knife. . . . "Have you heard about Thiessens' Anna? . . . "Warkentins' Naetke is working for Edigers. . . ."

By midafternoon the pork sausage, the liver sausage, and head cheese were heaped on the big table set up in the granary. Men were stuffing sausage casing and curling it into huge round tubs. Peter was stirring the bubbling mass of chopped fat for cracklings with a big, flat paddle, in the huge iron rendering kettle that had been moved to one end of the granary.

Hannah, curious and tired of washing greasy pans indoors, bundled up in Pa's old brown coat and trundled out to watch. The hams, trimmed of their fat, lay clean and salted on the table, ready for the smokehouse. Hams. Heavy and plump. Just right for her wedding. . . .

Peter's laughing eyes crinkled at her. "What will John Penner think of his bride now, coming to look the hams over? If they are not just right, will she call the wedding off?"

"What—" Hannah started, then sauntered slowly toward him, sniffing the pungent odor of bubbling meat in the kettle. "I—Peter, do you think the Smiths always have enough to eat? The way Maggie and Sammy—look like starved rabbits. And their cows are always so thin. . . ."

"Stop thinking about the Smiths!" Peter said sullenly, his gray eyes flashing. "It was bad enough for you to chase after Dan, before you were promised to John. Now—"

"Chase after Dan!" she cried out hotly. "I didn't ever do that, Peter! He—" *He kissed me—and I liked it. . . .*

Peter grinned sheepishly. "Dan liked you, Hannah, and Dan can be friendly if he wants to be. But Dan is cruel, too. Watch out for him. I'm glad you will marry John Penner."

Dan cruel? The lean kine and the fat. . . . Dan can be friendly—when he wants to be. . . . But I am going to marry good, steady John. . . .

"March 2, 1899"—Hannah thought two weeks later, just before slipping into the creamy wedding gown— "My wedding day—to John Penner. Dear Lord, let me be a good, dutiful wife to him all the rest of my days!"

It was a prayer from her heart. She would be a good wife, no matter what happened.

The snow had almost disappeared after a few mild days. However, the ditches were still laced with a few reluctant, dirty snowdrifts, that turned the roads into bottomless mudholes.

The church was almost filled that afternoon when John came for her in the shiny, black-painted buggy. Her white dress, covered carefully with clean, dark lap robes, weathered the mile-and-a-quarter drive in the deep-rutted roads.

John looked almost handsome in his new black suit and spotless white shirt, his brown hair slicked back from the middle part to neatly trimmed edges above his ears. The scar on his chin like a cleft added distinction to his plain face.

He looked at her solemnly. "You look very nice, Hannah. Everyone will say what a nice couple we make!"

As he helped her off the buggy and up the steps of the church, he touched her shoulder gently, somberly.

"Hannah—I do like you—very much. . . ," he said shyly, and disappeared into the men's cloakroom.

Hannah's hand caught at her throat. John liked her. He'd said so! Better than Emma? But—a sudden memory crossed her mind like a stab of pain. Dan's passionate kisses, raining on her face, her lips, her neck. . . . "*I love you, Henny—love you—love you. . . .*"

She shook her head and passed her trembling hand over her forehead, as if to wipe out the painful thought. She tacked a smile onto stiff lips and set her shoulders resolutely. Not on her wedding day—she must not think of Dan! It was time she and John walked down the aisle together.

Elder Harder preached for half an hour and Brother Dyck for the next hour—the choir sang—and then came the vows. . . .

"Will you, Hannah, take Johann Penner. . .?"

Hannah hesitated only briefly. "*Ja. . . .*"

They knelt to pray. John's voice, strong and vibrant, poured out to God his thanksgiving "for such a woman as this wife," while tears streamed down her face in response.

"Help me . . . to be a good wife to John . . . ," she stammered, "and bless our home. . . ." The die was cast. She was John's wife. Forever.

During the wedding reception around the long, narrow tables, guests supped on cold boiled ham with mustard, zwieback—those round globs of bun dough topped with a head—cookies and coffee, when everyone tried to talk at once, amidst all the bustle and stir.

Looking over the gift table, Hannah's heart swelled with gratefulness. There was a beautiful blue Wedgewood plate from Emma; a deep-green pitcher-and-water-glass set with fluted edges; gray enameled cookware; a dark red glass sugar bowl and butter dish; the

70

sturdy crockware of dishes. And an opalescent hen bowl—from Maggie Smith. . . .

The feast was over, and John led Hannah outside for their ride to the Kliewer farm. A group would come over in the evening for the "after-wedding."

As John and Hannah stepped from the porch, a sudden smile quirked John's somber face. Hannah laughed lightly at the sight of the buggy. Someone had taken one large back wheel from the rear and exchanged it with one of the smaller front wheels, and the buggy stood dejectedly lopsided in the muddy churchyard.

Young people on the porch rocked with laughter, and Hannah felt very conspicuous as she and John stood gazing bewildered at the spectacle.

"We'll be over tonight for the shivaree, don't forget!" someone shouted, and Hannah turned to wave dutifully to her friends after Father Penner drove up with the family carriage in lieu of the bedizened bridal buggy.

John assisted Hannah carefully into the carriage, and presently they rumbled down the muddy road toward home.

"Will they shivaree *bad?*" John's sister Anna asked with an alert twinkle in her blue eyes.

Father Penner's brown beard bristled and he looked stern. "Let us hope not! The guitar-playing and the hymn-singing are good. It's when young people go making such bad noise that it gets unchristian! But—" he shrugged his big shoulders, "what can we do about it?"

Yes, what could they do about it later, when the hymn-singing and devotions were over, and the whole outdoors of the Kliewer yard clattered and screamed with noise!

John and Hannah stepped out onto the porch to acknowledge the noisy crowd which clamored for their presence.

Dim lantern-light invaded the dark yard, now milling with grotesque shadows. The Leppke boys, the Enns *bengels*, the Hieberts and Harmses, and a host of others Hannah couldn't readily recognize, thronged the yard, shooting firecrackers and banging hammers on old plowshares.

In a circle of yellow light Hannah thought she saw the dark, mocking face of Dan Smith, and she caught her breath sharply. Dan hadn't been at the wedding, she was sure, although Maggie, her stringy hair in a wispy bun under a shabby brown velvet hat, had come shyly to congratulate them at the reception.

Quickly Hannah turned her face away and riveted her attention to the spading sounds of a pit being dug in the center of the yard.

"Come here, Penner!" someone jeered. "This one's really going to stop you!"

The careful English—Dan's. *Dan can be cruel*—Peter's words.

Hannah grabbed John's sleeve lightly. "Stay here, John. Don't go!"

He turned to her. "But Hannah, if I don't—"

"No! Don't leave me!"

"Come on, Penner!" the jeer became a snarl. "Let's see you stop this one!"

John paused and looked at Hannah in the dim light from the large south window that flooded the porch, gripped with indecision.

His eyes dropped and he turned and jumped from the porch. At that same moment a charge of gunpowder exploded from the pit and a cry tore through the night—a cry of stark terror and agonizing pain.

Hannah rushed forward, her creamy white skirts brushing through the muddy, rutted yard toward the pit. The full light from a lantern fell on the tousled head and bloodied freckle-face of Sammy Smith!

9

For the last time Hannah lay in her old walnut bed, staring at the darkened ceiling. John, curled up beside her, had been sound asleep for some time. Her thoughts were in turmoil. The flickering lanterns on the muddy yard, the noise, the clamor. And then the thunderous burst of gunfire, and gawky, fifteen-year-old Sammy Smith, his freckled face lacerated and torn from the impact, writhed grotesquely on the ground. . . .

Come on, Penner! Let's see you stop this one. . . . Dan's voice. She couldn't forget the pugnacious overtones, the thick snarl, the murderous gleam in the black eyes in the dim light of the yard. It lay embedded in her mind and racked her, driving away all thought of sleep.

John was calmly sleeping beside her. *Let's see you*

stop this one . . . stop this one, Penner. . . . Dan is cruel . . . cruel. . . . Dan wanted to hurt—maim—*kill*—John! The sudden fact broke through the surface of her turbulent thoughts and she trembled violently.

Oh, how could she have been so blind as to think she had ever cared for that dark, handsome—*devil!* A feeling of revulsion toward Daniel Smith gripped her and burned out any emotion she'd ever held for him. She was done with thoughts of him forever.

John. Good, plain, steady John. Ordinary, yes. But clean and good. A rush of tenderness swept over her and almost overwhelmed her.

She reached out her arm and flung it lightly over John's broad shoulder.

"John—John—" she whispered huskily in the darkness. "I—didn't say it before because I didn't know. But I—I love you. . . ."

He slept on, heedless of the battles, the victories that pulsed through Hannah's soul on her wedding night.

At last she dropped into a fitful, dream-fogged sleep and slept until dawn.

The breakfast table was full of Low German talk, with Mahm so obviously presiding as she hovered over them all, plying the hearty eaters with more apple pancakes generously doused with sugar.

"First of all we'll go to the church and clean everything up," Pa said decisively, dabbing at the last sprinkle of sugar with a bit of pancake, his neatly trimmed beard wobbling. "Then after dinner we'll move everything to your place, children. I'm giving you the big Holstein cow for a present, and you can

keep her calf. I think Mahm will give you a dozen
hens. Just make sure there aren't any clucks among
them," he called out toward the kitchen.

Mahm bustled into the dining room, her ample figure
enveloped in a huge black-and-white checked apron,
carrying another heaping platter of hot apple pancakes.

"*Evoh!* I know how to pick out the hens, Pa!" she
said plaintively. "I'm also setting some clucks for
Hannah so she'll have baby chicks later on. Are
Penners giving you some chickens, Johaun?"

"Both chickens and ducks," John said blandly. "And
two cows. I think—"

At Fromm's insistent barking he paused. Hannah
looked up to see Maggie Smith's drab figure flying to
the door from the small buggy at the hitching post.

Peter jumped up and opened the door and let her
in. She hung in the doorway like a brown reed bent in
the wind, her eyes tear-stained and her stringy hair
straggling from her gray-shawled head.

"It's—Sammy!" she wept. "He is burned bad, and
he's—dying. He—wants you, Hannah. Can—can you
come—right away?"

A tremor seized Hannah at the thought of going to
the Smith place. John was on his feet and placed a
hand on her shoulder.

"She'll come right away. Go with Maggie, Hannah.
Later, I'll come and get you."

Dully, Hannah pushed herself away from the table
and staggered to her feet. Once Sammy had saved her
life when she had stepped on the fork. Now she must
go to him.

Dutifully, John held out the dark blue coat Pa had

bought for her, and she slipped her arms languidly into it. Tying a black scarf over her braided hair she followed Maggie weakly out into the yard.

"Don't forget. I'll come after you," John said, assisting her into the buggy.

A few minutes later the buggy rolled out of the lane and turned south, Maggie's thin hands taut on the reins, her narrow face grim above them.

Hannah stirred uneasily. "I—am very sorry for Sammy," she said in her hybrid English. "He should not have jumped on the pit when the gunpowder was not gone off yet."

"I know," Maggie nodded tearfully. "But Sammy was afraid—John would come, and get hurt. . . ."

Sammy! Sacrificing himself for her sake? She tried to swallow the lump in her throat.

Maggie's silence disturbed Hannah. She tried to make conversation.

"The hen bowl you gave us for a wedding present is very nice, Maggie. I'll keep it so I can remember you with it."

A faint smile tugged at Maggie's drawn mouth. "It's something that's been in the family for years and years. Belonged to great-grandmother Smith. I—I wanted you to have it," she added shyly.

Hannah reached over and pressed the careworn hand. "I'll see that it always stays in the family."

Was it a prophetic word? Hannah caught herself wondering after she'd said it. Or was it just a brash promise?

The buggy was spinning up the winding lane and rumbled ominously over the plank bridge and then squeaked to a stop before the lone hitching post beside the house.

Hannah stepped from the buggy and hopped over the broken boards toward the sagging porch. She swallowed hard as Maggie opened the door and led her inside the bleak kitchen. The same stale odor of dead tobacco ashes and manure-encrusted boots seeped into her nostrils. She brushed it aside and followed Maggie into a small, shabby bedroom.

Sammy's white face stared up at her from the narrow iron bedstead with its lumpy mattress and ragged covers. His frightened, pain-filled eyes darted to her face and she hurried to his side and knelt down, scarcely recognizing the elder Smiths huddled tearfully around the sickbed.

"Sammy," she whispered softly, "you wanted something?"

The burns and lacerations had been partly bandaged, she noticed, but the despair and pain that wracked his brow were plainly visible.

He barely nodded. "Hannah—I—I'm gonna d-die— and I'm s-scared. Could you—could you help me? Once, when I was teasing Abram and—Johnny they said—they said that people who didn't go to the Mennonite Church—couldn't get to heaven. I—said it wasn't so and I busted into them, and we had to s-stay after school. They said if I didn't be-believe it I should ask—you. Is it—true?" The words hopped like stringent bottle corks from his swollen lips.

Hannah buried her face in the tattered comfort. *Oh, God, what can I say? Help me. . . .*

"Sammy—" she lifted her face and began gently,

"we go to church to hear the preachers tell us how to prepare for heaven. But anybody can get ready whether he's in church or not. All have sinned, the Bible says."

"But—I'm not a Mennonite! The Mennonites don't need to get rid of their sin—because they don't sin!" he protested feebly. "That—that leaves me out—doesn't it?"

Hannah shook her head staunchly. "No, it leaves no one out. Everyone has to get rid of sin if he wants to get to heaven. Mennonites as much as anyone else. Sammy, after you pulled out that fork from my toe I grew very ill because the fork was rusty. I knew I couldn't die and meet God that way. God loved us so much that He sent Jesus to die for us. We need to tell Jesus we'll turn away from sin and He'll cleanse us. I did, and He changed me. He—"

"But I—don't—understand," he whispered thickly. "How—could He save—poor me?"

"Sammy—" she went on anxiously, "just like you jumped in the pit and tried to stamp it out, so my— my husband—wouldn't get hurt, like that Jesus took our place on the cross so we wouldn't need to die. *He took your place, Sammy!* Do you understand?"

Sammy's eyes, clouded by pain and anguish, stared dully at Hannah. She strained to catch the words, faint and grim, from his swollen lips.

"He—took—my place—yes, thank you!"

Then his eyelids dropped suddenly and he lay still.

Shaking, Hannah arose stiffly from her knees and would have swayed to the floor if someone behind hadn't steadied her. She turned, and looked into a pair of leering eyes in a pale face framed by bobbed blond hair. At the girl's sullen stare, Hannah regained her balance.

"I—I'm sorry," Hannah said hesitantly. "I didn't mean—"

"Never no mind. Can't bear to see a full-grown hussy like you faint!" the voice hissed low in Hannah's ear.

Hannah shrank back from the girl and looked about wildly for Maggie.

The wispy-haired Maggie, her eyes red with weeping, wasn't aware of Hannah's readiness to leave. Hannah moved silently toward the door and slipped to the foul-smelling kitchen. The arrogant, sullen-faced woman followed her.

"So you did your dirty duty, didn't you?" the words were like hissing cracks of a whip. "Only that senseless, colorless fop of a cousin Maggie would have had the nerve to haul you down here, after what happened las' night."

Hannah's hand flew to her throat. "What—what do you mean? Sammy—kept away my—my man from the pit. I was glad to come. . . ."

"Yeah, I bet you were. But maybe—maybe if it was your man who'd just died like Sammy did now—maybe the story would'a had a different endin'. Cousin Dan could'a got you then!"

Hannah fumbled blindly for the doorknob and let herself out onto the porch as quickly as she could. *I've got to get away—fast. . . .*

A vise-grip tightened on her arm and she looked up. Dan's mocking face with a stubbled growth of beard

shadowing his chin leered down at her, the heavy scent
of liquor fogging his breath.

"So Henny is back again," he snarled. "Come back to
gloat over my brother's broken body—"

"No, Dan . . . no!"

"To show us Smiths that you Mennonites are too
good for us!"

A sob caught in her throat. "Dan—Sammy is dead,"
she said dully.

He stared at her unbelievingly, pushed her aside
roughly, and swaggered into the house.

She steadied herself as stormy, turbulent tears
streamed from her eyes, and she made her way across
the mud-spattered yard to escape the horror of the
moment.

"John—oh, John—" she wept as she stumbled down
the long muddy lane. And as if in answer to an un-
voiced prayer she heard the rumbling of his buggy
toward her.

10

John and Hannah moved into a small, two-room farmhouse in the middle of a field, five miles away from her parents. On either side of the house fields stretched away into brown infinity, hovered over only by a small henhouse and a tumbledown barn.

The house smelled dusty and tired and moldy, as if it had been shut up for a long time. Its "front room" boasted of two windows and the only door to the outside. Its walls were dull gray, and the bare board flooring scrubbed white. A small, sturdy square table, covered with a brand-new red-and-white checked oilcloth, stood against the north window. In the center squatted a valiantly polished "monkey stove," with two black-lidded holes, its oven built partly into the chimney. In the corner cupboard Hannah set the white pottery dishes with the brown rims and clover leaf designs in the center; the blue Wedgewood plate from Emma; and the green painted pitcher with the fluted edge. The opalescent hen bowl from Maggie she placed carefully on the top shelf.

The small bedroom contained a high, maple head-board bed and marble-topped dresser. On the two square-paned windows Hannah hung fragile, creamy lace curtains which Mahm had dug out of the old trunk in the attic at home. She hammered a nail into the murky brown south wall, and hung the sampler she'd painstakingly cross-stitched in the past months. It read simply:

Befiel dem Herrn deine Wege, und Hoffe auf Ihn— "Commit thy way unto the Lord; trust also in Him. . . ."

In the opposite corner loomed the big chest that Pa had built for her. On it she laid the velvet-covered photograph album. The newest picture in it was of Albert standing in a chair, wearing a long, lacy white dress. Their wedding portrait would fill the next page.

As she paged pensively through the album, John tiptoed into the room. "What are you doing, Hannah? Already homesick?" he teased, the cleft in his chin dimpling.

Hannah started, then closed the album and laid it back onto the chest. "*Na*, John! Am I a baby to cry for Mahm so soon?"

He took her by the shoulders and gazed at her intently. "I wasn't so sure when you came from Smiths crying the other day! Was it all so bad?"

"Bad?" she echoed gravely. "Oh, John, you've no idea! Sammy lying in death—and then this—this *shlutty* woman—their cousin Irene, talking mean to me. John, how could she talk like that anyway?"

"I have always said the Smiths were no good. Maggie and Sammy didn't do so much to show it. But that Dan!"

Hannah dropped her gaze. To think I once imagined myself in love with him!

She smiled wanly. "I am so glad that Sammy is with Jesus. I wish our church could have had the funeral for him. But the Smiths aren't Mennonites. So it couldn't be."

"That's the way it is," John said firmly, releasing his hold on her and turning toward the kitchen. "It's better we have nothing to do with that kind. They never would fit in anyhow."

Hannah walked slowly across the room and placed her hand on the doorjamb. "But why couldn't they fit in, John? Someday, if they believe on the Lord and want to be baptized and join our church—"

"The Smiths Mennonites?" John laughed harshly as he stoked the monkey stove. It belched angrily as though that closed the subject. "*Ach*, this stove. Someday, Hannah, I'll buy you a better stove. I promise!"

Hannah was busy as the weeks and months sped by, with cooking and baking, gardening, and caring for her brood of baby chicks.

John, sweating in the wheat fields astride the tottering Minne binder, came home tired and grimy at night. It was only after Hannah plied him with fried ham and gravy, fresh bread, and crusty mulberry pie that he dragged himself into the tiny bedroom for a few hours' sleep.

84

One particularly hot, humid day which John had spent helping Hannah's older brother Isaac with wheat "bindering," he came home and dropped wearily onto the front stoop and sighed.

"I think you'd better go help Isaac's Marta tomorrow, Hannah," he said after she had seated herself beside him. "She doesn't look so good. Her time is almost up, Isaac says. But her folks aren't around to help out. Little Gerhard isn't well either."

Hannah glanced at John shyly. "Should I maybe bring little Gerhard here? You would like a—a child in the house like Gerhard?"

John stroked his cleft chin thoughtfully. "If you want to. Someday we want lots of children, Hannah. But now we must help Isaac out."

Kind, thoughtful John. She stared tenderly at his tired, stubbled chin under the quiet stars and smiled wistfully. Someday she would give John the children he wanted.

Early the next morning, after John was off to help Isaac with the rest of the cutting, Hannah went into the kitchen and finished the breakfast dishes, hanging up the tea towel on the line behind the house. Then she got out a panful of apples from the damp cellar and began to peel them for an apple roll. The spicy aroma filled the small kitchen with its tangy fragrance. After she set the pan into the oven the heat from the monkey stove pressed around her temples and wrung the sweat from her face. She closed off the tiny bedroom to keep it cool for the night.

Slipping off her apron, Hannah jammed a blue slat bonnet onto her braided hair. Wrapping the still-warm apple roll into a fresh tea towel, she hurried out and caught Nell, the brown mare, and hitched her to the buggy. Then she drove lightly toward Isaac's small, neatly kept farm four miles down the road.

She hoped Marta would be feeling better today. If she offered to take little Gerhard with her, it should help Marta considerably. She'd leave the apple roll with Marta for afternoon lunch.

When Hannah arrived, Marta was bending over the washtub in the kitchen, rubbing aimlessly at one of Isaac's gray shirts on the board. The swish-swish of the clean-smelling lye soap punctuated the quiet kitchen like the ticking of the kitchen clock.

"Here, let me do that, Marta," Hannah said, edging her sister-in-law gently aside.

Marta looked up, her face gray and haggard. "I—just —can't seem to—get all my work done," she said wearily. "And Gerhard sick—"

Hannah scrubbed at the threadbare collar effortlessly. "What seems to be the matter with little Gerhard?"

"I don't know. He has—the fever. . . ."

"You go lie down, Marta, and let me finish your wash," Hannah said briskly, picking up a pair of Gerhard's brown, homemade trousers. "Then I'll cook the dinner for the men. After that, I'll take Gerhard home with me so you can rest better."

"But—"

"No, I mean it, Marta!" Hannah said staunchly, straightening up for a moment and looking at the Seth Thomas clock, which ticked ponderously on the shelf. Its slow beating heart sounded ominous in the hot, steamy kitchen. Time for rinsing and starching, and then it would be time to put potatoes on for dinner.

Gerhard drooped listlessly during the noon hour, and when Hannah tried to spoon a bit of chicken broth into his mouth he sputtered it all over his thin, blue shirt.

The boy really is sick, the frightening thought struck Hannah. But maybe if she put him to bed in the little south room at home he would sleep if off.

Mahm always put much stock in "sleeping off a sickness," especially if accompanied by a generous glassful of warm camomile tea.

After Hannah had finished the dinner dishes and hung the last of the wash on the line, she picked up the feverish little Gerhard and stole softly into the bedroom to look in on Marta. The woman on the bed opened her eyes dully.

"Now, you just rest easy, Marta. Let me take Gerhard home with me so you can have it easier. There is apple roll for lunch, and all you need to do is make coffee."

Marta sat up suddenly. "It was nice of you to come, Hannah. But I—I don't want you to take Gerhard. I want him with me."

"Well, you need to rest, Marta. I'll take good care of him, I promise!"

"After the baby comes, I'll feel better again," Marta smiled feebly. "*Ach*—" she reached over and touched Gerhard's hot, wizened face gently—"thank you for wanting to take care of my boy. Maybe that would be best anyhow."

"It's time I learn to take care of children," Hannah laughed shyly, "so that when I get some of my own I know how!"

The sun beat hot upon Hannah as she carried her burden to the buggy. She touched Nell lightly with the reins and the mare trotted easily down the road.

Gerhard, his face flushed and damp, lay limp and warm against Hannah's body. She pressed him closely to shield him from the brassy sunshine that filtered through the buggy's seamed top.

If only Gerhard were hers—and John's! They wanted a large family—wonderful, soft, sweet children. Like Gerhard. Hannah smiled wistfully at the thought of her dreaming.

She slowed down at the driveway and Nell sped toward the house.

Was Gerhard less feverish? The small body felt less damp, cool and limp against her.

Hannah glanced at the still features, and then her face whitened. Gerhard— Oh, God, no!

She dropped the reins and swayed dizzily as Nell trundled to an effortless stop before the kitchen door.

For a long time Hannah sat unseeing, clutching Gerhard's lifeless body to her breast. Gerhard—dead. *And I killed him—I insisted when Marta said no*—she whispered wordlessly—*I am not fit to be a mother— never—never—I killed Gerhard. . . .*

11

The century turned, and the years simmered past. Hannah, still plagued by the memory of the lifeless form in her arms that first summer of their marriage, hadn't been able to consider conceiving a child of her own. The thought had been reduced to a piteous crying within her.

Although many a chilly wind had moaned and warm spring rains had caressed the neat little mound in the cemetery, they had served only to withdraw her more and more to herself.

Now the rain drummed ceaselessly from the eaves, lashing against the small house, rattling the windows and bending the trees with the weight of their dampness.

Hannah stood moodily by the north window and looked out. She fingered the cretonne curtains absently, watching the dull clouds hang like ballooning gray blankets over the earth.

Suddenly the rain stopped, as though some unseen faucet had snapped shut. A light wind scurried through the trees, showering the imprisoned drops to the ground. The starting mists clutched at the treetops with long white fingers, catching the opal light which swept swiftly through the skies until the clouds in the east turned golden pink.

In the west, cloud was piled upon cloud like vast cathedrals built for worship to the throne of God.

John pushed himself away from the dinner table and came to stand behind her. He turned her sorrow-tinged face toward him, and chucked her chin into his palm.

"What you need is a child, Hannah," he said frankly. "We have been five years married now. I thought we wanted a big family."

She looked at him dismally. "Oh, John, I do—I did! But—how can I have a child of my own when I couldn't take care even of my brother's?"

He looked at her miserable face intently. "Hannah—Hannah, are you happy? Am I not making you happy? Or have you been sorry you married me? I sometimes thought—"

"No, John—I'm not sorry. I—just feel bad because I can't—"

"It wasn't your fault that little Gerhard died!" he said fiercely, his gray eyes clouding. "He was sick already when you decided to bring him home with you. Isaac knows that, and so does Marta. They have never felt bad toward you. Don't you know that?"

Yes, she knew. But still the blame nagged at her and made her unwilling to conceive. Was God punishing her for having insisted on taking the little sick boy away from his mother? She had asked herself the question a thousand times. Or had she gone on blindly, marrying John, when he might have wanted someone like—like Emma Peters?

What had Mahm said? "I always thought she liked your Johann Penner. It's good we got him first. . . ." *Sold. To the highest bidder. . . . But I didn't love John then. I thought it was Dan I loved. . . . Now I know better.* And hadn't John said he liked her? But she looked so nice as a bride—"People will say what a fine couple we are." People always love brides. . . .

John dropped his hands abruptly. "Let's go to town this afternoon, Hannah. We're doing fine with our farming, and next year we will be able to buy us a bigger farm. But I want to get you something now. How would you like—an organ, maybe?"

"An—" she echoed, speechlessly. "You mean—you want to buy me—an organ? But—but—"

He nodded, and the cleft in his chin dimpled. "With bellows and pedals and stops. I saw a good used *Shonringer* at Klassen's Furniture Store. Shall we go look at it?"

Hannah surveyed the tiny house with bewilderment. They would have to put it on the east wall of the small bedroom. But it might be nice to have a place on which to put the wedding pictures. And the tall red vase with the gold flowers John had given her for Christmas last year. She hoped the organ would be stylish so that there was a place to set coal oil lamps on carved round shelves. . . .

Dazed, she followed John meekly into the store an hour later. There it stood, dull mahogany, with its mirrored top and frescoed trim. The stops marched round and firm behind the ivory keys—*forte, dulciana 8', vox humana, diapason 8', flute 4'.* . . .

Hannah's breath quivered. "Oh, John, it's beautiful. . . ."

Still shaken, she left Klassen's and hurried down the boardwalk to pick up some thread at Cornelson's General Store.

Inside the dimness she moved toward the counter. "I want, please, some thread—white," she said with a catch in her voice.

"Jane P. Coats?" A mocking voice whispered in her ear. She whirled around and stared into the dark, arrogant face of Dan Smith, his mud-and-grime-streaked clothes emanating with the odor of stale tobacco.

"J 'n P Coats," she said stiffly, her face red. She started to move away.

He grabbed her arm roughly. "Well, well, well! So it's the little bride of—five years, is it? I thought Mennonites believed in being fruitful," he said with a derisive laugh. "But I see Henny's arms are still empty. Too bad. Don't tell me John's less of a man than wicked Dan Smith!" And he twisted himself around and swaggered out of the store.

Hannah stared after him, her fury mounting. So Dan thought she wasn't able to have children. I'll show him, she vowed firmly. The year was 1904—the "year of the organ"—and a child—if she could help it!

Visions of little Gerhard's lifeless form faded in the

months that followed. For Hannah, in her new determination to show Dan, joyfully paged through Mahm's Jones & Company catalog for baby things that fall. She still hated to sew, although Mahm and Sush wouldn't be denied the privilege of clothing the coming child.

Just before Christmas, Hannah presented John with a tiny brown-haired daughter, who was promptly named Alice.

"It's such a fancy name!" Hannah admitted shyly when Mahm questioned the wisdom of departing from the traditional Bible names.

Before the first of March, John and Hannah moved to the substantial farm just south of the church.

Hannah reveled in the roominess of the sturdy frame T-house, with its ample kitchen, the pleasant, bay-windowed dining room, a separate "parlor" for the organ and a set of used rockers and a settee, and a large airy bedroom. Plus three rooms upstairs.

One lazy May afternoon when the air was fragrant with budding lilacs and the sun leaned over the young corn, nestling in the rise and fall of the furrows in newly awakened rhythm, Hannah laid the baby gently in the yellow-painted cradle and stepped onto the porch of the parlor's east door.

The garden was drenched in midafternoon shade, with a small blue butterfly, silver dust on its wings, quivering over the clumps of dandelions that clung to a clod. Soft *thee-thee* bird notes twittered in the elms, and a light breeze lifted the new green leaves of the cotton-wood tree by the milkhouse, undersides gleaming.

A whinny on the driveway sent Hannah scurrying back into the kitchen to make sure it was tidied up.

Maggie Smith's drab, stooping figure hopped from the buggy and looped the reins around the hitching post.

Hannah, taking a fresh apron from the cupboard drawer, tied it firmly about her waist and waited at the door for Maggie.

"Hullo, Maggie," Hannah called out cheerfully, opening the screen door for the thin, colorless woman. "Come in! It has been such a long time since I've seen you. Can I do something for you?"

Maggie smiled feebly, standing hesitantly in the doorway. "I came to see your baby, Hannah. Sarah tells me it's the most beautiful thing she's ever seen. I wanted—to see—for myself."

Hannah beamed as she led Maggie toward the bedroom. "Sush almost eats that baby up! Well, she is getting married herself this summer—to Ben Hiebert. The one Emma Peters almost married. She's getting ahead of Abram and Hans even!"

Alice, her blue eyes wide, cooed as she kicked her fat little bootee-clad feet into restless gyrations in the cradle.

Stooping over, Hannah picked up the plump figure and straightened the long full skirt.

"See? Here she is. How do you like her, Maggie?"

For a moment Maggie's eyes filled with longing tears. "Oh, she's beautiful! She's—like a glass doll. And you have her so neat and clean—not dirty and filthy—like —like Irene's little Fidelia."

"Irene?"

Maggie laughed weakly. "Our light-haired cousin. Her baby's a few months older. Irene spent several weeks with us last February. But her baby isn't sweet, like your Alice. Irene is—well, she doesn't much care. The baby—smelled bad and she cried a lot. Maybe it was us. I don't know. Our home isn't—it's not pleasant. And you know Dan. Bitter and sullen and lazy. And how he drinks! When he gets drunk he's awful. . . . Keep away from Dan when he drinks, Hannah!"

The words dug sharply into Hannah's peaceful world and she glanced forlornly at Maggie. *Keep away from Dan.* . . . Then, with an effort at cheerfulness she laid the baby in Maggie's arms.

"Here, you hold Alice while I fix us some coffee and fresh bread with butter. Come, sit here in the rocking chair by the window while I go to the kitchen."

It amused Hannah to see how Maggie carried Alice —like a fragile glass doll. *Careful, like I handle the opalescent hen bowl.* . . .

The two women chatted long over their coffee cups while Alice dozed and the afternoon waned.

Suddenly Maggie rose to her feet. "Look at the time! It's been so nice with you, Hannah. I can't tell you how much I've enjoyed it. But I must hurry home."

"You'll come again, Maggie?" Hannah asked, filled with a passionate pity for the drab, colorless figure. She had carried the baby back to the cradle, with Maggie like a faithful puppy at her heels.

Maggie's thin lips worked back and forth. "May I?" she asked shyly.

"Yes. I want you to."

A gracious, adoring look swept over the faded eyes. "I'll come. And thank you."

With that, Maggie hurried out of the house and untied her horse. Hannah stood in the doorway and watched her leave.

When the clopping of the hooves and the clatter of buggy wheels had died away, she knew that her life would be long entwined with that of the Smiths!

12

Ruby and Henry followed Alice into the cradle in rapid succession, and Hannah's hands found no time for idleness.

Alice, shy with curly brown hair and gray eyes, had apparently inherited Sush's dutiful nature. She would rock baby Henry in the old yellow cradle by the hour while dark-haired, impetuous Ruby was quick to ferret out Hannah's hoarded treasures.

"Ruby, you leave Mamma's glass dishes alone!" Hannah scolded, taking away the Sunday best sauce shells from Ruby's damp fists. "Why can't you behave nice like Alice?"

Or she'd get into the button box and spill all the varicolored buttons onto the new rose-sprigged dining room linoleum. And Hannah would have to lower herself to her knees and scoop them up. Finally, at the first clatter of the cascading contents, Alice in her calm motherliness would leave the cradle and squat down on the floor and pick them up, one by one.

Once Ruby had even discovered the opalescent hen bowl, the precious gift from Maggie. It had almost slid from the childish grasp when Hannah had come upon her unexpectedly. She'd had to find a safer place for it. Hannah almost despaired of keeping order.

"How will I ever bring up my children if they act so *schlunsig?*" she wailed often.

When Alice marched off to school that first fall, Hannah felt as though she had lost her right arm. Ruby and her impetuosity managed to steer Henry into continual scrapes. "Ruby . . .! Henry . . .!" It seemed her shouts were constant and more shrill than ever, and Hannah wondered if things would ever change.

Henry, unlike Ruby, throbbed with quietness, like his father. His dark blond hair and blue eyes decreed him "a genuine Penner," as Mahm would say. "He always is so still."

And that "quiet Penner," his lean shoulders slightly stooped under the heavy field work, was forced to deal with the youngsters' frequent escapades.

Alice, a sturdy seven, preferred peeling potatoes and chopping up cabbage for *borscht* after school to doing her arithmetic sums.

"Why don't you work at your schoolwork, child? Your teacher says you don't read so good."

Alice, her blue eyes teary, shrugged her plump shoulders. "But it's so hard, Mamma! The words don't come right. I guess I wasn't meant to go to school."

"Alice is just hard learning," Hannah told John later. "We can't push her."

Later Hannah wondered if Alice's lack of interest in academic things was what prompted John to consent to serve on the school board.

He was no less concerned with the work of the church. "I wish we'd elect a few more deacons. Brother Leppke and Brother Foth are having it too hard. Planning everything for the festivals shouldn't fall on just two men."

Maggie, on one of her rare visits to Hannah who was canning May cherries, beamed with interest.

"I can't see how your husband can do so much, Hannah!" she said, pulling up a chair in Hannah's kitchen and picking up a panful of the pale pink cherries. She began to snap off the stems briskly. "I hear he helped Reimers cut alfalfa the other day. Of course, Mr. Reimer isn't well."

"Reimer has cancer, they say, and he can't do the work alone. Someone had to help," Hannah said casually, putting a kettleful of cherries on the new Home Comfort range to cook.

"But John has enough work of his own, doesn't he?"

Hannah laughed. "John isn't happy unless he is busy. I guess he will always be that way."

"I see," Maggie said soberly, nodding her wispy head. "No wonder your place always looks so—so neat. I wish—well, my father's got that bad leg, and he can't do much . . ." her voice trailed off lamely.

"And—and Dan?" Hannah asked quietly, politely, one eye on the cherries bubbling on the stove and the other on Ruby who was sneaking undetermined handfuls of cherries from the pail beside Maggie.

"Dan—" Maggie sighed, and her colorless voice quivered. "Dan's a lazy lout. Don't know what he does—or where he goes. But he's gone so much— and the cornfields and yard are full of bindweed. . . ."

Hannah pushed the kettleful of cherries to the back of the stove, remembering how Pa would always sweep his hayrack after threshing the Smith wheat, making certain none of the bindweed would escape to the Kliewer farm by mistake.

"Well, these are done. I'll be saving a bucketful back for—Ruby, you keep your hands out of those cherries! You've had enough now. Go on and play! Enough back for the feast next week. My, how that child gobbles the cherries up! She's a regular pig!"

"She's a pretty child, Hannah. Those dark blue eyes—"

"Ruby?" Hannah laughed. "Her face is too narrow and her nose too long to look purty. She looks like John, don't you think?"

Nodding, Maggie got up, set down the panful of stemmed cherries, and wiped her thin hands carefully on Hannah's old apron that all but drowned her slight figure.

"Well, that finishes these cherries. Ruby will break men's hearts someday!" Maggie said with a short laugh. "John was never that way, was he?"

No, John wasn't, Hannah thought. Plain, steady, easy-going John. None of the girls had ever really fallen for him. Except Emma Peters. . . . "Ruby isn't a bit like John," Hannah added pensively. "But I think she will do better in school than Alice. I guess you knew

Alice flunked the first grade? She's hard learning, Alice is."

Maggie arose. "Too bad. But she'll make someone a good wife. She's so motherly. I'd better be going now, Hannah," she said moving toward the door. Then she added hesitantly, "You're having a festival Sunday?"

"We'll find out for sure tonight," Hannah said, dipping the pale pink cherries into the hot, clean jars. "We're having *Brodaschoft*—business meeting. Deacon election first and then we decide about the feast—or like you say it, festival. Missions in the morning and Sunday school convention in the afternoon. For dinner, cherry *moos* and ham. It will be a full day."

She was tired when evening came, for she was heavy with her fourth child now. But when she saw the rows and rows of freshly canned May cherries on the kitchen table, she breathed a satisfied sigh.

After John had left for church, Hannah washed the last of the sticky canning kettles and put the children to bed.

She dropped into the rocker by the bay window and closed her eyes. It had been pleasant having Maggie come over and lend a hand with the cherries; yet, somehow, seeing the drab, colorless woman never ceased to disturb her. Maggie's thin figure always looked hungry and unfed, and her pathetic eagerness to share Hannah's life was vaguely disquieting. She didn't know why. Maggie wanted desperately to belong someplace; yet there was no real niche for her in this strict Mennonite community.

When John came home from church shortly after

nine, Hannah stirred sleepily in her rocker. He looked so solemn Hannah wondered what his news might be.

Languidly she rose from her chair and walked heavily toward him. "Is anything the matter, John?"

He looked deeply into her eyes and said gravely, "Hannah—they elected me deacon tonight. I am a very human, ordinary person—to be God's servant! Hannah, why should they choose me? Will I be able to do my duty?"

"Oh, John—" she leaned her head against his shoulder and whispered tremulously, "John—you're always good and kind and generous. The people know that. Like helping Reimer with his alfalfa—and so many others you have helped too. No wonder they chose you. The Lord will help you."

He nodded and stroken his chin thoughtfully. "I guess you're right. But it's a big job—to make right decisions. . . ."

"You'll make it fine. Don't worry," she added, wiping her eyes and blowing her nose. *I'm not worthy of him. He's so good, so fine. . . .*

John moved toward the round oak dining table and picked up the well-worn Bible, leafing through it aimlessly. She set herself clumsily across from him and sighed.

"You look tired. Finish all your canning?" he asked.

She smiled wanly. "All done. If Maggie hadn't come to help— That reminds me, John. Have you decided which Sunday will be the mission-fest?"

"We're not having it on Sunday this year, Hannah."

"Not on Sunday!" she echoed. "But we always do! Why not Sunday?"

His forefinger traced the yellow leaf design on the oilcloth. "We're having it on Wednesday of next week. We're all farmers, and we can come. If we have it on Sunday, all the Englishers come just to eat. That's the only reason they come. They—"

"But John, are we going to shut the church doors to them?" she interruped quickly. "We can never win them to the Lord—"

"They would never become Mennonites anyway," he said decisively, "and if they don't learn German, they can't understand our services."

"What if we'd start having our preaching in English, John? Then they could—"

"Hannah!" John burst out in alarm. "You can't mean that! Why, that would never work!"

"Why wouldn't it?" she pursued stubbornly. "Why should we shut out people like Maggie Smith and—"

"The Smiths!" he scoffed. "Thieves—that's what they are! Didn't Jesus cleanse the temple of thieves? Didn't He? Right here, in Matthew, it says—" he paged through the Gospels.

Hannah winced. "What makes you so sure the Smiths are thieves, John Penner? Just what have they stolen? Tell me one thing!"

John looked at her without flinching, his finger on the Bible passage. "Hams. Reimers are missing two big hams from their smokehouse. Do you know of anybody else in the community who is hungry like the Smiths? Now, I don't mind you having Maggie come here, Hannah. But don't tell her everything—like how many hams we got, and when we butcher a beef, and what you've canned. Things like that."

"I don't believe it," Hannah said dully. "Maggie would never—"

"If she is hungry, she would," John said emphatically, looking down at the Bible and beginning to read aloud.

The fat kine and the lean—Hannah's thoughts weren't on the Scripture passage John was reading. Someday the lean kine would devour the fat. . . .

And when that time comes, dear Lord, do help me to be strong. . . .

13

Hot July days rushed upon Hannah, and with them the harvest. Hannah had struggled through the long, tedious hours of wheat cutting and shocking, miraculously keeping on her feet as the days dragged by.

Today it was "threshing day." Already the big steam engine had lumbered up the drive pulling the large separator behind it, and coming to a ponderous halt near the barnyard gate by the stock tank before it chugged off into the wheat field north of the barn.

Hannah's contribution to the busy day included cooking a huge dinner for thirteen hungry men, besides preparing substantial morning and afternoon "lunches."

Isaac's Marta had promised to help, only to call up early in the morning to tell Hannah that she'd sprained her ankle and couldn't be on her feet.

"But maybe Sush could help," Marta suggested timidly. "Or Liesbet?"

"Sush is helping Ben's mother today," Hannah said in a disconsolate voice. "And Liesbet is working elsewhere this week, Mahm said."

"How about Emma?"

"Emma Peters? Emma is working for some English people in Hilton."

Marta was silent for a moment. "Well, is there anyone else? I'm very sorry, but I stepped into the fence post hole. . . ."

"I'll think of someone," Hannah said tonelessly. "There is always Maggie—" and she hung up.

Maggie was delighted to come, she said, when Hannah called her. "I'll be there as soon as I can," she said wistfully.

In the meantime Hannah cut up five chickens for frying, and was in the midst of rolling out the pie crust when a shriek sounded from across the yard.

Dropping the rolling pin and wiping her floury hands on her apron, she hurried to the opened north window and peered out.

Hayracks still poured over the yard into the barn lot toward the wheat fields, creaking ominously as they rounded the bend.

Near the stock tank Alice was holding on to Ruby, who was straining and screaming to break away.

"I wanna go along!" Ruby shouted, yanking her hand away from Alice and starting after the men on the racks. Alice darted after her and pulled her sister back.

"No, you don't, Ruby!" she yelled. "Mamma said we

were s'posed to stay on the yard. I'll tell Mamma on you, if you don't mind!"

"Tattletale!"

Hannah sighed and returned to her pie crusts. She could trust Alice to watch impulsive Ruby and little Henry, but she wished Maggie would hurry and come to help. All the pies to be baked, the rolls iced, and the coffee to be made for the morning's lunch and she was tired already.

She bustled as fast as her bulky figure permitted, sugaring the apples she'd sliced into the crusts in the tin pans, and sprinkling a bit of cinnamon over the tops. She dotted them with butter and slitted the top crusts and spread them with deft, easy strokes.

"I hope the children behave," she told herself breathlessly, peering at the clock with one eye and out to the yard with the other. "That Ruby is such a lively one. . . ."

Just as Hannah almost despaired of receiving any help, she heard Maggie's buggy creak up the driveway. Maggie could fry the chickens and peel the potatoes, and if she had time she could also snap the beans—

She padded to the door in her bare feet, pushing back the damp hair that straggled into her face as she walked.

"Come in, Maggie," she called out diffidently. "I—"

Dan stood at the screen door, a twisted grin on his handsome, stubbled face. "I brought Maggie over," he said evenly. "She stopped to kiss your littlest one's toe."

"Henry?" Hannah smiled wryly. "I don't have time to mind my children this morning. There is much to do—"

"Can I help?" he asked guardedly.

"Oh—Maggie and I—can manage," she said weakly. "But—when is your threshing?"

He laughed shortly. "Don't have a threshing rig of my own, you know. Must wait until these—these thriving Mennonites ever finish theirs before they'll get around to mine. You ought to know!"

Hannah turned slowly, grateful that Maggie stepped into the screen porch at that moment and let herself in.

"Why don't you keep an eye on the children, Dan?" Maggie suggested as she tied a skimpy, mended apron over her faded brown dress.

Dan swung around without a word and swaggered across the yard, and Hannah and Maggie busied themselves in the kitchen.

Hannah shoved the last pie into the oven and thrust a paring knife into Maggie's hands.

"Here, you can start peeling those spuds in that pan. I'll fry the chickens and you can tend to them. It's almost lunchtime, and I have to fix the coffee. . . ."

Maggie looked up quickly from the potato she was scraping. "You're tired, Hannah. You look all in!"

"It's just—well, my baby is almost ready to come, and this is such a busy day. . . ."

"I'm sorry I couldn't get here sooner, but I had to wait until Dan had the chores done. He says he wants to use the buggy later."

Hannah's tension mounted. "Chores—at nine-thirty in the morning?" she flung out brusquely. Then, realizing her abruptness, she softened. "I'm sorry, Maggie. I know you couldn't help it—but I'm so—tired —already."

Poor Maggie, Hannah thought, dipping the chicken into the pie tin with flour and placing the pieces into the hot grease in the skillet. She can't help it if Dan is so exasperatingly slow and undependable. . . .

Milk . . . sugar . . . lemonade . . . the crusty rolls . . . coffee . . . twelve cups—Hannah checked off the items as she placed them into the large peach basket to be taken to the field. John would carry the food with him the next time he came in with a load of wheat to be shoveled into the granary.

The gray enameled range in the kitchen poured out waves of shimmering heat, coupled with the blistering breeze that pressed through the open doors and windows. Flies perched on the food, and on her hot, damp forehead. Her hair drooped listlessly, plastered against her head in sticky sweat.

She lugged the basket to the porch, hardly daring to lift it with her arms. If only this nightmare of a day were over and she could fling herself into bed!

Just then a wagonload of new wheat lumbered through the gate and creaked toward the granary. Hannah looked out to see if John was there, when she spied Dan and the children near the gate by the stock tank.

The odor of flying chaff and fresh straw surged through the humid morning and Hannah pressed her hand over her hot, flour-smudged face. If I can only hold out until tonight, she thought wearily, walking clumsily toward the granary. Her apron billowed over her heavy body like a tent at the county fair, and she tried to hurry. Mahm always warned her about being as inconspicuous as possible during her pregnancies—

especially if strange men were present. She must catch John so that he could take the lunch to the field.

He swung out of the granary just then, his straw hat pushed back from his grimy face. He waited until she reached him.

"Lunch is ready, John," she said simply. "It's waiting on the porch."

He took off the sweat-stained straw hat and ran his fingers through his thinning locks. "In a minute, Hannah, when we finish unloading. We're having a good harvest. The wheat was never better!"

Hannah nodded mechanically. "That's good. Well, I'd better hurry back. . . ."

"You look all in," he said suddenly. "Are you all right?"

"Oh, I'll be fine—after we get done with today!" She turned, and waddled slowly back toward the house. Now, to see if the potatoes were boiling and the beans stemmed and snapped.

She had barely reached the house when Alice burst in, crying bitterly.

"Mamma, Mamma! Henry—fell in—the tank. . . . He fell—"

Electrified, Hannah whirled around, and pushing Alice aside she propelled herself out of the door. Oh, dear Lord, don't let Henry—

Dan swaggered across the yard toward her, carrying Henry's limp, wet body in his arms.

"Henry—" Hannah's voice was a piteous groan as she flung herself trembling at her son.

Dan held her off with one hand. "I think the tad's going to be all right, Henny. He—was sitting on the gate. Then—wham! there he lay in the water. I got him out quick. He—Look, he's trying to open his eyes now!"

The damp-lidded eyes flickered and flew open, and he coughed slightly. A great wave of thankfulness swept over Hannah.

"Oh, Dan—Dan— Bring him in the house. Dan— If it hadn't been for you—oh, Dan—"

She followed him meekly as he carried the wet, sturdy little frame through the door and laid him on the big bed in the bedroom.

Kneeling clumsily at Henry's side, Hannah stroked the wet face gently, murmuring softly, "There, there, baby! You will purty soon be all right. . . ."

Alice stood white-faced at the opposite side of the bed, staring at little Henry, her childish lips shut tight and thin.

Weakly Hannah smiled at her. "Why don't you help Maggie set the table for dinner? The men are coming in soon, and I must change Henry."

Like a ghost, Alice moved toward the door, pausing to look back at Dan who stood in the center of the room. The look was almost one of terror, of hatred. Then she hurried out of the room.

Hannah noticed Alice's strange behavior only briefly, for the next few moments she was busily stripping off Henry's wet trousers and shirt, and dressing him in clean, dry garments.

He lay on the bed, looking at her silently. Then he shut his eyes sleepily.

"You must be tired, child," she said gently, forgetting her own weariness. "You go to sleep now, while I fix dinner for the threshers."

With a squeeze of his tiny damp hand, Hannah smiled and walked toward the door. Dan stood in the doorway, blocking her exit, his lips curling scornfully and his hands on his hips, glancing toward the dining room.

"Tad reminds me of—your husband, Henny. Doesn't have the fire your second one has! Say, that one's all *you*!"

With that he whisked around and strode abruptly out of the room and vanished out of the house.

Hannah felt a new awareness of Dan. He'd been kind—kind, not cruel. Dan had been kind. . . .

Still trembling, she splashed cold water over her face and speared the last of the chicken from the skillet. The men were already washing themselves in the washbasin on the little bench under the elms. She poured off the excess grease from the chicken fryings and dumped in enough flour to brown for the gravy.

The rest of the day went better. Somehow, Hannah felt fresh vigor after the ordeal she had just weathered, knowing that little Henry was alive—and that Dan had been there to save his life. The child was sleeping soundly and even the girls had agreed to a nap.

After the mountainous stacks of dishes had been washed and dried, Hannah dropped into the rocker by the window and motioned Maggie beside her. She picked up a newspaper and began to fan herself.

"Here, let's sit and rest a spell. This has been a hard day and I'm tired."

Maggie slid her thin figure effortlessly into one of the dining room chairs and sighed. "I'm tired, too. But the dinner was delicious, Hannah. Those men ate ravenously. You have such a big threshing crowd."

Hannah smiled wanly. "Ours is a company rig. Eight farmers belong to it. We take turns threshing, one day for each family first, and then the second round. It's a big machine and threshes fast."

"Can I help you again when the second round comes here? I'll try to come earlier!"

Hannah was about to answer when she felt a warning twinge in her abdomen. The baby? Coming now? But it couldn't! It—

She rose languidly to her feet. "Maybe, Maggie. I—I guess we'd better fix the lunch real quick. My—my baby—is going to come—soon, I think. . . ."

Automatically Hannah counted cups, measured out sugar for the lemonade, and tried to time the stabs of pain that came all too often now.

If only it wasn't threshing time! But she knew it had been the strain of all the work, the shock of Henry's accident. Maybe she should call Mahm right away. Mahm would know what to do.

Between packing up buns and tending the children, Hannah struggled through the next hour.

Alice was balky, which was strange for the usually placid, motherly child.

"I don't wanna stay at Groszmahm's," she wailed, after Hannah hunted out a clean percale frock for her. "Not until *she* goes!"

"Until—who goes?" Hannah ground out under her breath, clenching her teeth as the pain grew in intensity.

"M-Maggie."

Hannah stared stonily at her eldest. "What do you mean? What has Maggie—"

113

"Not Maggie. That—man Dan. He—"

The pain that knifed through Hannah sent her staggering into a chair.

The next hours were lost to Hannah. She remembered seeing Mahm's blurred face and that of Dr. Hoyle bending over her.

Alice's words, somewhere in the echoes, beat against her head—her spirits—like the surging of breakers against the rocks. . . .

"He pushed—Henry . . . into the water. . . . I saw him . . . I saw him . . . saw him. . . ."

Like a drifting fog the formless words enveloped her, and her hands went out before her, pushing . . . stumbling through the murky, moss-grown water of the stock tank. . . . And the lusty cry of her newborn child was lost in the throbbing of the words. . . .

14

"Now you're all ready, Ruby!"

Hannah patted the last dark braid into place as she kissed the newest first grader and shoved her gently toward the door.

Alice, her scrubbed round face ringed with brown curls, stood patiently on the screen porch. "Hurry, Ruby, or we'll be late for school."

In the doorway Hannah watched the two girls skip lightly down the driveway, now sparse with leaves of early fall coming down through lacing sunlight.

At the baby's demanding cry, Hannah hurried to the cradle. Tiny, beautiful Jenny, her light brown hair in a dark fuzz against the round firm head, kicked her sturdy legs impatiently. Undoubtedly, she was hungry. At seven weeks they knew exactly what they wanted.

Henry stirred sleepily from his crib in the corner. Then he sat up and blinked. "Ma-ma?"

"Yes, Henry?" Hannah went over to him and riffled his dark blond hair.

He squirmed, now fully awake. "I want eat. I hungry."

She picked him up and held him close, remembering how narrowly he had been spared to them the day Baby Jenny was born.

Alice had told her all about it later. "We were watching the wagons driving through the gate by the tank, you know, and Henry climbed on the gate. This man Dan—he came close by and—and he rocked Henry up and down, up and down, and Henry laughed. Then this man Dan laughed a horrible bad laugh and he—he just gave Henry a push. Henry slipped sideways and splashed into the water. This man Dan just stood and looked mean. When Henry didn't come up I pulled on his arm—and he looked like he hated me. Ruby—she pinched him hard and told him to pull Henry out or she'd scream. Then he grabbed into the water and dragged Henry out. . . ."

This man Dan . . . cruel, Peter had called him. Spiteful—sadistic—

Hannah hadn't wanted to mention it to John—or Maggie—or anyone. After all, it could have been an accident. Only, she didn't believe it was. She wondered if Dan had a decent bone in his body.

Now she sighed as she carried Henry into the kitchen and plopped him onto the high, backless stool.

"Oatmeal for you, child, and milk for Baby Sister!" she said brightly, gratefully, scooping up a bowlful of hot cereal and pouring a generous portion of cream over it.

Jenny's wails became hoarse with insistence. It was time she nuzzled her bottle.

I wonder how Ruby likes school, Hannah thought as she warmed the formula of cow's milk and brown syrup for the baby. The teacher was new this year—new and rather inexperienced. Miss Selma Bartel was a Mennonite teacher, one of the few qualified teachers in the area. She had had two years of normal school which had made her seem very well educated. Hannah hoped it would be enough to help the slow Alice.

Hannah dressed the two youngsters and made them comfortable and began to straighten up the house. There might be time to fix a peach cobbler before dinner, if she hurried. And of course, she'd have to remember to bake a batch of sugar cookies. With two school lunches to pack, a sugar cookie or two tucked on top of the homemade bread-with-syrup would be just right for recess snacking.

Mahm had been quite upset when Hannah had mentioned school lunches. "*Evoh!* You just live a few steps away from school, and you don't let them come home?"

"The children like to eat with the others. It does them good!" she'd said brightly, remembering her own times of sitting in the north ditch with Emma Peters and Lehn Toews, nibbling at corn bread and apples, spiced with happy laughter and chatter. Her own children would benefit from the social aspects that "eating together" gave a person.

The day passed by all too swiftly. Hannah missed Alice's motherly assistance with the little ones, and now it was four o'clock and the wash was still on the lines.

Just as she pulled on her shoes and began to pad

across the kitchen floor, the screen door burst open and Alice and Ruby rushed in.

The tin dinner pail clattered into the corner, followed by a couple of itinerant schoolbooks, as the girls scurried to Hannah's side.

"Mamma, Mamma," Ruby shrieked, her dark braids awry and her once-clean blue-checked dress rumpled and soiled. "Do we have to go to school tomorrow? Can't we stay home?"

Hannah paused, looking from Alice's miserable face to Ruby's defiant one. She caught her breath sharply. "Ruby—Alice—what's this? Your first day of school—"

"It's Fiddy," Alice tried to say it matter-of-factly, her plump features struggling for composure.

"F-Fiddy? What's Fiddy?"

"She's a new girl. A bad, mean girl!" Ruby burst out vehemently.

"Now, listen here, girls," Hannah came toward them with slow, deliberate steps. "We don't go around saying mean things about new scholars the very first day! How do you know—"

"Mamma," Alice interrupted tensely, "you don't know Fiddy. She—she pulled away Joey Klassen's chair so he sat flat on the floor. He—he was still hurting by the time school was out. She—"

"She hid Amy's dinner pail and wouldn't tell Amy where she put it," Ruby added grimly. "And she—"

"She threw ink on Elsie Ediger's new pink dress!" Alice took up the refrain.

Hannah eyed her daughters sternly. "Now, who is this—this terrible 'Fiddy' person you're talking about anyhow? We don't have anybody in this school district

118

by that name! Are you sure you're not making all this up?"

"Mamma!" Alice cried in a horrified tone. "Fiddy's —she has real dark, fuzzy hair, and she—she goes home east from the church. We—we don't have to go back tomorrow, do we?"

"You certainly do!" Hannah said firmly. "I'm 'shamed of you, carrying tales like that! Don't you let me hear another word out of you. You hear?"

Alice, her blue eyes tear-stained, nodded woodenly.

Ruby, her impetuosity unrequited, began to protest. "But Mamma—"

"I said no!"

Hannah marched outside with grim, measured tread. How ridiculous! Why should the girls make up things like that? No doubt, it was just another figment of Ruby's healthy imagination, because it just didn't make sense. No one in Plainfeld school did things like that. They just didn't. Swiftly she unpinned the diapers from the line and tossed them into the slatted peach basket.

Sobered and quiet, both Alice and Ruby had little to say at the supper table.

John tried to draw them out. "Well, how was school today? You're going to like it, Ruby, do you think?"

She shot Hannah a quick look and replied somberly. "I get to sit behind Leppkes' Linda. She couldn't even read the first word of 'Little Red Hen,' like I could. But Fiddy—" she broke off suddenly.

"Mamma, I think Miss Bartel is going to teach me real good," Alice said abruptly. "She—she is teaching us by sounds—you know, *r-eh-d   h'-eh-n* . . . like that."

The Little Red Hen had been the beginning of the girls' reading experience. Although Hannah heard no more of the mysterious "Fiddy" for days, she nevertheless found herself seated between her two first graders nightly, hearing their lessons from the stained-brown reader.

The story the girls seemed to enjoy the most was *Chicken Little*. Hannah sat between them under the yellow lamplight at the dining room table and heard them read. It was plain that energetic, impetuous little Ruby was going to surge ahead of plump, motherly Alice when it came to academics.

Ruby's dark head, bent over the tattered Winston Primer, soared away on wings of expression and imagination, in a detached, otherworldly way. The simple words took on new meaning for Hannah as Ruby read them.

> One day Chicken Little went for a walk.
> Something fell on her tail.
> "Oh, oh!" said Chicken Little,
> "The sky is falling!
> I will go and tell the king."

> On the way she met Henny Penny.
> Henny Penny said,
> "Where are you going, Chicken Little?"
> Chicken Little said,
> "Oh, Henny Penny,
> The sky is falling!
> I am going to tell the king."

> "Who told you?"
> asked Henny Penny.

Later, as Hannah lay in bed, willing sleep to come but not finding it, the words swirled through her head. The night seemed full of words. *The sky is falling . . . I must tell the King . . . the sky is falling . . . falling . . . with sudden wings, shrilling . . . cows lowing . . . the lean kine devouring the fat. . . .*

It wasn't until one day when Ruby came home lethargically from school with a black bruise on her forehead that Hannah sensed something amiss. She took the child to task immediately.

"What's the matter with you, Ruby? Did you have a fall? That bump—"

Ruby drooped into a chair and shook her head dully. "No, I—didn't fall. . . ."

Hannah looked quickly at Alice, who turned away abruptly and ran toward the cradle to play with Jenny.

"What's the matter?" Hannah demanded, pulling Ruby toward her not ungently.

Ruby's lips quivered. "Mamma—"

"Come on. Tell me. You didn't have a fight, did you?"

"N-no, Mamma," Ruby said, tears trickling down the narrow face. "It's just that F-Fid—"

Hannah dropped her hands in exasperation. "Not that again! I thought I told you to forget about that Fiddy-business!"

She turned and walked deliberately into the kitchen and began with supper. Sausages and noodles were good fillers, and Ruby loved them. Maybe she'd get over acting so mysterious about the mythical "Fiddy." If there was anything Hannah couldn't stand—

"Mamma," a tearful voice called from the dining

room. "Teacher's coming up the walk. She'll want to see Papa."

Wiping her hands on the towel hanging on a nail by the kitchen door, Hannah smoothed out her apron and hurried into the dining room just as the hesitant knock sounded on the screen door.

Miss Selma Bartel stood in the doorway facing her, the broad face resolute but weary with only a faint trace of tears in the clear gray eyes.

"Come in, Miss Bartel," Hannah said graciously, opening the door and ushering the teacher into the dining room.

She motioned the teacher to the rocker. "Sit down and rest a while. You look tired. Have a hard day?"

Miss Bartel looked about swiftly, and seeing only the distraught Ruby slumped in a chair, cleared her throat.

"I suppose Ruby and Alice have told you what happened in school today," she began gravely.

"To tell the truth, Miss Bartel, they have not. I have tried to find out but all I get out of them is gibberish!"

Ruby stirred listlessly in her chair. "But you wouldn't listen, Mamma, when I wanted to tell you! You said—"

"Let Miss Bartel tell it, Ruby!" Hannah interrupted tartly. "It's why she came, I guess."

"Yes, that's why I—came," the teacher replied wearily. "I suppose they have mentioned Fidelia Gibbons and her—her escapades. She has been making a shambles of school this year, especially in the lower grades. Frankly, Mrs. Penner, I—I'm at my wit's end. . . ."

Hannah caught her breath sharply. Fiddy—Fiddy—Fidelia—that name. Where had she heard the name before? Maggie's flat, colorless voice. *Your baby is neat and clean—not dirty and filthy like Irene's little Fidelia. . . .* "She goes home east from the church"—Alice had said. So this—this "unholy terror" was the Smiths' cousin Irene's daughter! Hannah's spirit groaned, remembering her meeting with the brassy Irene years before when Sammy died.

She breathed slowly. "I see. What—what happened in school today?"

The teacher rocked gently before answering.

"Fidelia—hit Ruby with a rock. Deliberately."

"But why?"

"Why?" Miss Bartel shrugged her broad shoulders. "Fidelia doesn't need an excuse for anything she does!"

"You've whipped her?"

"Oh, I've tried," Miss Bartel said with a wry smile. "But she bites—and kicks. She—"

Hannah noticed the teeth marks on the teacher's left arm. "I see. Well, you leave it up to me. John's on the board. He'll go to Smiths tonight and have it out with them. Don't worry, Miss Bartel. I'm very glad you came."

After the befuddled teacher had left, Hannah took Ruby into the kitchen and bathed the lump on her forehead with cold water, her mind in a whirl. Why couldn't she have guessed something was going on? The girls' reluctance to go to school, which she had attributed to Ruby's overactive imagination; their hesitance to talk about it, after she'd told them to forget all about the mythical "Fiddy."

Ruby began having hysterics almost as soon as John left for the Smiths that night. Hannah had all she could do to calm the child.

"Don't let them hurt Papa!" Ruby shrieked as she lay fully clothed on the trundle bed. "That man Dan is awful mean! He will hurt Papa, like he tried to hurt Hen—"

"Sh-sh-sh!" Hannah's own fears were aroused, but she mustn't let on. "No, Ruby. Your father can take care of himself. Just—just lie down and let me take your shoes and stockings off. It's time you went to bed anyhow."

After a bitter struggle when the girls had finally given in and gone to sleep, Hannah dropped languidly into the rocker and waited for John.

When he came home an hour later, he looked haggard and spent. She arose and went toward him, laying an arm on his shoulder and pushing him gently into the rocker she had just vacated. Then she drew up a chair and folded her hands on her lap and waited for him to speak.

Silent and tense, he stared straight ahead, avoiding her probing gaze.

"John?" she ventured with a tightness in her throat. "What happened?"

He shook his head laggardly. "It didn't do a bit of good to talk to them! Dan—he got terrible mad and said the Mennonites just have it in for them. This cousin Irene, the child's mother, was the hardest thing I have seen in my life. Her language was as bad as his—how they can swear! They claim the children drive Fidelia into being bad. Only Maggie showed some sense. When she tried to tell me differently, this Irene slapped Maggie's face and Maggie ran crying from the room."

"Poor Maggie!" Hannah whispered. "But what did you accomplish?"

John's lean face hardened for a minute. "Nothing. Fidelia has as much right in school as anyone else, as long as she lives in the district."

"And that was all?"

He shook his head savagely and drew his hands over his face. He got up and started toward the bedroom. His voice drifted to her from over his shoulder.

"No, Hannah— Please tell me—you didn't, did you?"

Fear pounded in her heart and she felt its brassy taste in her mouth. "I didn't what, John?" she choked in a small voice.

John paused and moistened his lips. "Dan said—you married me—only because your folks made you. That you loved him—and always had! I wondered why you so suddenly said yes!"

Hannah stumbled toward her husband and tried to throw her arms around him. "I didn't love Dan! John, I tell you—I—never did!"

He held her off and stared at her hard for a moment. Then he said brokenly, "Now I'll never know what to believe!"

She watched him go, a terrible feeling of uneasiness surging through her. *The lean kine had begun to devour the fat!*

15

All night long Hannah lay in bed beside John, listening to the moaning of the late October wind through the leafless trees. Her heart was sore and bleeding; as though calloused feet had trampled upon it and battered it to a pulp. John—good, steady, dependable John, doubting her love! Yet, how could he know otherwise?

She remembered their wedding night, and how all the dross and doubts had burned out of her soul and her love for John had emerged. She would tell him about it in the morning, she told herself staunchly. She would tell him everything.

But when the gray ribbons of morning unfurled, Ruby raged with fever and Hannah had no time to think of her personal problems.

Dropping Alice off at school and leaving Henry and Baby Jenny with her parents, Hannah and John took Ruby to see Dr. Hoyle.

After a thorough examination the doctor shook his head. "I'm afraid she's had a slight concussion. She'll have to stay in the hospital where we can watch her and where I can check her more thoroughly."

"Hospital? But only really sick people go to the hospital!" Hannah said dully.

Hannah stayed with Ruby in the small, antiseptically white room while John drove home.

Ruby lay back against the pillows of her hospital bed, her eyes closed. The dark braids dropped over the narrow face and Hannah pushed them away gently. She stroked the pale forehead which was partially bandaged, and a shudder gripped her.

To think that a mere child—a wanton, reckless child —could cause such distress!

Marrying John had not freed her altogether of Dan, she grimaced. Dan's inconsistencies, his sadistic reasoning, had dogged her all through the years of her marriage. And now, this little Fidelia, daughter of his slatternly cousin, had carbon-copied the warfare.

"Where will it end, dear Lord?" she whispered tremulously, her heart constricting with fear. "Where will it ever end?"

"Mamma?"

Hannah reached for Ruby's thin white hand and pressed it gently. "Right here, Ruby."

The eyelids fluttered and a faint smile touched the thin lips. "Mamma—why didn't—God take care of me? Why did He let Fiddy hit me? Fiddy doesn't—go to church, like we do. She—"

"Why—" Hannah groped for words. How can one tell a child that time and chance happen alike to all? "Why?

Maybe—maybe He wants us to show love to—to Fiddy, even if she is mean. Like Jesus did. Remember how the people spit on Him, and nailed Him on the cross? Still, He loved them."

"But I hate Fiddy!" Ruby spat out vehemently. "She —she's mean! She—" the child tried to raise herself.

"Please! Ruby, you mustn't get upset. Lie back now. That's fine. Now, you listen to me. We must love our enemies. That's what—"

"That's what the Mennonites say! Fiddy says we are just—just cowards when we don't fight back. She—"

Hannah shook her head steadily. "No, Ruby. If we love Jesus, we will love those who hate us. The Bible tells us that."

"But—" Tears blurred Ruby's deep blue eyes. "But I don't wanna love Fiddy. She—"

"It's because we don't love Jesus that we can't love Fiddy. God says, 'Without Me, you can do nothing.' And if we don't love Jesus, we will get hateful too."

Ruby lay silent for several minutes and stared at the fine cracks in the ceiling. Then she turned imploringly to Hannah.

"Mamma, I wanna love Jesus. Maybe then I'll love Fiddy too. Would you show me how I can learn to love her?"

Hannah fought for breath. Ruby's so young, she thought. She is only six, and she can't possibly understand what it means to commit one's life to Christ. But if I don't tell her now when she wants to know—Help me, dear Lord.

She picked up the thin white hand and squeezed it gently. "Just ask Jesus to come and live inside of your heart. Ask Him to put His love in you, because you remember how the Bible says, 'For God so loved the world, that he gave his only begotten Son, that whosoever believeth in him should not perish. . . . ' Can you understand, Ruby?"

The narrow face nodded perceptibly. "It's like He's saying, if you love God with His kind of love, everything's going to be all right."

Hannah's eyes filled with glad tears. Ruby had understood. *Everything is going to be all right*—with Ruby and God; with herself and John; with the Smiths—She had to believe that someday it would.

When Dr. Hoyle's quick stride sounded down the corridor, Hannah looked anxiously toward the door. She tacked a smile onto her lips when he entered Ruby's room.

"Well, how's my favorite patient this morning?" he asked pleasantly, flipping his stethoscope on the flat little chest and listening intently. "Looks like you're doing fine. Saturday we'll let you go home. How's that?"

Ruby's eyes searched Hannah's and she grinned impishly. "I like that! I think nobody else in Plainfeld school has been in a hospital. Nobody in the first grade, f'sure."

Dr. Hoyle chortled. "You'll be a celebrity, all right. But don't let anyone hit you on your head again. Next time you might not get off so easily."

Ruby smiled wanly. "I'm gonna love Fiddy, even if she's bad. I hope she never gets wicked as that—that man Dan. He's too bad for God to forgive, I betcha."

Hannah's hand flew to her throat. *Have I let my children believe that? Has he the right to terrorize us*

129

all? Now, even John believes there was something be-
tween us. . . .

Hannah's resolve to tell John everything was driven aside by the busy days that followed Ruby's return from the hospital.

Motherly little Alice began to wait on Ruby hand and foot, letting her play with "Bena-dolly," the long-legged, cotton-torsoed "best doll," a privilege clumsy Ruby hadn't dared indulge in before.

The impressive square of bandage on Ruby's forehead was a real badge of honor, and Hannah laughed to herself as she noticed even young Henry fingering it solemnly.

"They's nobody of us got such nice-smelly salve on our heads!" he wailed after he'd caught a whiff of the pharmaceutical medication. "Why do we use goose grease on our sores, Mamma? Why can't we use real doctor-salve?"

Mahm and Pa, over on a Sunday afternoon visit, weren't quite as impressed.

"Doctor-salve costs money, Henry," Pa said tersely, his gray beard bristling. "We have goose grease for nothing! I still can't see why the doctor had to keep Ruby in the hospital. She had no surgery. Lay in bed she could have done just as well at home."

Alice, off in one corner of the dining room, was carefully pressing Bena-dolly's pink ruffled dress with a toy iron. She glanced up pensively.

"We got some nice-smelly salve from the medicine peddler once. It burns."

"Men-t'lati-um," Mahm said absently. "It stings. It isn't as good for wasp stings as soda. It's—Alice, don't

130

you know it's sin to iron on the Sabbath?" she reprimanded sternly.

Alice looked up in bewilderment. Ruby, picking up the doll from its tiny cradle in the corner, and rocking it gently in her arms, laughed boisterously.

"Now, Groszmahm, don't you think God knows this little iron isn't hot?"

"Ruby!"

Hannah glanced firmly in Ruby's direction. That child's impetuosity would get her into real trouble someday. It was time she learned to respect her elders.

Alice promptly thrust the little iron back into the toy box with a quivering sigh. Then she laid the dress carefully into Ruby's lap and hurried into the kitchen.

Hannah arose slowly and started after her. It was time to put the coffeepot on for *faspa,* as they called Sunday afternoon lunch. As she opened the kitchen door, she heard Alice's muffled sobs from behind the pantry door.

"Alice?"

The sniffling stopped, and one teary blue eye peeped through the crack.

"Alice, come here," Hannah commanded gently. "You can help me fix *faspa.* Run down to the cellar and bring up a jar of peaches. Then you can put the zwiebacks on this big plate. . . ."

Sensitive Alice blew her nose noisily behind the pantry door and marched out importantly to bring up the fruit.

Ruby soon caught up with Alice in reading again, and by now, according to the evening sessions with the

Winston Primer, Chicken Little had caught up with Foxy-Loxy.

"You know who makes me think of Foxy-Loxy?" Alice ventured one evening after the two girls had gone over their lesson twice.

Hannah, bending over her mending in the yellow lamplight, smiled. "Who?"

"Fiddy. She's just as sneaky and mean and—"

"But we're s'posed to love Fiddy!" Ruby interrupted quickly. "The Bible says so. Doesn't it, Mamma?"

"But—but—" Alice sputtered. "Fiddy shoved you out of line yesterday at recess, and she 'rased off all Teacher's words on the blackboard."

Fiddy . . . Fiddy. Hannah shook her head helplessly. Would they ever be relieved of the slatternly child? And would she ever understand her two oldest? Sensible, motherly Alice, and bold, unpredictable Ruby. How could two sisters be so different?

Winter swooped down on them with a spell of biting cold weather. As Hannah entered the kitchen one morning, there was ice in the water bucket. She blew upon her fingers before she shook the grate in the gray enameled cookstove, and threw in a few cobs soaked in kerosene. Then she lit a match, and after the fire began to burn briskly she placed the thin pieces of hedge-wood atop the flames and felt warmth seep into the frigid corners of the kitchen. Coffee . . . oatmeal . . . school lunches—

The girls were deep in Christmas secrets, divulging little of the school program activities. Alice begged for a tablecloth for the "play" she was in; and Ruby dredged in mystery as she hunted through old boxes upstairs for a long dress—"for the mother in 'The Pink Scarf,'" she admitted reluctantly.

"What about the pink scarf?" Hannah asked curiously. "I have that old shawl I got years ago which you could—"

"Oh, we're making them out of pink outing flannel," Ruby stated blandly.

"Them?" Hannah echoed, caught up in their whirl of excitement. "You mean, there is more than one scarf?"

Alice leaned over and whispered, "Well, this girl—that's Ruby, see?—she wants a pink scarf for Christmas. So everyone gives her a pink scarf. Fiddy is the mother—if she'll do it. That's why Ruby wants the long dress."

Trust Ruby to be generous toward her erstwhile enemy, Hannah thought trimly. This was a sign of her change of heart.

The Penners arrived early at the schoolhouse on Friday evening for the program so that John could light the two gas lamps dangling grotesquely from the streamered ceiling. As they entered, the smell of pine mingling with the acrid odor of coal fire in the large heater and the tangy odor of apples in a basket rushed out to greet them.

Alice and Ruby scurried with their mysterious packages toward the popcorn-cranberry-strung tree, and moved importantly behind stage. Ruby, her green wool dress with its Peter Pan collar banded in tan braid, looked like a wood nymph, proudly nonchalant; while Alice, her embroidered blue serge setting off her brown curls like a frame about the plump face, was the picture of little girlhood.

The teacher came forward and the murmurings and buzzing of voices from the crowd ceased.

Alice and Ruby, standing primly timid and important, sang lustily with the other girls.

> "In a low manger bed, lay a Baby asleep;
> In the heavens bent above Him, angels close
> watch did keep;
> Holy Christ-Child, divine. . . ."

Another Christmas of yesterday nagged at Hannah's memory as she pushed it back warily. "I love you, little manger Baby. . . ."

Just before "The Pink Scarf" was to be dramatized, Miss Selma Bartel stood before the crowd apologetically.

"I'm sorry to tell you," she began, and Hannah caught the relieved tone of her voice, "that one of our characters has up and gone. Fidelia Gibbons, who was to have played the part of the mother in our play, left this afternoon for her home in Kansas City. . . ."

A general sigh of relief swept over the room, and Hannah found herself smiling without effort now. With Fiddy gone, school would be a happier place for everyone. As if it would close a chapter in her life. Or, if not close, it would undoubtedly postpone the unpleasantness which might follow.

Her smile crinkled the corners of her eyes as she turned to John. He looked at her intently, then grinned back at her.

PART TWO

16

Cold rain sluiced down from soggy skies and beat relentlessly against the windowpanes as fresh-budding lilac twigs tapped rhythmically on the sill.

Hannah stood at the window of the doctor's waiting room and peered out at the dreary landscape. Puddles of dirty water on the street threw back the dismal reflection of passing motorcars and buggies. People walking down the wet streets seemed isolated by the small worlds of their umbrellas, while lighted street lamps wavered through the driving rain.

Her thoughts gyrated around the complexities that had enveloped the family during the past years. It was 1918. The United States had entered the World War the year before, and had conscripted Hannah's baby brother Albert with it.

Albert, twenty-two years old, had with some indecision gone into noncombatant service. The fact that Mennonites did not believe in killing coupled with the strong feeling against German-speaking people had made the Mennonite community of Plainfeld most unpopular with the patriotic masses.

"When you go in public," John had warned the family sternly, "be sure to speak English. Anybody speaking German—or even Low German—is looking for trouble."

Pa had disagreed violently, his gray beard wobbling. "But what does it matter what we talk, as long as we are loyal to our country? I can't speak English so well. If I want to talk everything in German, I will!"

"How will people know on whose side you are, if you keep on *brummeling* the German?" John had persisted.

"I am a naturalized American citizen!" Pa had declared vehemently.

But it wasn't enough, especially since the Mennonites believed in nonresistance. Albert was now languishing at Camp Funston, cleaning out filthy tents and doing KP for the regulars.

The outer door to the waiting room opened and Hannah felt a breath of cold, damp air against her ankles. She turned.

The stubbled, sallow-faced dirty-wet figure of Dan Smith swaggered into the room. Hannah's fists clenched involuntarily.

"Well!" the mocking voice greeted her harshly. "So we meet again. Haven't seen you for a good long time, Henny Penny. You been too busy fighting the war?"

She looked at him closely. The unshaven face, the

137

dark, uncut hair, the sulky features—nothing was changed. A faint smile touched her lips.

"Have you?"

Cold steel crept into his eyes. "Look, I'm too old to fight. But my brother Sammy would've enlisted, if he were alive, that's sure. And he wouldn't have been a coward, like your yellow-livered brother!"

"Albert is doing his duty. He is serving—"

"Doing what? Polishing the captain's boots? What's so noble about that?" he flung out bitterly. "Other soldiers go to the front and get their brains blown out. But you Mennonites—"

"We Mennonites believe war is wrong," Hannah said calmly. "The Bible says, 'Thou shalt not kill'— and 'love your enemies' and 'be good to them that hate you.' Our first allegiance is to God. But Albert—"

"So you let your fellow countrymen do the job in making this world safe for democracy! Hiding behind your religious skirts, that's all. Why, I bet you jabber German at home and at church all the time! How can you pretend to be against the enemy by doing that? Is that how you 'love your enemies'? And how kind are you Mennonites to us 'Englishers'? Bah!"

Hannah moved back and seated herself in a chair. She drew a deep breath and stared gloomily out of the window. It was no use to argue with Dan, and she knew it. She was tired. Not only the endless beating of the wind and rain but the child she was bearing had drained her of all energy today. She was grateful for Dan's silence now, for she was in no mood for further disparaging conversation.

For weeks she'd been so tired and listless that even

138

Mahm's home remedies had failed to perk up her spirits. John had suggested she see Dr. Hoyle, and at his insistence she was here.

School had closed just last week, and the children were home alone. Plump, motherly Alice was fourteen now, and Hannah hadn't a moment's worry.

She hoped this new baby would be as good as Jenny. Jenny, with the fringed blue eyes and the brown curly hair, was her "angel-child." Not only was she the most beautiful, but also the happiest. She danced around with a sort of buoyancy that permeated her very being. Hannah often thought she had never seen a child so completely happy and carefree.

No wonder Jenny had been Albert's favorite. He could entertain her by the hour on Sunday afternoons, and laughingly threatened to kidnap her. Hannah thought that of all his family, Albert had been most loath to leave little Jenny.

She had clung to him stubbornly when he had come to say good-bye before he left for camp. She'd wept as though she'd never see her beloved "Uncle Abba" again. For some time now he hadn't written, but he would be due for a furlough soon. Surely the war would be over before long.

At that moment Dr. Hoyle called her name and she walked heavily into his inner office.

"Well, Mrs. Penner, what can I do for you?" he asked briskly, pushing her gently into the chair by his desk.

Hannah sighed ponderously. "I—I always am tired, it seems. And with the new baby coming—"

After a preliminary checkup the doctor patted her

shoulder lightly. "You are run-down. Nothing more. There is an epidemic of influenza sweeping over some parts of our country, with most of the cases being mild. Still, I think we'd better see to it that you keep from getting it. I'll prepare a tonic for you, and I'd like for you to stay in bed for a week or two. Think you can manage that?"

She nodded. "Yes, Alice—that's our oldest—she can take care of things. I don't want to get real sick."

"Good. You keep cheerful now, and whatever you do, don't get panicky. This world's in enough of a mess as it is, without our civilian population coming down with this grippe."

Hannah felt happier as she left the doctor's office, the bottle of tonic clutched tightly in her hand. Dan had gone when she walked through the waiting room and she was glad she didn't have to face him again.

The rain had stopped, and behind the fresh-budded elms fuzzy clouds scudded frantically across the sky.

Driving home in the new motorcar John had bought last year, Hannah breathed deeply of the clean-washed air. The pungent odor of boiling chicken greeted her as she came into the house.

Alice was chopping up vegetables for *borscht,* while Ruby's lanky twelve-year-old legs were furiously pedaling the organ in the parlor as she wrenched agonizing chords from the old Shonringer.

Henry looked up from the Tinkertoy set on the floor and grinned at her. Jenny flew into her arms.

"Mamma, Mamma," she cried, "we got a letter from Uncle Abba!"

Hannah's face lit up. Ruby stopped her playing and

brought the square white envelope into the dining room and thrust it toward her mother.

Tearing open the letter, Hannah began to read:

"Dear Hannah and everybody (speshly Jenny)," Albert wrote in his large, wide-spaced scrawl. "I gess its time I rite you a letter once. We bin very bussy lately and I dont get time to rite to everybody. Gess you can here when I rite to the folks. the letter is for you all. How is my little Jenny. Still the prettist girl in church. I sure miss her. I am helping in the infirmy now. I have to help take care of sick soldiers, we have gripp here but I did not get it yet. I gess I am prety strong, ha. Gess what. One solder he thought he was going die and he was fraide. I said why don't you believe on Christ as your Savior and he wanted me to read him the Bible and he said God be mercyfull to me a sinner and he died happy. I was glad I helped him. It makes it easier when the others call us yello. . . ."

Hannah's eyes brimmed with tears long before she had deciphered the last of the letter. God was using Albert in spite of persecution for his religious convictions.

Later in the summer there was another letter from him. He seemed very cheerful.

"I count the days when I can come home and play with Jenny. After my furlow I will get transfred to the coast, maybe overseas. Did not know I would get to see the world yet, ha. Lots of sickness here. Still the flue. Am thankful I dont get it yet. . . ."

The summer wore on, with harvest and threshing, and the inevitable long hours of backbreaking work, and with it came Hannah's baby—a lovable, lively bouncing boy. John promptly dubbed him *levendich*, which meant lively in Low German.

"He is so *laeflich*—lovable," Hannah added with a slow smile as she watched the kicking of the sturdy little legs and the aliveness of the round face.

The girls shortened the name to Lafe—and in spite of Hannah's mild protests, the name stuck.

Jenny prattled on and on about showing off her baby brother to Uncle Abba when he would come home on furlough.

Little Lafe was two months old when the word came that Albert had succumbed to the scourging influenza pandemic. This second wave was particularly severe, resulting in thousands of deaths.

The severe chill and high fever which characterized this flu strain was apparently aggravated by secondary infections of pneumonia and other respiratory infections. Albert's colonel wrote optimistically of his "flunky's" condition.

"Private Kliewer has been most conscientious and unselfish, giving of his extra time and energy to help the sick. But many have recuperated. We believe he will do the same."

Ruby and Alice scrambled to the dictionary to look up what "recuperate" meant.

"It means to get better!" Ruby shrieked, grabbing Hannah's hands in glee. "Uncle Albert's going to get well."

That night the Kliewers received a grim message over the phone. "Private Kliewer passed away peacefully at six o'clock this afternoon. His body will not be viewed, due to the nature of his illness. Please notify us as to arrangements."

142

Albert gone! Hannah's baby brother—the lively little tad whom she had helped nurture through babyhood. . . .

Hannah felt numb. It couldn't be. Dear Lord, it just couldn't be!

17

The sod had long blossomed with spicy wild roses and blue field daisies over Albert's grave, and it was as though the whole solemn service had never been. The war was over now, and the world was trying to forget the awful scourge it had left. Albert's cheerful face around the family table gradually blurred and dimmed, and four years had all but erased the heartache.

Crowds had attended the memorial service and people had come away impressed by Albert's silent witness. Although his casket had not been opened, he had spoken as surely as though he had raised himself up and moved his lips.

Maggie had told Hannah about it later, her flat, colorless voice tinged with emotion.

"At first I thought Albert was a coward for not wanting to take up a gun," she said sadly, "but the fact that he volunteered to work in the infirmary and exposed himself to the awful flu shows he had real courage. Most boys who were drafted were forced to face danger. But your brother did it because he wanted to. That took real spunk."

Writhing on her bed now, waiting for her sixth baby to be born, Hannah recalled Maggie's words. Courage. How many times had she lacked courage to be a witness for the Lord? She had failed with her own children.

Quiet Alice, at eighteen, still hadn't made a commitment to Christ, although Ruby pinpointed her salvation experience back to those drab days when she had lain in the hospital and found she could forgive Fidelia Gibbons.

Her labor was more difficult this time, Hannah thought, as the slow, painful process of giving birth was taking place.

"If I make this, dear Lord, I'll not rest until all my children are in Thy fold! But I need grace, dear Lord —grace. . . ."

And Grace it was, when the tiny infant made its appearance half an hour later. Puny and thin, with a ragged birthmark on her forehead, Baby Grace struggled valiantly for life.

Somehow, when Hannah tried to nurse the enfeebled child she was left with a feeling of inadequacy. For the narrow blue lips seemed too weak to suck. A high, thin cry wrenched from the scrawny throat, then simmered into a faint gurgle.

John, seating himself on Hannah's bed, stroked his chin anxiously. The scarred cleft left a harsh outline when he dropped his hand.

"What will we do about her, Hannah?" he asked solemnly, his brow furrowed like a winter cornfield. "She's too weak to get her milk."

Hannah shook her head and stroked the tiny bundle at her breast. "I don't know, John. She—she's so little—so helpless. . . ." Her heart broke at the pitiful sight.

Mahm, ambling languidly into the bedroom an hour later, was trying to be her old efficient self, despite her creeping years.

"Evoh! Don't be so alarmed," she said curtly when she caught sight of the tiny wizened face. "Go to Kasper's right away and get a jar of goats' milk, John! Then we boil it good and put in a little bit of brown syrup. You got any empty medicine bottles around to use?"

Just how Mahm did it Hannah didn't know, but before the afternoon had waned the thin, piteous crying had ceased and the baby slept soundly. From then on the preparation of the goats' milk formula became a daily part of Hannah's routine for weeks to come.

Autumn stole over the landscape with a blend of drying hay, wild grapes, and ripening apples. A tinge of gold edged the elms along the driveway as though summer, putting on bright raiment, were looking back over her shoulder, reluctant to leave.

Hannah, spooning a thinned gruel of oatmeal into Baby Grace's mouth, paused at the sound of a car rumbling onto the yard.

The rattle and screech boldly announced the Smiths' Model T, and Hannah laid down the spoon and put the baby into the old yellow cradle. Then she walked with slow, deliberate steps toward the door.

Dan and Maggie, seated stonily in the car, made no move to get out.

At last Maggie eased herself out hesitantly and plodded toward the house, her plain face grim and sorrowful.

Hannah opened the door and motioned her wordlessly inside to the dining room. Silently Maggie took the proffered chair and sank into it like a broken reed. Hannah stood by the table and waited.

Taking a grimy handkerchief from her faded blue sweater pocket, Maggie blew her nose, and a wave of pity stirred in Hannah's heart.

"Is it—your father, Maggie?" she asked softly.

Maggie nodded woodenly. "Father died early this— this morning. We—Mamma and I—wondered if—if we could maybe have the funeral in—in your church, instead of at the house. Since your John is a deacon—"

The funeral of Hobart Smith in Plainfeld Mennonite Church? Hannah felt herself grow limp at the thought. The Smiths almost never attended church, unless there was a festival. "And then they come only for the eats," John maintained stoutly.

Now they wished a Christian burial for their tall, rugged parent. Hannah knew what the answer would be, even before she told John about it.

She tried to soften the blow. "I'm very sorry, Maggie. We have great sympathy for you. But—" she laid a trembling hand on the thin, drab shoulder—"let me talk about it to John. I don't think—you see, we Mennonites are very strict. Your father wasn't—a church member; so—"

147

"So that makes it impossible for us to have the service in church, doesn't it?" Maggie asked in her dull, flat voice.

Hannah hesitated. "Well—I'll tell John and see what he says. But—"

Maggie arose slowly, with great effort, and propelled herself toward the door.

"Never mind. I—I understand. It's just that we'd so hoped—Mamma and I. . . . Dan told us we'd be wasting our breath. . . . He was right, of course—"

Shame and pity stabbed Hannah's heart at the words. *What kind of testimony do we have in our community when we refuse the unbelieving entrance into our church?*

"Maggie—wait!" Hannah cried as the grieving woman plodded sadly back toward the rattletrap vehicle. She turned around and stared at Hannah for a moment, then hopped into the car. Dan flashed a mocking, hate-filled look at Hannah as he cranked up the car. With an explosive roar, it careened crazily down the driveway.

Hannah watched them go, her spirits low. Why did the Mennonites have to be so narrow? Yes, it was all right to "live separated" "be not *conformed* to this world"—but was being kind and sympathetic toward an unbeliever *conforming to the world?* Hannah wondered how many good, staunch church folk had ever visited or bothered to approach the Smiths with the gospel.

When she talked to John at the dinner table about Hobart Smith's funeral, he looked thoughtful.

"We just can't start letting the Smiths into the church," he said almost indignantly. "Next thing you know we'd be burying atheists in our churchyard!"

Hannah smiled to herself. Small chance there'd be of having an atheist burial service in the church!

"Maybe—maybe we ought to offer our men's quartet to sing at the funeral anyhow," John conceded. "Maybe Brother George Wiens could even say a few words in English. He's gone to college and he can speak English better than our preacher can."

"All at the house, of course," Hannah murmured dryly.

"Yes, of course. At the house."

At first Hannah doubted that the Smiths would accept such secondhand help, but to her surprise the grief-stricken widow and the colorless Maggie seemed almost pathetically grateful when John approached them.

"Could you also supply the pallbearers?" the tear-stained face lit up quickly.

John nodded gravely. "Yes, yes, of course. We can bring over some folding chairs from the church for the people to sit on, if you want to."

Hannah was in no mood to accompany John to the funeral service. But upon his insistence she agreed reluctantly to go—for Maggie's sake.

Dressed in her second best blue crepe with the dark satin collar, she hurried out to the garden at the last minute and picked a bouquet of bronze chrysanthemums and arranged them into a fan-shaped spray. The coffin would boast of few enough flowers as it was, she was sure.

The Smith place, more tumbledown and decrepit than she remembered it, stirred vaguely with the few cars on its littered yard. The house itself had been swept and dusted, yet unmistakably impregnated with the strong odor of stale tobacco and barnyard manure.

The cheap gunmetal brown coffin at one end of the drab little parlor stood aloof with a gray sense of hopelessness. Hannah carried her spray of golden mums and laid it gently on the coffin, aware only of the women's piteous sobbing in the background and Dan's sick, mocking gaze upon her back.

I shouldn't have come, she told herself grimly, because I'll never forget the feeling of—of utter despair. . . .

The men's quartet sang in solemn, quivering voices:

> "Jesus, Savior, pilot me
> Over life's tempestuous sea;
> Unknown waves before me roll. . . ."

The grimness, the awfulness of death overwhelmed Hannah and she clamped her lips tightly as she sat stonily beside John through the brief service. The body, when the coffin was opened for the last time, was as stark and cold in death as it had been in life. . . .

"Did anyone know if he was converted?" Mary Reimer whispered noisily into Hannah's ear just before the benediction.

She shook her head woodenly. "What did *we* care? None of us tried to show him to the Lord."

For days deep grief held Hannah in its grip and she could think of little else. Hobart Smith had gone to a Christless grave. And the Mennonites had been to blame!

"Someday," she promised herself firmly, "I'm going to tell them—myself! Maggie—her puny little mother

—yes, even Dan. They are going to learn what it means to be a Christian!"

But before the day had ended she was sucked into her own whirlpool of grief. Mahm's strident voice sounded tearful over the phone as she called Hannah at five-thirty. Pa had passed away very suddenly while milking in the barn. . . .

When John and Hannah hurried to the homeplace to throw their comforting arms around the ample figure, Mahm sniffed and smiled through her tears.

"Now Pa has 'overcome'! He is sitting now on God's lap!" Of course, being a staunch Mennonite, Mahm believed Pa had that special privilege.

And how different was Pa's funeral from Hobart Smith's a few days before! It seemed almost like a victory service, Hannah thought. The choir sang music that was both triumphant and comforting.

"Safe in the arms of Jesus, safe on His gentle breast. . . ."

Elder Harder's German message rang with joyous assurance: "I am the resurrection, and the life: he that believeth in me, though he were dead, yet shall he live!"

And the vast crowds that filed past the rich, gray-velvet coffin smothered with flowers, saw the peaceful smile under the grizzled beard. . . .

After the committal service in the cemetery the whole congregation met in the church basement for a fellowship lunch of zwiebacks and coffee.

Amid the bustle and clatter of coffee cups, friends and kin wandered toward the family table to offer their condolences. Again and again Hannah heard the words:

"Your father has finished his course and kept the faith—we all know that!" And it was comforting to know that all was well with her parent.

Jenny and Lafe squirmed and wriggled and begged behind the tables until Hannah sent them outdoors.

"You stay outside until I call you. But be careful so you don't get yourselves dirty!" she ordered.

And she resumed her soft murmur of acknowledgments as the sympathetic voices continued.

Suddenly it was time to go home for the chores. She slipped out of the basement to call the children.

As she stood by the battered door looking up and down the church grounds, she felt a rough hand on her arm.

She turned. Dan Smith's dark intense face leered down at her and she caught her breath sharply.

"So your father had a funeral too—church, choir, two preachers—everything!" he said angrily. "But my father was just scum. Dirt for you Mennonites to gossip about! Well, let me tell you, Henny Penny. Your fine, big Mennonite heaven is big enough for my father, too! He never pussyfooted around in mortal sin like you people. He was good and honest and true to my mother. Not like you and your good deacon husband! He—"

"Stop!" Hannah cried in alarm. Dan was upset. He—

"No, you listen to me!"

His fist bit into her arm and she clenched her hands in pain.

"Please, Dan. Let me—go—"

"Not yet! I just can't stand you people acting so good and fancy when you're not. You didn't know there was something between your deacon-husband and that wishy-washy Emma Peters, did you now? Did you?"

Hannah's face whitened. "No—no . . . ," she whispered.

"Oh, yes!" he went on relentlessly, his mocking grin bearing down at her. "I saw them myself, not more'n two weeks ago. There's that woodlot close to our place, remember? I was walking through it on my way to the north field when I saw them near the road. They were standing real close together. . . ."

Hannah tore herself away from Dan and ran back into the basement. But the noise, the bustle and talking and clatter of dishes were not enough to drown out her turbulent thoughts.

18

The gray November skies were bleak with undisclosed promise. The high, immeasurable, everlasting wind swooped up between the elms along the driveway and gusted around the corner of the granary.

John was hauling feed, loading the tepee cornshock bundles onto the hayrack, stalks flapping, then lumbering up the barnyard where he deposited them patiently into cone-shaped stacks.

Hannah, in the warm, spicy kitchen, was rolling out noodle dough paper-thin, flouring her rolling pin and pressing hard, listening to the whir of the sewing machine in the dining room.

She hadn't forgotten Dan's angry words about John and Emma, and they had nagged at her for months, making her heartsick and weary. But she had to believe that John was faithful. It couldn't be any other way.

And anyway, now there was sad-faced Alice to think of.

Ruby was attending high school in town while Henry and Jenny struggled through the daily grind at Plainfeld district school.

Lafe and Grace bent over the toy box and Hannah could hear their mumbled laughter intermingled with childish prattle above the thump of her rolling pin.

Suddenly the monotonous whir of the sewing machine ceased. For two days now, Alice had been busy sewing. Harve Enns, a rugged young farmer with the too-pointed chin and sparse brown hair that refused to lie flat, had pressed his suit relentlessly. Alice, happily in love with him, had given her affirmative answer. Now she was making practical print dresses, sturdy cotton slips and nightgowns, and gay-rickracked aprons. If all went well, the wedding would take place before Christmas. If all went well—

"Harve doesn't want to marry me until I'm a Christian, Mom," Alice had told her gravely.

"But Alice—"

"Yes, I know." The plump face was strangely drawn. "I've tried and tried to be a Christian. But I just can't."

Hannah listened for the sound of the sewing machine now, but it remained deathly silent. Laying the noodle sheets on floured newspapers to dry, she went in search of her eldest daughter.

The brown, well-molded head was slumped over the yards of dark blue print, and Hannah thought she. heard a muffled sob.

"Alice?" she asked gently, placing her hand on the stooped shoulder. "Is anything the matter?"

155

Alice lifted her tear-stained face. "Oh, Mom! I do so want to marry Harve. But why can't I be a Christian? For years now, I've tried. I've gone forward at every revival meeting in church. I've cried and I've prayed. Yet nothing happens."

Hannah pursed her lips gravely and seated herself near the machine. "The Bible says we must not be unequally yoked with unbelievers. Why can't you believe?"

"But I do! I do believe that Christ died for my sins, Mom," Alice insisted stubbornly. "Yet when I cry and pray, nothing seems to happen."

Hannah tapped her fingers on her lap thoughtfully. "That's the second time you said that, Alice. What do you mean—nothing happens?"

"Well—" Alice blew her nose and swallowed. There's no voice, no light, no rolling away of burdens inside of me. I've waited—and waited—Mom," she burst out, terrified, "do you think—maybe God doesn't *want* me?"

"God doesn't—" Hannah gasped. "You mean, you think the dear Lord doesn't want one of His creatures? Oh, Alice!"

"But why doesn't something happen to me then?" Alice buried her head in her arms again and sobbed.

Hannah pressed her lips together firmly, pondering for a moment. How she wished she could lift Alice bodily and bring her to the Lord in person! But she knew that was impossible.

Alice had always been good and kind, motherly and helpful. It was hard for her to realize what sin was, to believe that the Bible insisted that "all have sinned."

How could she answer her daughter? For years she had hoped and prayed for this full commitment; yet because salvation was so simple it was hard!

"Alice, you say you believe that the Lord took your sins away. Do you believe that He did this for you—yourself?"

Alice lifted her disheveled head. "Why—why, of course, Mom. He took my place upon the cross, and He forgave my sins."

Hannah looked at her daughter pleadingly, daringly. "Then that's all there is to it. You've confessed Him to me, child. Not everyone has a special feeling, or hears a voice, or sees a light. The main thing is faith."

"Faith," Alice savored the word longingly. "I see. Oh, I do see! That's it—that's it!"

Quietly Hannah arose and tiptoed back into the kitchen, leaving Alice alone to revel in her newfound faith.

The wind had died down, and only a few ragged clouds scudded across the murky sky. She put a chicken on to cook for supper and began to map out the week's work. For she was certain now there'd be a wedding in the family in a matter of weeks. A large church wedding. They would give Alice the best.

As the days sped by and autumn lengthened into winter, Hannah sat at the sewing machine, pedaling furiously as she ripped and stitched by turns the long, filmy white satin gown for Alice. No one would have guessed she had hated to sew as a girl!

One Saturday when matters piled up particularly heavy, Lafe and Grace were restless and constantly underfoot.

157

"Mamma, can we lick out the cake pans, huh?" Lafe pouted, his sandy head cocked over the cabinet in Hannah's way.

Hannah, worn out from the endless days of planning and sewing, said irritably, "Don't bother me, Lafe! I have all the floors to wash and wax. Tomorrow we're having Harve's folks here for dinner and I have so much on my mind. If you'd just keep out of my way—"

John, standing at the water bucket with the dipper in his hands, tilted it to his lips.

"Little ones in your way?" he asked tolerantly. "Why don't I take them along with me to town? Maybe you can work in peace."

She sighed audibly. "Oh, will you? I just can't get everything done. First it was Grace waking me up early this morning and wanting to know what the time was."

"I didn't hear her."

"Oh, she whispered real quiet. She said she didn't want to wake me up!"

John burst into laughter and Hannah's irritation mounted. She fairly shooed John and the two youngest out of the house.

Next week she had to make Jenny's dress and Grace's coat, and help Ruby fit her dress. The final week there would be the last-minute things to do—the servers to contact, cakes to bake, and the zwiebacks to assign. . . .

She hoped Ruby would wait a while before getting married. Not that Ruby seemed interested in anyone in particular. But her impetuous vivacity captured every teenage boy's fancy, in spite of Ruby's too-long nose and her too-narrow face.

Of late her chatter had been full of Eric Schroeder.

158

Eric was dark, reckless, and full of life, and reminded Hannah painfully of Dan. The same mocking gleam lurked in his open gray eyes, and the jeering laughter exploded very half minute. Next year Ruby would enter college, and begin normal training. Perhaps she would find a more tractable boy to talk about.

Hannah finished daubing the last bit of paste wax on the dining room floor when John and the two little ones returned from town.

"I left them with Aunt Amelia while I went to the store," he told Hannah mildly. "They've been there before, but when I left them off in front of Aunt Amelia's house this time they got mixed up and walked into the wrong house. You know, the square white one with the little porch that looks like Aunt Amelia's? Well, I guess they found out pretty quick they were in the wrong house!"

She only half heard John's recital as she called after Jenny and Henry to hurry up and slide on the wax. The paste wax didn't want to take on a shine unless it was skated on with stocking feet. And the linoleum simply had to be shiny for tomorrow's guests.

The day of Alice's wedding dawned cold and bright. Hannah stretched herself languidly in bed as she turned over wearily for more sleep when suddenly she remembered. There was still so much to do.

Grace had been coughing intermittently all night, and was feverish by morning. Now what? Surely, she wouldn't come down with a cold on the day of Alice's wedding! Well, it was only a cold. Everyone had colds during the winter, and nobody would mind Grace's dry, hacking cough.

Lafe drooped listlessly in his chair at breakfast but he slapped a wide grin on his face. "I'm not gonna miss Alice's wedding!" he boasted. "Hey, Mom. Can we sit up on the church balcony? You always say Preacher Dyck preaches over our heads anyhow!"

Hannah snorted. "No smart cracks, young man! You will sit downstairs in the front with us, right behind the happy couple. And you'd better sit straight up, and don't slump like you're doing now. This is a wedding we want everybody to remember."

She didn't know that her words were prophetic. It wasn't until the long service was over and Grace leaned herself against Hannah's green crepe arm that she noticed the fine sprinkling of red on the flushed face. . . .

With a startled exclamation she looked across John's lap at Lafe who lolled glassy-eyed on John's arm. He too was peppered with red dots. Then she remembered the day two weeks before when John had taken the children to town and they'd entered the wrong house. . . .

Measles! Well, it was a wedding everyone would remember, all right!

19

Ruby came home from college over the weekend. Her long dark hair was combed straight down from the middle and bunched over her ears in two round chignons. Her eyes sparkled as she whirled around Hannah.

"Well, how'd you like it?"

"Ruby!" Hannah, bent over the ironing board, burst out quickly. "What have you done to your hair? It looks so—so—"

"Different? Well, we call 'em 'ear puffs.' Newest style."

Hannah shook her head helplessly. "But isn't it—worldly?"

"Oh, Mom!" Ruby laughed gaily. "Worldly? Well, it's still long. Or do you want me to cut it? Annie Siemens came to school the other day with her hair bobbed."

"No!" Hannah was shocked. "Just remember, she

gets put out of church for this. No Christian is separated who bobs her hair. Your father will see to that!"

Ruby placed her hands on her slim hips. "But why, Mom? What's wrong with having one's hair long or short? You must spend at least ten or fifteen minutes a day braiding your knot; and I know it takes me nearly that long to rat my ear puffs. But you take Annie now. She can run a comb through her hair and be ready in minutes. Maybe she has more time to read her Bible."

"Ruby!" Hannah retorted sharply. "Read the Bible? You mean, Annie would cut her hair and then read the Bible? But don't you understand? It's sin to cut one's hair. Our church rules—"

"Just because our church rules say so doesn't make it sin, Mom. And anyhow, I still have mine long. Eric doesn't like it the old way, with the plain bun. He likes the bangs—and the spit curls. . . ."

"Ruby!"

"Oh, all right, Mom. I don't have bangs and spit curls—yet," Ruby went on blithely. She dropped into the walnut rocker and sighed. "Honestly, if Eric had his way—" she paused.

Hannah laid down the dress she was ironing. "Had his way, then what?"

"Oh—" Ruby sighed with a dry laugh. "We'd get married. But—" she shrugged her thin shoulders.

Hannah picked up a white shirt from the dampened pile in the peach basket and shook it out. "But what?"

"I don't know," Ruby said gravely. "He's full of dash and fun, and I like him a lot. His parents are good Mennonites, but Eric doesn't care about church. I guess

162

that's one reason. And anyhow I don't know if I love him. How do you know when you love someone, Mom? Is it when it's exciting to be with someone you like? Is that enough?"

For an interminable time Hannah didn't answer, remembering her own past. Life had been exciting when Dan was around. His kisses were warm and passionate, his arms stirring. But the real warmth, the steady trust and respect weren't there. As it had been with John.

"Ruby," she said slowly, "when you love someone you'll just know. It doesn't need to be exciting, although I guess in a way that is there, too. You'll want to do what he wants—really want to. But be careful. Don't marry someone who isn't a believer. The Bible is very strong on that."

Ruby looked across at her mother, her blue eyes wide. "But why should you be so concerned, Mom? You married a Christian. Don't you think Eric could become one, too?"

"He—the way he acts—brash and—and mocking—I just wish you wouldn't flirt anymore with Eric!" Hannah pleaded desperately.

"But why not, Mom? I'm just having fun with him."

Hannah hung the freshly ironed shirt on its hanger and paused. "You could get yourself hurt. And you don't want to turn into a flapper yet!"

"Flapper! Oh, goodness me, Mom!" Ruby's tone was incredulous. "Me, a flapper? Ridiculous!"

Grace melted into the room, cuddling an unkempt doll in her arms, and the subject was closed. Grace, her small face framed in blond curls, with the livid brown birthmark on her forehead—Grace who always entered a room unobtrusively. Grace, a moody, thoughtful child.

"Mamma," the gypsy eyes were pensive. "I wish we had a baby once. Everybody has babies, but we never do. Why don't we ever have a baby?"

Hannah laughed as she shook out a green-striped apron and laid it on the ironing board.

"But you were all babies once, Grace! You—Lafe, Jenny, Henry—all of you. If—if you wait until next fall, then maybe Alice and Harve will have a baby. I think you'd like that, wouldn't you?"

"Alice—a baby?" Grace echoed, aghast.

"That would make you an auntie!" Ruby said gaily, jumping out of her chair and stretching herself languidly.

"A baby!" Grace repeated unbelievably. "Old people are aunts, like Aunt Sush and Aunt Liesbet. What's an aunt, Mamma?"

Lafe, cavorting into the room at that moment, broke in jovially, "An aunt's a lady uncle!" And with that he darted up the stairs.

Hannah and Ruby exploded into laughter while Grace drifted out the same fluid way she'd come in.

Summer drifted into fall and life was full and busy. The children were growing up; the family was prospering as John bought more farmland; Ruby would graduate from the normal course in another year and go into teaching.

Hannah and John were awaiting their first grandchild and were serene and happy about it. In the middle of October, Alice's first daughter was born, whom she named Louise.

Hannah had never believed in spoiling babies, but

with grandchildren it was different. Every moment she could spare she spent helping Alice. It seemed she hadn't seen anything of Maggie for weeks, and wondered idly if Dan was still drinking heavily.

One morning at the end of October the news came over the little battery radio. The New York stock exchange had collapsed! The panic it created was the prelude to an economic depression with worldwide implications.

John, with the newly purchased land to be paid for, was very grim.

"Maybe I was in too big a hurry, Hannah," he said soberly. "Wheat prices are dropping and I don't know what's going to happen. And there's Ruby's college tuition to pay. . . ."

"We'll manage somehow," Hannah murmured consolingly. Instead of buying materials for new clothes, she began to salvage what she could from odds and ends. Ruby's outgrown dresses were cut down for Grace; John's old Sunday trousers became cut-downs for Lafe. Mahm turned over her hoard of Pa's clothes to her family, and the "swap-pile" among the families grew popular.

Ruby looked glum. "But how can I finish college when there isn't any money for tuition?" she pondered seriously. "I'll just quit school and get married."

Mahm's figureless form appeared from nowhere. "*Evoh!* You won't stop school to get married! I'll pay for your college myself and you can pay me back when you teach school. But forget about that—that Schroeder!" she stated tersely in her stringent voice.

But when school neared its spring closing and Ruby

searched frantically for a teaching position, there didn't seem to be any.

"Everybody wants experienced teachers," she said dejectedly. "These are a dime a dozen. Seems like experienced teachers are glad to teach for almost nothing these days. Yet how can we get experience if no one hires us?"

"Have you tried Belltop school north of town?" Hank suggested casually. Everyone knew Hank paid frequent visits to one member of Belltop district. Ann Hiebert could cook and bake well enough to take blue ribbons at the state fair.

"They already hired Miranda Lenski. You ought to know!" Ruby retorted. "And that old Greta Flaming is teaching Comstock school. Three pupils!"

Hannah's brow wrinkled. She was afraid Ruby might give in to Eric and get married if she didn't get a school. She tried to sound reassuring.

"I'm sure someplace a school will turn up. Maybe not around here. But someplace."

"It's hopeless, Mom," Ruby said dully. "I just don't know—"

Eric's persuasiveness will win, Hannah thought painfully. Eric, with the dashing ways, the charm and good looks of Dan Smith. . . . *Dear Lord, help us!* she prayed earnestly.

"Ruby—" she began hesitantly, feeling her way through her jumbled thoughts. "Ruby, promise to wait until next week—before you think about marrying Eric, won't you?"

Ruby's narrow face sagged for a moment. Then she smiled wanly.

"All right, Mom. I might as well practice my faith a bit longer. Sure, I'll wait."

Hannah gave a faint sigh of relief at Ruby's words. The Lord would come through, she was sure. With one week of school left, there was always a chance that something would turn up.

On Monday evening when Ruby called home from college she sounded jubilant. "Guess what, Mom!" she cried ecstatically. "I've got a school. In Meade County. In Western Kansas! A little country school with fifteen pupils—at forty-five dollars a month!"

Hannah, her hands clammy with relief, was speechless. Then she swallowed. "That's—that's fine, Ruby. That's just fine!"

20

Fall wore into winter and into spring, and another two years had passed.

Hannah squinted at the pale, hot sky one morning and glanced at the scrawny wheat that looked ripe too soon in the unseasoned drought and heat. She wondered idly how many days like this the pasture could stand before it turned prematurely an autumn brown.

The wind. The immeasurable, everlasting wind. Ever since the dead of winter it had been blowing, whipping the fine dust off the bare fields, slipping it under doors and around windows, and settling it on tables and bedspreads, not to mention peppering the food on the table.

The heat flickered down from the vacant sky as from an overhead broiler, relentlessly cooking the world.

Jenny, seventeen and vibrant, looking like a fragile

china doll with her translucent skin and dark eyelashes, was Hannah's standby that hot summer. Her buoyancy and happy, carefree spirit permeated everything she did. Today she had gone to town with her father to help him pick up the few groceries they had to buy.

"I won't splurge—I promise!" she said breathlessly. "But how I'd like to eat some store-bought cornflakes for breakfast for a change!"

Times were still hard, and Hannah had even created their own breakfast cereal. "Grape-nuts," the family called it. Soaking home-ground wheat bran in molasses and toasting the panfuls slowly in the oven tasted unprofessionally amateurish, but it was thoroughly nourishing when generously doused with milk.

"We need things worse than cornflakes," Hannah said stoutly as Jenny ran out of the house and hopped into the car.

Poor children, Hannah mused as she puttered and dusted, mopped and cleaned out the corners. Of course, it didn't do much good to clean, but it gave her an excuse to sort her thoughts. If it wasn't one problem, it was another.

For weeks now, Ruby's letters had been full of one Tyler Hammond, a young wheat farmer in Western Kansas. She had met him at a school function last December, and he seemed to be all she could ask.

"He's tall and lean and brown, like cornstalks in September," her letter had stated with her usual imagination, "and he's fun to be with. I'm glad now I didn't marry Eric, for he doesn't begin to compare with Ty—"

It disturbed Hannah. At least, Eric came from a good,

staunch Mennonite background. The name Hammond was as strange to the Low Germanic Mennonite as Smith. And probably equally as repulsive. . . . What had Pa always said? A husband must: (a) be a Mennonite; (b) be thrifty; (c) be a Christian—in that order.

Ruby had been fascinated by the gay, dashing Eric, and Hannah wondered if Tyler Hammond had the same persuasiveness that Eric possessed—that Dan had. . . .

She sighed. Impulsive Ruby who believed in having a gay time, a social time. Would she consider Tyler's religious beliefs?

"Not if she's that fascinated with him!" Hannah thought grimly. "I thought if she would teach away from home she would forget Eric, and she has. But this Tyler is no Mennonite. If only I knew what to think!"

Grace melted silently into the room and handed Hannah the mail methodically. Then she drifted outdoors again.

Deftly Hannah sorted the mail. The weekly *Mail and Breeze,* a few advertisements, a letter from the loan company which was probably about interest to be paid on the land they'd bought four years ago—and a letter from Ruby.

Hannah drew the old walnut rocker into the bay window to catch a stray breeze and tore open the letter with trembling fingers, fanning herself with the envelope as she began to read:

"Dear Mom and Dad," Ruby wrote in her round, childish script. "I guess I'd better plunge right in and tell you the good news. Ty and I were married last night at the Baptist parsonage. He's so wonderful, so good—oh, Mom, I really do love him! You were right. You said if a woman truly loves a man she'd know it—like you did. And that's the way it is with Ty and me. Times are hard; so I'm going to keep on teaching. That's why I didn't want the fuss and expense of a big church wedding for you, like you had with Alice. Wish you could come and see us. You'd like Ty, I'm sure. . . ."

The letter dropped into Hannah's lap. Ruby married! And to this—this utter stranger. A man who'd talked the impetuous Ruby into a hasty marriage. . . . She groaned aloud. They knew so little about him. What was he like? Charming and dashing like—like Dan Smith had been? And what was life for Ruby that he'd make her go on teaching school instead of settling down and letting her be a housewife? Remembering the dilapidated Smith place, Hannah shuddered. Ruby —Ruby—

Her mind was numb and she sat like a statue in the rocking chair, not daring to think.

The door burst open and Jenny flew in, her brown hair curling damply from the hot wind.

"Mom—oh, Mom!" she cried breathlessly. "Guess what! I met Aunt Sush's Linda in town and we had such fun just roaming up and down main street. She's got a green dress with *puffed sleeves* and boy, is it ever pretty! She got it from the lady who clerks at Cornelson's. And I didn't buy cornflakes anyhow. I hope my next dress can have puffed sleeves, too. Well, we met Daddy in front of the hardware and asked him for a nickel apiece so we could buy ourselves each an ice-cream cone, but he said he couldn't afford it. So I said OK. Later, when we walked past the drugstore there

171

sat Daddy at the soda fountain eating a banana split. We just about had ᴀ fit—Linda and I. And we said—Say, Mom, aren't you listening?" Jenny paused suddenly in her vivacious recital.

Hannah started. "Wh—I—yes, go on, Jenny. What happened next?"

"Nothing—much. Something's the matter. Are you sick? Can I get you something, Mom?" Jenny was anxiously noticing Hannah's absorption.

Hannah shook her head stoutly. She held up Ruby's letter. "Here. Read it. Your sister was married the other night."

"To that devastating Tyler Hammond? Boy, how exciting!" Jenny's exuberance knew no bounds.

"Exciting," Hannah said spiritlessly. "What do we know about him, except that he has a wheat farm in the dust bowl? And Ruby will have to keep on teaching."

John looked grave when Hannah told him about it later, while she was preparing supper.

"Well, it's done now, and we can't undo it. The question is, What kind of a man is this Hammond? I wish I knew."

"Will this put Ruby out of church for marrying somebody who isn't a Mennonite?"

"Depends. If this Tyler Hammond is a Christian, then maybe not. Although I can't see why she couldn't have found herself a Mennonite. At least, then we'd know she'd be safe."

"Would you have liked it if she married Eric Schroeder?" she asked acidly, her hands busy with chopping up fresh cabbage for slaw.

John let out a long sigh and stroked his chin. "At least, Eric is from a Mennonite family and he is saving and hardworking. Look here, Hannah. After harvest, why don't you go to Western Kansas and visit Ruby and her new man and see for yourself what he is like?"

She paused, knife suspended above the cabbage head. "But can we afford it? The trip on the train, I mean?"

"We'll make out somehow, Hannah," he said contemplatively. "We've got to know about Ruby's man!"

The next morning Hannah awoke to the noise of rain on the roof. The windows glistened from the wetness. As she prepared breakfast, she saw water standing in puddles on the yard, and heard it gurgling down the rainspouts.

Jenny laughed and laughed at the breakfast table, toying with her bowl of "grape-nuts." "Guess what I dreamt last night. I dreamt Papa had died and we put sliced bananas around his grave!"

The laughter caught on, and despite the eerie implications of the exuberant Jenny's dream and the unwelcome news of Ruby's marriage, the day dawned happily. Yet somehow, Hannah found it hard to write to Ruby and wish her happiness.

Harvest and threshing came on abruptly, then disappeared into the mists of the past.

John looked pleased as he came into the house after hauling the first load of wheat to the elevator.

"Wheat's going up, and I think we'll make out all right this year. I'll even be able to pay a little off on the land. And you'd better start packing for your train trip, Hannah."

173

"Maybe I should take the bus," she said. "It would be cheaper."

"I guess it would. But a bus bumps so."

She smiled wanly. "I don't think I'll mind too much!"

Three days later she was seated on the transcontinental as it jogged down the hot asphalt highways toward the West. The wind that blew in through the open windows seared her arms and face, and caked her tongue with its stifling breath. Flies buzzed over the bone-weary bus occupants and lighted surreptitiously on the crumbs that lay scattered in the aisles. The whimper of a restless child, the monotonous whisper of a newspaper fan, rose faintly above the lazy purring of the motor.

Hannah leaned back and shut her eyes tightly. Her brown-and-white print which had been fresh and clean when she started this morning, was now limp and damp from the heat.

She ached to see Ruby, and she wondered if her daughter already regretted her marriage to this lean brown stranger.

She might've waited around for somebody of our kind, Hannah thought dully. *But she just didn't want Hank to get ahead of her.*

Hank, a tall, quiet twenty-three, was marrying Ann Hiebert next month.

"On a shoestring!" Hank had laughed when Hannah had asked how he was going to support a wife. With a few cows and an old broken-down tractor he was renting the Reimer place across from the Smiths. Hank would make out. And he loved Ann.

Hannah opened her eyes, and noticed the dust that

surged over the ground as the whistling wind picked it up. A weird blue-green color palled over the murky cars on the highway. She was glad Meade was the next stop.

As the bus lurched to a grinding stop at the small, dusty station, Hannah's eyes searched the place for Ruby's tall, narrow figure.

A slender brown man came toward her briskly. "You must be Mom Penner," he said simply, taking her small rough hands in his strong ones. "Ruby described you so well. She said—she said you were neat and clean and always wore your hair in a braided knot! What would've happened if you'd worn a hat?"

She laughed heartily at that, and stopped. Was this easy, friendly young man Ruby's husband? There was none of Eric's charm, his dash—just a clean, eager likableness. . . .

"You are—Tyler, Ruby's man?" she asked tremulously.

He nodded briskly. "Very happily so. Let me take your bags."

He picked up the battered black suitcase and the paper sack that contained a few jars of apricot jam and a small ham, and led her to a modest car that had seen better years.

Opening the door, he helped her in gently, then went around to the other side.

"I'm sorry Ruby couldn't be here to meet you, Mom," he said as he started the car and it leaped forward. "But she had promised to speak at our church this afternoon."

"Your—church?" Hannah echoed.

"Yes. Faith Baptist. The women had a missionary society meeting and it was Ruby's turn to discuss the missionary lesson. They're studying about God's will in a person's life and she has such good ideas. We'll stop and pick her up when we drive by there a bit later. I hope you'll let Ruby join my church."

Hannah caught her breath sharply. Why, Tyler Hammond talked about church almost as freely as though he were a Mennonite!

He scanned the darkening sky anxiously, then went on. "It's the dust storms that have plagued us these past few years. Seems as though mountains rise up in the skies and descend on us. . . ."

Hannah noticed the sifted soil banked against farm buildings and fences. The wind began to tumble in high billows now, flinging up clods into its maw. Pitch black at the bottom, smoky yellow at the top, it boiled toward them.

And then it hit—total, utter darkness. And smothering silence with only the hiss of twisting silt in the background. . . .

Ty had stopped the car and laid his head upon the steering wheel. He reached out for Hannah's hand and pressed it gently.

"Well, there it is. A poor welcome for you, Mom. But then, God doesn't always promise the easiest things in life, does He? I'm so thankful that He gave me Ruby. She's a wonderful wife, Mom. I know her family must be great, too. It means so much to me that she loves the Lord."

Hannah stirred uneasily as the storm turned the car windows to ebony and dust sifted into the folds of her dress. Yet there was an exultant note in her voice as she spoke.

"You mean—you're a Christian, Tyler?"

She couldn't see his nod, but she felt the reassuring pressure of his hand. "'For by grace are ye saved through faith; and that not of yourselves: it is the gift of God: not of works, lest any man should boast' (Ephesians 2:8, 9). My verses. I also trust Him to bring us out of these dust storms. He always has and He will again. Someday Ruby and I will have one of the finest wheat farms in the state!"

This was the West, he told her, and west was where there was space. He needed space to let his heart grow, not to mention his dreams. As soon as he'd seen all this flat, yellowed prairie leaning itself against the sky he knew this was where he belonged.

Her heart grew light. There was something so genuine, so refreshing, about Ruby's young husband that she couldn't help believing in his dreams.

The wind was dying down now, and only a brown pall seemed to hover in the air. A few minutes later a feeble splinter of sunlight needled its way through the murky sky.

"Look!" she burst out gratefully. "The sun's trying to peek through. Does it always stop so sudden?"

He laughed boyishly. "Sometimes! Except that when we get home we'll have black pitchers of milk in the icebox and dirt floors in the house. We've gone to bed during a storm with soaked towels over our faces. Luckily, we weren't home today."

Ruby, never mentioning this black scourge in her life, had loved Tyler and everything about his dreams.

"Whither thou goest, I will go. . . ."

Amidst the heavy pall and the choking dust Hannah breathed a prayer of thanks.

21

"Mom, I got another letter from Paul Harms today!"
Jenny cried as she tore open a neatly penned envelope
and perched herself on the arm of the old rocker. Her
blue eyes shone and her red lips were parted in the
wonderment of her love letter.

Hannah, busy with cutting out a summer dress for
Grace from the pink dotted voile spread over the oak
dining table, looked up quickly.

"Don't tell me you are falling in love with Paul
already! Where does he live anyway?"

"Oklahoma." Jenny jumped up, stretched herself
lazily, and tucked the letter back safely into its envelope, then slipped it into the pocket of her light blue
frock. "He was visiting Myrna Richert—that's his
cousin—and that's how we met. I think I told you.
Then last Sunday he came again for the Kansas-

Oklahoma song festival. Oh, I think he's the handsomest guy I've ever seen!"

The soft snip-snip of Hannah's shears interrupted the gentleness of Jenny's outburst. Hannah threaded a needle and began to baste the side seams together.

She pursed her lips thoughtfully. "Well, just don't get married as quiet as your sister Ruby did, although Ruby's man is as good as any we could expect."

"For an Englisher!" Jenny added flippantly.

"Well—yes. I guess you could say that," Hannah replied mildly. "Although you might even say he is lots better than some Mennonites. But don't ever tell your father I said so!"

"Wonder when Ruby'll settle down and raise a family. Hank and Ann have a boy; Alice already has two girls!" Jenny said pensively, and Hannah thought Jenny's face looked a bit paler than usual.

The May weather had been ideal this year, after a stormy winter. Now it seemed as though the spring plowing had turned the dark months under at last.

Jenny, always a spontaneous, happy child, seemed particularly restless, Hannah thought vaguely. But then, she was probably imagining herself in love. And that, for the lovely Jenny, wouldn't be at all unusual. She'd fallen in love with half of the boys in high school, it seemed.

Hannah looked up at the clock ticking ponderously on the shelf.

"Jenny, would you run to the field and bring your father a drink of fresh water? Also, stick a few cream cookies in a sack—not the ones with the butter icing —he doesn't like that kind—but some of the others.

He'll like a bit of lunch about now."

Jenny whirled from the room and Hannah heard her clattering around in the kitchen and then there was the slam of the screen door and silence.

The telephone rang and Hannah laid down her basting to answer it.

"Hannah? This is Maggie. How's everything at your place?" the flat, colorless voice reached over the thin wires.

"We're fine," she said placidly. "I am sewing Grace a dress, and Lafe is working for Hank today. John is finishing up some spring plowing. Next week there'll be the alfalfa to cut. How's things with you?"

Maggie laughed shortly. "Like usual. Mamma isn't a bit well, and I have my hands full with trying to cheer her up. She misses not having Mrs. Reimer close, I think."

"Mrs. Reimer was such a nice person. I wonder where she is by now."

"Didn't she go to California to be with some of her children?" Maggie asked. "Irene wrote something about having met her in Shafter once."

"Irene?" Hannah asked, visions of the bleach-blond hair and sneering voice. "I thought she lived in Kansas City."

"Oh, not for a long time," Maggie said flatly. "She and Fidelia have been at Shafter for about five years now. But Fidelia keeps talking about coming back here. Irene does anything that stupid idiot wants!"

Hannah smiled as she turned away from the phone. The "stupid idiot" was no less unpredictable than the unmotherly Irene, if she remembered correctly. She only

181

hoped the Gibbonses wouldn't hang around too indefinitely in Plainfeld community. That would just stir up trouble.

Jenny dragged herself in and dropped listlessly into a chair.

"Whew! That walk wore me out!" she panted. "Think I'll go lie down a while. Call me when you need me for anything."

She got up languidly and walked slowly up the stairs. Hannah watched her go. Was it sultry enough to sap even Jenny's buoyancy? Maybe a good rest would do Jenny some good. If John wanted to, they could go to town for ice and make homemade ice cream tonight after supper. She'd have to remember to keep back enough sweet cream when John separated the milk.

When Jenny came down she was full of her usual bounce and energy. She sang as she peeled the boiled potatoes for frying, her rich voice vibrant with feeling.

"In the gloaming, oh, my darling,
    When the lights are dim and low. . . ."

That Jenny was falling in love was obvious. One of these days they would have to write Paul and ask him to come visit them.

The days lengthened into weeks. Busy, Hannah grew suddenly aware of the dark circles that etched Jenny's fringed blue eyes. She moped and drooped until Hannah took her to task.

"What's the matter, Jenny?" she asked one day. "Are you sick or something?"

Jenny shook her dark head lethargically. "It's—Paul. He—hasn't written for—almost two weeks now. . . ."

"Maybe he's busy with field work. Maybe—"

"I don't know, Mom," she said listlessly. "But I know I love Paul. It's so—hard on me—when he doesn't write—"

The day Jenny's gums began to bleed Hannah grew alarmed. "You're sick, child. I'm taking you to the doctor this afternoon!"

Jenny shrugged her off. "It's—nothing, Mom. If Paul would only write—"

But that wasn't all, and Hannah told her so. "Let's get something for those gums, anyhow. Maybe you'll feel better. And when you hear from Paul you'll get back your pep and bounce."

On the twentieth of May, Hannah took Jenny to Dr. Hoyle.

He asked questions, thumped and tested, then said casually, "I believe we'd better do a blood count. Maybe being in love is all that's the matter with Jenny, but I'd like to be sure."

Jenny grimaced at his words and bit her lip as the nurse took her into the examining room for the blood sample.

Hannah sat in the waiting room and leafed through some old magazines. She was amused at the lovelorn column in one rather battered edition of the *Topeka Daily.*

"Dear Emily," the letter began, "my boyfriend hasn't ever kissed me good night. The reason is, Pop always leaves the porch light on and that spoils things. How can I make Pop leave the porch light turned off?"

Hannah laughed heartily at the seemingly silly question, and began to read the answer when the nurse called her.

"Mrs. Penner, Doctor would like to see you for a moment in his office."

Laying down the daily paper, Hannah arose and walked into the doctor's private office. He looked a bit grim, Hannah thought as she slid into the chair opposite his desk.

"Mrs. Penner," he said gravely as though taking a plunge into a cold pond. "I hate to tell you this. But the blood count shows that your daughter has a—a serious blood condition."

A faint premonition of fear nagged at Hannah but she pushed it aside. "Well, of course, she's active. Maybe a good tonic—or a special diet—"

Dr. Hoyle shook his head slowly. "I'm afraid it's more serious than that, Mrs. Penner. It's a disease of the blood-forming organs, although I'm not sure yet in just what form it is."

The gravity of his voice disturbed Hannah. She toyed with the strap of her handbag.

"Go on," she said dully, her heart racing with trepidation.

"Your daughter has—leukemia, Mrs. Penner. Do you know what that is?"

She moistened her lips. "No, I don't think so. These big-sounding names always mix me up. If she needs to go to the hospital for treatment, I guess we can manage that. We—"

"No," the doctor said quickly. "She won't need hospitalization—yet. You see, leukemia is commonly called—cancer of the blood."

Cancer of the blood! Hannah felt as though a chill hand were clutching her heart and squeezing the life out of it. But it couldn't be! Vibrant, happy, beautiful—not Jenny! *Oh, dear Lord, don't let it be!*

But the doctor's face was serious as he waited for her to recover from the shock of his statement.

"That means—it's hopeless?" she stated rather than asked.

"There's no cure for it, although much research has been done."

Hannah struggled to her feet. "How—how long does she have, doctor?"

"Maybe six weeks—maybe three months. It depends on how fast it goes," Dr. Hoyle said kindly, taking her elbow and piloting her out of the office. "But let's not tell her just yet. Keep her in good spirits, if you can. Later will be time enough for her to know."

Keep her in good spirits! Hannah groaned aloud. *How can I accept this myself?* her heart cried out piteously.

Woodenly she walked into the waiting room. Jenny sat in one of the chairs, browsing through a magazine like a carefree schoolgirl.

With great effort Hannah forced a smile to her lips. "Well, Jenny, I guess we'd better go home and make supper. The family will be—hungry."

Hungry? *I feel as though I can never eat again,* she thought, as Jenny followed her out into the late afternoon sunshine to the car.

22

Jenny spoke little as the days went by. If she was any more tired than usual, she didn't complain. It seemed as though her spirit had grown subdued, but perhaps it was because she hadn't heard from Paul for weeks now.

"I just can't bring myself to tell her that she's going to die!" Hannah cried to John in secret day after day. "I guess I keep hoping Dr. Hoyle is wrong. Jenny does seem almost her usual self. . . ."

John stroked his chin thoughtfully. "Time will tell. We can still pray for a miracle. Our God is able, don't forget!"

Yes, He is able, she agreed mentally. But is it His will?

She hadn't told anyone else—except Alice. The fewer people who knew about it, the better, she felt.

Alice had been aghast. "Leukemia? Oh, Mom, that's awful! But why should it hit our Jenny? Why couldn't it have happened to someone else? It just doesn't seem fair! She's so much to live for. If there's anything I can do to make Jenny's last weeks happier, then I'll do it!"

Hannah shook her head. "Really, Jenny's such a happy person. She doesn't need anything else—except —except—"

Except Paul Harms. But Jenny was going to die, without ever belonging to Paul. . . .

A sudden idea burst into Hannah's mind. Why not write Paul and tell him to come see Jenny? If he could make her last days happier by pretending to care for her—

Hannah's pencil flew over the pale blue lines of her tablet as she dashed off the letter. Surely, Paul couldn't refuse!

Each day she watched for the mail. If Grace appeared quietly with the daily delivery before Hannah had tramped to the mailbox herself, she made certain Grace handed the mail to her. Mostly, it seemed these were bills and papers, or a letter from Ruby and Ty.

Three days later Paul's letter came. He sounded genuinely sorry but he had fallen in love with another girl and Jenny meant nothing to him. That was why he hadn't written for so long. Surely she ought to realize that!

Hannah's head spun. Why couldn't he have shown more compassion, more concern for the dying girl?

Jenny, her large blue eyes luminous with secret pain, smiled wistfully as Hannah thrust the letter into her apron pocket.

"I've given up waiting for P-Paul," she said tremulously, her chin quivering. "Either he—never cared for me, or else I just mistook his interest as personal. But I guess it's hit me hard. I keep feeling so—so drained. Does love do that to a person, Mom?"

Hannah turned away quickly. She didn't want Jenny to see the tears that welled up in her eyes.

"Jenny—" Hannah said, after she could speak, "maybe—maybe—it's because you aren't feeling too good. Maybe after you get your bounce back—"

"Then you don't think it's love?" Jenny's eyes widened painfully. "But Paul means everything to me! He's sweet and good and I want him to share my life, like I want to share his. Surely that is loving, too, isn't it?"

Oh, child, child! Hannah's heart cried within her, *if you only knew—if Paul only knew. . . .*

Resolutely, she wrote another letter to Paul, begging him to come and see Jenny.

"She's dying, and she doesn't know it," Hannah wrote in her precise script. "But she loves you so. Why can't you come and pretend you care for her? It would make her last days so much easier. . . ."

Three days later Jenny went to bed. She seemed oblivious to the heat that pulsed through the house and penetrated the walls. Chills plagued her and she begged for blankets. Hannah finally put her downstairs in hers and John's bedroom.

"Mom—" she called weakly from the bed and sought Hannah's face imploringly with her large, sunken eyes. "Mom, I wonder what's wrong with me. Do you s'pose I have the flu? I wonder if this is what—this is what

Uncle Albert had—when he got so sick and died? Oh, Mom, Uncle Albert was always so swell to me, the way he carried me around in his strong arms. I wish I could see him again—I wish—"

Hannah stroked Jenny's brown curly hair and pushed it away from the white forehead. "Uncle Albert loved you very much, Jenny. You always were his pet. But I'm sure—I'm sure you don't have the flu—" her voice caught in her throat.

She left the room quickly because she was afraid she'd burst into tears right in front of Jenny. Since they were low on bread, she decided to stir up a batch of *schnetke* for dinner. She patted the biscuit dough flat, cut it into narrow strips, and rolled them into ridges. She heard the car roar up the drive and she peered out of the window.

Presently John strode into the house and perched himself on the kitchen table.

"Well, I guess Eric Schroeder finally got married. It was about time, too. The way he has chased the girls in church, it was getting to be a shame. And him not even a Christian."

"Who did Eric get married to? Anyone we know?" Hannah said absently, placing the panful of pastry into the oven.

John smiled mysteriously. "Hold on to your head, Hannah. Two of a kind, I'd say. Fidelia Gibbons!"

"Fiddy!" Hannah gasped. "That 'stupid idiot'! But— she at least won't make trouble for the Mennonites. Or does she expect to become a part of us because Eric folks are good church members?"

"Maybe—" John began solemnly, "maybe we ought

to warn Schroeders about her."

Hannah shook her head feebly. "No, John. Maybe Schroeders can—can do her some good. Just think, if it were our—Jenny—" her voice broke and she wept softly.

John put an arm around her shoulders. "Hannah, don't! We still have Jenny with us. I'm still not giving up on her."

At Jenny's weak call, Hannah blew her nose on the corner of her apron and hurried into the bedroom. The blue eyes burned in the marble-white face. "I feel so—nauseated, Mom. I wish I'd get over this soon!"

Hannah returned to the kitchen for a pan and set it beside Jenny. "Just you relax, child. You'll feel better after a while," she said consolingly, anguish tearing in her breast.

At the sound of a second car on the yard, Hannah went into the dining room and peered through the dotted curtains.

A tall young man with a shock of dark hair that fell into his eyes, came hesitantly up the walk.

Hannah went to the porch to meet him. He thrust out a sinewy hand.

"I'm Paul Harms. You must be Jenny's mother."

"Oh—" Hannah's hands flew to her throat, and she trembled slightly. "I am glad you came, Paul. Jenny doesn't know she is—is dying. She—she is feeling very low today. So I'm sure she'll feel better when she sees you. If you could just tell her that you—care for her—"

He looked at her sharply. "It's like I wrote you, Mrs. Penner. I'm in love with another girl. I came only because you sent for me. But I'll do what I can to make Jenny's last days easier. Yes, I'll even tell her I love her, although I'll be telling a lie."

"Thank the Lord, you've come," Hannah added tearfully, leading him to the dining room. "Let me go on ahead and see if she is ready for visitors."

She hurried into the bedroom and drew the sheet up to the white face.

"Mom—" Jenny whimpered. "I feel—so—bad. . . ."

Hannah went to the walnut dresser and picked up a comb. "Let's comb your hair, Jenny. You have a visitor. One you've waited for for a long time."

Her blue eyes widened. "Paul?" she whispered tremulously. "To see me? Oh, Mom!"

"Yes. Paul is here," Hannah nodded gravely. "Shall I send him in?"

Jenny's thin hands flew to her hair and she smiled wryly. "I guess I must look a fright. Did you tell him I'm a bit under the weather? He doesn't mind, does he?"

"I'm—sure he—doesn't," Hannah said in a choking voice, motioning for the tall young man to come in.

She went back into the kitchen and left the two alone together. The panful of *schnetke* were cooling on the windowsill now, and John had gone out to the barns. Her heart pounded with questions. Was it right, begging Paul to come see Jenny, pretending to love her, when his heart belonged to someone else? But Jenny's glad cry of "Paul!" still rang in her ears. Yes, it was the only thing. Of that she was sure.

She puttered around the kitchen, opening a jar of corn for supper, flouring a young fryer and putting it on to fry, and then she began to peel the potatoes.

A few minutes later Paul came in search of her, his face set and grim.

"Well, I did what you asked me to, Mrs. Penner. I told Jenny I—I loved her. Her face just grew radiant. Then she wanted to know when we could get married. I—I told her as soon as she—she was well!"

Hannah laid down the raw potato in her hand. "That was very nice of you, Paul. Would you like to stay for supper? I think it would be good—"

"No, thank you," he said stiffly. "I don't think I'd better. I'll just go to Cousin Myrna's and then back to Oklahoma tomorrow. Just so all this won't get me in Dutch with my girl at home!"

Wordlessly Hannah saw him to the door. "I'm sorry about that," she said painfully, finally, "but this means so much to Jenny. You'll never be sorry for making her happy like this."

He nodded thoughtfully, and his hair tumbled over his forehead like a dark visor. "Yes, I hope—I have made her happy."

Then, looking at Hannah intently for a moment, he swung around and strode swiftly to his car and was gone. She watched him leave, scarcely seeing the dark as it washed like water color over the late afternoon.

She started woodenly for the kitchen, then decided to look in on Jenny before she finished preparing supper.

The sick girl was sitting up in bed, her blue eyes staring dreamily into space. She turned abruptly as Hannah came toward her.

"Oh, Mom! Paul loves me—he said so!" she cried joyously. "We'll be married as soon as I'm better. I'll get well fast now, you just wait and see if I don't! I'll begin by getting up and eating supper at the table with the family tonight."

Hannah winced. "Are you sure you should? Your nausea—"

"All gone. Forgotten. Oh, Mom, I'm so happy!"

Tears touched Hannah's eyes. To see joy blooming in Jenny's pale face, the radiance— If it were only real and not a fake on Paul's behalf.

A sudden clap of thunder shook the house, and lightning rolled like fire across the window. To Hannah, it seemed to mark the beginning of the end of everything!

23

The days that hot summer simmered past reluctantly. Jenny, with her remarkable buoyancy, was up and about within a few days after Paul's visit. She floated through the house like a blithe spirit and lifted her heart in singing.

"Look, Mom!" she cried one morning, her voice vibrant with love and hope. "You'll have to start making my wedding dress. If I can persuade Paul, we'll be married next month. Have you written Ty and Ruby about us?"

"What—" Hannah's heart cavorted crazily inside of her. Jenny seemed so much better. The doctor must have been wrong. And if she actually went ahead with her plans for marrying Paul, what would happen if she found out he'd been steam-rollered into his false declaration of love?

When she told John about her fears, he stared at her darkly. "You mean, Paul Harms was putting on about loving our Jenny? But why would he do a stupid thing like that?"

Hannah moistened her dry lips with her tongue. "John, it was my idea. I knew Jenny loved him, and I thought if it would help her to die happy—"

"Your idea!" he exploded. Never had she seen the calm, easygoing John as angry as he was now.

"Hannah, what are you trying to do—pretend you're God? Now look what you've done. Jenny's getting better, and she actually believes she is going to marry Paul Harms. And Paul doesn't even love her! Have you lost your senses? What's the matter with you anyhow?"

"But I only wanted—"

"You've made a mess of Paul's life, and you'll make a bigger mess of Jenny's when she finds out Paul only pretended to love her to let her die happy. Now that she isn't going to die—"

"How do we know she isn't, John?" Hannah asked with a dull ache in her throat. "Dr. Hoyle was so sure she had leukemia."

"When was the last time she was in to see him?"

"A week ago yesterday. He still said there was no change."

John stroked his chin thoughtfully. "Well, maybe you'd better take her in again. She seems so much better. See if she's getting over it. And if she is, you'd better tell her the truth about Paul!"

"And if she isn't getting better?"

He looked at her curiously. "What makes you think she isn't? Haven't we been praying. . . ?"

"But the Lord doesn't always say yes to our prayers, John!"

"What's the matter with you, Hannah?" he demanded. "Where is your Christian faith? Don't you believe God has healed our Jenny?"

She swallowed, the hot, dry tears making it hard to speak. "Of course, John, I have faith! But we must face facts. We must—"

"Just because you're facing facts doesn't mean we can doubt God. I think He is healing our girl. And if you were right toward God, you would believe it too!"

"Me—right. . . ? John, what do you mean?" she almost gasped.

He frowned, the dark furrows of his thoughts penciling his forehead. "I have known for a long time there was something between you and that—that terrible Dan Smith. You've always stood up for them and their shameless ways! Well, God alone knows what it was, for there must have been something—"

She had been shaking her head furiously as he spoke. Now she talked, her words a mere whisper above her breath.

"I swear to my God, there was nothing. . . ."

He stared at her unbelievingly. "I—don't know, Hannah," he shook his thinning head dully. "I can't—see it—yet. But about Jenny. Take her back to the doctor and make sure."

She nodded slowly, her face white. "Yes, John. I will. This afternoon."

When Hannah talked to Jenny about seeing the doctor, the girl rebelled.

"What for? I'm doing great, Mom! And anyhow, I

196

wish you'd hurry up and get my wedding dress made. A fine wife I'll be for Paul if I can't even wear a pretty dress!"

Hannah shook her head despondently and decided to speak to the doctor herself.

"Is she really improving or did you diagnose wrong?" she asked hopefully when she went into town that afternoon.

Dr. Hoyle tapped his fingers on his desk. "She has what you call a remission. It means her sickness has reached a standstill. But it won't be for long. Just don't get your hopes up, Mrs. Penner. There is absolutely no cure for her condition."

The same sense of hopelessness swept over her spirit and dragged her into the mire of despair that had plagued her the first day. For she also knew that the time had come when Jenny would have to be told of her fatal illness.

"But I can't do it, dear Lord!" she wept bitterly. "I just can't tell her!"

Jenny was lying down upstairs in her room when Hannah returned from town. Her face looked transparent and her eyes large and luminous. She smiled wanly at her mother and tried to shrug off the look of lethargy.

"Now, would you look at me! Here I am, a bride almost, and what do I do but lazy around in bed!" Then a look of near panic clouded the blue eyes. "Oh, Mom! What's the matter with me? I thought I was getting along so well. And now I feel so miserable —again. . . ."

Tell her, the voice inside of Hannah hammered

fiercely. *Tell Jenny she's dying!*

A half sob escaped her. "Dear Lord—I can't—I can't—"

"You can't what, Mom?" Jenny said in a strange little-girl voice. "Then you do know what's wrong with me. You—"

Hannah sank to her knees beside Jenny's bed and wept soundlessly. Her little angel-child, the vibrant, happy one. How can I give her up, Lord? Help me, she pleaded silently.

Children are an heritage of the Lord. . . . The Lord gave, and the Lord hath taken away—the words poured soothing oil over her troubled spirit. She took a crochet-trimmed handkerchief from her pocket and blew her nose. Then she sat down on the edge of Jenny's bed and picked up the thin white hand.

"Jenny—" Hannah fought for composure. "Jenny, you are—you aren't going to get well—ever. You have a— a sickness—a blood sickness that the doctors can't cure. . . ."

"Leukemia—" Jenny murmured in a lifeless tone. "I'm going to die. . . ."

Hannah nodded wordlessly. What can I say that will ease the reality of it for her? she thought weakly.

"But I can't die!" Jenny cried out suddenly, her fists clenched. "Oh, Mom, I just can't!"

"But you're ready, child," Hannah pointed out carefully, reaching for the hand again. "You are a child of God. . . ."

"Yes, yes, I am!" Jenny said fiercely, sitting up suddenly and flinging her mother's hand aside. "Mom —It's Paul—just when I'm going to marry him. . . . I

198

love Paul. I love life. It just isn't fair!" Tears rained down the thin pale cheeks and the stricken girl made no move to stop them.

Helplessly Hannah sat by, her own heart crying piteously within her. To see Jenny's hopes and dreams shattered like this—how could she bear it? Hannah groaned aloud. *Why, Lord, why?*

At last Jenny ceased her sobbing and wiped her eyes with the back of her hand.

"I—I'd like to be alone now, Mom," she said in a wretched voice that cut through Hannah like a scalpel. "This—is such a shock. I—need to think—about it."

Hannah arose, her throat constricting with misery, and slowly left the room.

She moved down the stairs in a daze, feeling like a traitor in leaving Jenny alone upstairs to face her fate. Jenny, who'd always faced everything with courage, with deep emotion—How would she accept this? *How can I accept it myself?*

She went dully into the kitchen and began to pack away the groceries. Salt. Coffee. Breakfast cereal—the coveted cornflakes for Jenny. . . .

She seemed to hear young Jenny's rapturous shouts of delight as she played with a fuzzy new kitten or chased the yellow butterflies among the early iris . . . the laughter of her blue eyes spilling onto her face like a rainbow after a shower . . . the ravishing beauty of her bright features on Christmas morning . . . her exuberance as she gamboled on the new grass in springtime . . . her transport of joy as she yielded her life to Christ . . . her winsome animation as she graduated from high school— And now— Soon it would be over. Soon Jenny would be snatched out of their lives forever. *Dear Lord, why? Why?*

Hannah was scarcely aware that she had dumped the salt into the sugar bin—it seemed so trivial beside the heaviness that threatened to sink her.

"Let's bring Jenny downstairs, John," she said somberly after supper as she returned from Jenny's room, the tray untouched. "It will be better for her if we are close by."

John went up without a word, and returned almost immediately, carrying the slight figure in his strong lean arms. He placed her on the double bed in the downstairs bedroom.

"Daddy—" Jenny's chin quivered as she tried to speak, "you're so—good to me. I wish I didn't have to—"

"Just don't mention it, Jenny," he said huskily, patting her thin shoulder. "We want you close by us."

The heat that pushed its withering breath through the house pressed against Hannah's temples and left her drained and exhausted after the first day.

Jenny's hot, vacant stare followed her around and unnerved her. That the girl was not resigned to death was all too apparent. Her love of life, her newfound love for Paul traced its bitter edge on her pain-ravaged face.

"Should we take Jenny to the hospital?" John asked with alarm after several ceaseless, wearying days. "You are going to give out, taking care of her, Hannah."

"No," she shook her head languidly, "as long as I can I want to take care of her myself. She needs me, John. She needs me—" her voice broke.

200

The long, hot nights when Hannah lay wide-eyed on the narrow cot near Jenny's bed were endless. The stifling breezes drifting through the open windows seemed only to fan the torture in Hannah's breast.

Tonight she shut her eyes tightly, willing them to sleep, but there was no slumber. In the laggard hours before dawn the stars hung pale and reluctant in the blackness of the sky, their beams prying at her eyelids.

Jenny, on the rumpled sheets in the large bed, tossed restlessly. *The heat,* thought Hannah wearily. *Jenny needs a fan. Maybe if she were in the hospital where there was electricity—*

The feverish tossing continued, as though Jenny were fleeing, racing, battling.

"Mom?" the plaintive voice called from the bed.

Hannah jumped up quickly and lit the lamp. She leaned over Jenny's turbulent figure.

"Yes, child? Are you hot? Did you want a drink of water?"

The sick girl whimpered querulously. Hannah picked up the thin, hot hand and caressed it gently.

"Just—hold my—hand—"

The agitation continued as the thin body trembled.

"Are you in pain, Jenny?" Hannah asked softly, her throat aching with pity.

Jenny shook her curly brown head ever so slightly. "It's a fight—between life and death, Mom. Paul—Paul— Oh, Mom—"

How can I help? her heart cried. *Oh, dear Lord, how can I help my child?* She sat by the bedside, holding on to Jenny's hand, almost willing her to win the battle.

Suddenly, as dawn began to seep dimly through the night, the relentless tossing ceased, and Jenny lay still.

For a long time Hannah stared at the quiet figure. Was she—

The transparent eyelids fluttered and Jenny's lips moved. Hannah leaned over to listen.

"It's over—the s-struggle. Tell P-Paul—good-bye. And that I—love him. If God wants to take me, then —then it's all right."

Exhausted, she lay still, and Hannah fought for composure. *How can I give her up?* she prayed weakly. She wished John were with her now. But he was upstairs, away from her. Away—

Wearily she closed her eyes and slept from sheer exhaustion.

Daylight streaked through the east window when Grace melted into the room with a breakfast tray and blew out the lamp.

"I fixed something for you to eat, Mamma. You must be hungry," she said in her quiet, liquid voice. "How is Jenny?"

Hannah stirred and sat up, perceiving the faint rise and fall of the bosom under the thin white nightgown on the bed.

"Jenny says she's going to be—all right, Grace," she said with a catch in her throat. "We'll take her to the hospital today. After breakfast. You stay with her 'til I fix something for Daddy and Lafe to eat."

Heavyhearted she picked up the tray and dragged herself into the kitchen. John came onto the back porch, a galvanized pail of milk in each hand. He paused in the doorway, a question in his eyes.

Hannah tried to swallow the lump that persisted to nag her throat. "Jenny's calmed down, John. She—" tears streamed down her cheeks as she remembered the pain-wrenched words. *If God wants to take me, then it's all right.* "She—she's going—to be—" *I can't say it,* she thought fiercely. *Dear Lord, I can't say it!*

Grace rushed into the kitchen, her eyes wild and staring, her birthmark dark and livid. "Mamma, Mamma!" she screamed. "It's Jenny! She just—just stopped—breathing—" and the moody little figure collapsed on the kitchen floor.

24

The late summer days dragged by like reluctant children off to school. Each day dawned bright with promise as before, and slipped away into eternity when night fell. Without a ripple. As though Jenny had never permeated their lives. . . .

Hannah wrenched herself through the long, weary days and the hot, sleepless nights after the funeral by sheer force.

There had been a short, polite note from Paul. He had written:

"I'm sorry you lost your daughter, and I'm glad she could go believing I cared for her. Even though I love Sue, I don't think I'll ever quite be the same for having known that Jenny loved me. She seemed so completely happy. . . ."

So completely happy. Yes, that described Jenny perfectly. No wonder Grace was more depressed and moody than ever. Life was like a candle that had suddenly been snuffed out by a gust of wind.

Hannah refused to be comforted. "Why, Lord, why?" she cried bitterly as the days wore on. "Why did it have to be Jenny? Was it because I didn't have enough faith like John said?"

The church choir seemed incomplete without Jenny's vibrant soprano, Hannah thought one Sunday evening as she sat among the women inside the stiffling church. It was Christian Endeavor night. Her green-figured voile clung damply to her figure and she picked up a fan, compliments of Metzler's Furniture and Undertaking, and batted the breeze around her tight, drawn face.

As the choir had finished the last resonant, "Sail on!" she followed the glance of the rest of the congregation to the couple that came late down the aisle to the front of the church.

The man, his lean, dark good looks reminding her of the Dan Smith of yesterday, was Eric Schroeder. The woman, her dark short hair curling in bangs over her forehead, clicked down the aisle on thin, spiked heels.

So Eric was bringing his new wife to church, was he? The high, aquiline nose and the jut of the chin were the same as Hannah remembered. Fidelia Gibbons hadn't changed much. Her low-cut white dress swirled around her rounded hips and shapely knees as she swung down the aisle after Eric. Anyone could see she still demanded to be the center of attention.

Apparently Fidelia's coming to church was just a gesture. Of defiance. Or of triumph. Hannah wasn't sure. But she was certain the insidious "Fiddy" had a purpose for stepping down the church aisle like a high-spirited horse.

"At least, it will please the Schroeders," Alice told her after church was out and they were standing on the cement porch talking.

Hannah balanced her youngest granddaughter on her arm tenderly.

"Does Eric have any notion about bringing her into the church? Like maybe getting baptized?" Sush, her latest baby squirming uncomfortably on her arm, asked brashly.

"Well, Hen Schroeders would like that. But as long as Fiddy isn't saved—" Alice began.

"Is Eric?" Hannah asked with a stab of remembering Ruby's conversation. "And anyhow, Eric knows better."

"Shameless wench, that's what she is!" Sush rushed on, rocking to and fro on her flat shoes trying to pacify her restless child. "A *shlut*. She doesn't care if people stare at her. Thinks because she married a Mennonite—"

"We can't keep her out, if she comes, as long as she comes to listen," Alice murmured, taking Marlene from Hannah's arms. "Well, I see Harve wants to go home. You all right, Mom?"

Hannah sighed audibly and pushed the damp gray hair out of her eyes. "You mean—on account of— Jenny? I have to be!"

Thinking about it later, Hannah wondered if she'd ever get over feeling emptied of life. Jenny's aliveness was gone forever.

"But I suppose I ought to be thankful she was ready

for God to take her. With Fiddy it would have been different."

Yes, the Mennonites did have something more than their English neighbors, Hannah decided quickly. Especially after Maggie came to visit her one hot August afternoon.

The two women sat outside on the big swing under the red maple to catch a bit of air. Hens cackled in the chicken house and the cottonwoods sighed against the milkshed. It was a peaceful day—and Hannah resented it.

"I wanted to see how you were, Hannah," Maggie said in her usual monotone. Her eyes were dull, her nose an abrupt round blob, and her mouth puckered like an autumn apple. Her head was topped with a sparse knot of grayish hair. "I don't see how you can do it—be so calm after giving up such a beautiful daughter. I know I couldn't have done it."

Calm? When she questioned God? Hannah smiled dismally and cleared her throat.

"The only thing that keeps me going is knowing Jenny is safe with the Lord. Otherwise I couldn't take it."

"I see," Maggie said tonelessly. "But how do you know where she is? I mean—is there a special place up in heaven where Mennonites go?"

"Special place?" Hannah echoed, rocking gently back and forth. "God has only one heaven. This for anybody who believes. If you were a believer, you could go there, too, when you died. Like Sammy did."

Maggie leaned forward, her dull eyes suddenly animated. "You mean, it doesn't make any difference if

I'm a Mennonite or not? I can make sure of heaven, too?"

"Why—yes, Maggie. The Bible says, 'whosoever.' I can't explain it very well in English but it's for anyone."

"I see," she repeated solemnly. "Maybe if Irene would've known more about this, she wouldn't have such a time with Fidelia. Of course, Irene encouraged her to marry Eric. I wonder if she didn't push her into it."

"Push her into marrying Eric?" Hannah asked. "You mean, Irene has a reason for it?"

"Sure," Maggie nodded slowly. "Eric's parents are well-fixed. Irene has nothing. So why not make her daughter marry a rich Mennonite? She'd be ahead in more ways than one."

"But I thought Fiddy had a very strong mind of her own," Hannah argued. "Nobody has told her yet what to do!"

"Nobody," Maggie added dryly, "but Irene. Just think of the prestige. Her idiot daughter becoming good enough to be a Mennonite!"

That figured, Hannah thought. *Trust Irene to nurture an idea like that.*

"But just marrying a Mennonite won't get her a ticket to heaven," Hannah said positively. "Does Irene realize that?"

"Irene?" Maggie scoffed. "Nor Fiddy, either. They never think of anyone but themselves. Not even of God," she added softly.

"And—and you?"

Maggie's drab face broke into a slow smile. "I'm

going to do what you said, Hannah. If your faith in God can make you so calm after burying your lovely Jenny, I want that kind of faith, too!"

A sudden release lever shifted inside of Hannah's heart. Years before she'd vowed to tell the Smiths about Christ. But she hadn't. And now it had taken Jenny to do the job for her.

The tears that sprang into Hannah's eyes were tears of joy, of resignation. And for the first time since Jenny's death Hannah was comforted.

25

Young, handsome Lafe Penner was on the phone. Hannah, peeling apples in the kitchen for pie, overheard snatches of his conversation.

"Look, Mary, I can come after you at seven. . . . No, no, I won't be late, I promise. . . . Well, I told you what happened. My car broke a tie rod and I had to walk home and get Dad's. . . . Of course, that's true! You needn't try that stunt again about getting into the first car that rolls on your yard! Get that! Sure, sure. . . . See you at choir practice tonight." He hung up the receiver and swooped into the kitchen.

Hannah looked up from the cabinet where she was quartering the last apple into a pie crust and motioned him into a chair.

"Mary mad at you?" she asked diffidently.

He shrugged his broad shoulders, and the thatch of

blond hair fell from his cowlick onto his forehead.

"Oh, you know Mary Harder! She's a good kid, Mom, but she likes to have all the guys fall for her. I thought all the time I was her guy, and then the other night when my car broke down and I got there late she was gone. With Eric."

"Eric Schroeder!" Hannah echoed. "But Eric's a lot older than Mary. And anyhow, he's divorced now. What does she think, running around with divorced guys?"

"I don't think she likes him all that much. It's just that since I wasn't around—"

Lafe has confidence in the old Lafe charm, Hannah mused as she sugared the apples and dotted them with butter.

"Mary is real pretty," she said guardedly, trying to feel her way through his confidences, "but she's also a flirt. Those flashing black eyes and that soft, slow smile, Lafe, just watch out so you don't get hurt!"

"Sure, Mary's a flirt," Lafe said defensively. "But I love her. When I'm with her I feel like I'm on top of the world, if you know what I mean."

Hannah nodded, her graying hair escaping from her braided knot. Ruby had pleaded with Hannah to cut her hair and get a permanent as other women were doing, but she'd scoffed and said that was just for girls. And besides, as a deacon's wife she had to think of her position in the church.

"Well, if the church has relaxed on cutting the hair they won't mind the permanent!" Ruby had laughed.

Grace wore her hair in a neck-length bob, but Alice still clung to her round, firm bun. It was true. The church no longer objected to short hair, although no one seemed to follow the latest hair fashions like pretty, vivacious Mary Harder. No wonder the boys flocked to the Harder home on Sunday afternoons and on choir practice nights.

John laughed at Hannah's fears about Mary. "Lafe is the best, Hannah. He is about the nicest-looking boy in the choir. And he has forty acres of wheat on his own. He's a good boy. Mary would be crazy if she turned our Lafe down for other boys."

"Especially for Eric Schroeder!" Hannah spat out the words. "That Fiddy Gibbons sure wasn't stuck with him long."

"That's because Eric wasn't able to get her into the church," John said deliberately, stroking his clefted chin. "His folks sure tried to get Fiddy saved but she just laughed at them. Thought she could become a Mennonite just by joining the church, but it didn't work."

"Well, it's partly Eric's fault," Hannah snapped. "He never cared much for church himself. I don't think he ever was saved. And now already he's divorced. He's such a sinner, let's hope Mary has sense enough to keep away from him."

John sighed audibly and his eyes narrowed. "Oh, she probably likes 'em dashing. Some women do. I can't help but think that Eric reminds me of Dan Smith. Sinners, that's what they are."

Hannah didn't answer. Nor could she help wondering if John had a reason for bringing Dan's name into the conversation.

Sometimes she didn't see the Smiths for months, although Maggie tried valiantly to attend church, for once in a while there had been a sermon in English now, and a few Sunday school classes were no longer held in the German.

The wooden bridge that spanned the meandering draw across the Smith lane had collapsed after the last big rain and Dan hadn't as yet rebuilt it. This meant driving through the washout with the car axle almost scraping the banks. Rather than be stranded, Maggie walked or stayed at home.

Now and then Hank and Ann brought her along to church, but it still meant she had to trudge down the long drive on foot.

"If I want to be a daredevil driver," Hank had announced defiantly, "I can do that elsewhere than on the Smiths' rat-holed lane!"

It was Maggie who phoned Hannah one morning several days later. "I wonder if you heard that Eric Schroeder eloped with Mary Harder last night."

"No!" Hannah's hand flew to her throat. "You mean, she actually did it? But Eric's already been married once. Mary will get put out of church for sure. It's going to be terrible hard on her folks."

"Oh, I don't know," Maggie said dully. "Her folks aren't much better."

"Harders? But Abe Harder is janitor in the church! They're there every Sunday. They—"

Maggie sniffed. "Which doesn't spell anything, Hannah. But I think you can be thankful Lafe didn't get Mary."

It would be a blow for Lafe. "I love Mary," he'd told Hannah just a few days ago. Mary was a flirt but perhaps in time she might have tamed down. Now Lafe was out of the picture.

When he came home at noon, Hannah knew he'd heard the news. His usually cheerful face sagged, and he merely toyed with the smoked sausage and *verenicke*—cottage cheese dumplings.

"I thought Mary knew better!" he glowered. "I was so sure she liked me. Sure, she's flirty, but all the guys know that. I thought she liked me special. . . ."

Hannah's heart ached for the hurt in her youngest son's life. Lafe had always been so lovable, so full of life—almost like Jenny. And now a coldness seemed to seep into his gentle ways and he grew silent and moody as the days went by.

"He'll get over it," John told Hannah confidently as she helped him with the milking one night.

But she wasn't so sure. At least, he wasn't showing any evidence yet. If anything, he was growing morose and more bitter every day.

The night Hannah smelled cigarette smoke on Lafe she began to worry, for Lafe had always been so set against smoking. Her concern deepened the night he staggered upstairs after three in the morning, half drunk. Hannah had been up in the rocker to wait for him as the dark hours dragged by.

"What's happening to our boy, John?" she said bleakly to John after Lafe had finally come in, bleary-eyed. "He was always such a good boy. Now look at him! Smoking and drinking and staying out all hours. All because of that flirty Mary Harder!"

John patted her shoulder gently. "You'd better come to bed now, Hannah. Lafe is facing a tough battle."

"But he's ruining his life!" she cried tearfully. "All we've ever tried to teach him is going down the drain.

Doesn't he see that?"

"What Lafe needs now is for us to stand by him. He's lost his balance, but he'll get it back. I'm sure of it."

But as the weeks wore on, Lafe made no effort to curb his bitter disappointment. During the day he moved around, depressed and resentful, doing his work only mechanically. He scarcely listened when anyone spoke to him.

Tearfully, Hannah tried to discuss it with John again. "What's going to happen? Lafe's always been a good Christian. Now the way he acts—is he getting unsaved again?"

A long, palliative sigh escaped him. "I don't know, Hannah! If he keeps this up, it can well happen that he'll get put out of church. If he'd just apologize once! Breaking church rules is a serious thing. We can't have that."

"But John," she protested weakly, "breaking the church rules isn't all. Lafe is also sinning against the Lord. If he isn't sorry for that—"

"Well, we know that Mennonites are supposed to live separate, if we don't, we must face the church!"

Heavyhearted, Hannah prowled around the house, pulling the shades against the thick, midsummer heat. In the parlor by the gray velour chair she spied a crumpled blob of brown, and remembered Maggie's visit yesterday. The sunbonnet without which Maggie never went anywhere.

I'll run over there and bring it to her, Hannah thought quickly. *I must get out of the house before I go mad.*

John was plowing and Grace was spending a week with Ruby in Western Kansas. Where Lafe was she had no idea. Lately he had taken off during the day and often didn't return until the next day.

Hurrying to the car, she backed it out of the shed and drove skillfully down the rutted country road. The wheels flung up wisps of dust which sifted over the upturned yellow sunflower faces rimming the shallow ditches.

As she passed the Harder place half a mile east of the church, a sudden feeling of revulsion welled up inside of her. What kind of people were they anyway, to permit their daughter to toy with the affections of a once-decent boy like Lafe? On her way home she'd stop at Ann's, she decided. She was anxious to see little Wayne.

When she reached the broken-down bridge on the Smith drive, Hannah got out and surveyed the deep tracks that cut through the washout. She didn't care to risk wrecking the car by driving through it. Picking up Maggie's sunbonnet from the seat she began to trudge slowly up the rest of the lane.

The woodlot to the north seemed ominously dark and shrouded with secrets, and she hurried past it as quickly as she could.

She reached the unkempt, weed-choked yard with its tall tangle of horseweed and cockleburs, and skirted the gray, weather-beaten barn which leaned over like a tired old man. The house seemed to sag toward her as she approached the crumbling steps.

Hesitating by the porch, debating whether or not to place her weight on the steps, she was startled by the thick, mocking voice behind her.

"Well, if it isn't Henny Penny! What a pleasant surprise!"

Whirling around, she peered into the dark, arrogant face of Dan Smith. Tobacco juice stained his stubbled gray beard and dribbled down the front of his torn blue shirt.

Helplessly she thrust the rusty sunbonnet toward him. "It's Maggie's. I thought she might need it already."

He laughed a short, harsh laugh. "I doubt it. She's gone for a few days, visiting Irene."

"In Kansas City? But she never mentioned—"

"Irene isn't in Kansas City. She's over in Moberly, with Fidelia and her new husband Fred Lawson. I suppose you didn't know about that?" he demanded, his mocking gaze riveted on her startled face.

"I—no, I didn't know," Hannah said in a small voice. "But why didn't Fiddy stick with Eric? Hen Schroeders are such good—"

"Oh?" he eyed her craftily. "Can you blame her? Fid's perfectly ready to become one of you narrow-minded Mennonites. But no—she's a Smith! She's an Englisher! She isn't good enough. So Eric heaves her."

"Eric wasn't much of a Mennonite himself," Hannah flung out with spirit. "If he was, he'd have been more careful of how he lived."

"I can't say that I blame him," Dan went on ruthlessly. "'Do this, do that, don't do this and that' —'don't smoke, don't drink'—and be careful you don't soil your hands on your English neighbors! No wonder Eric rebelled. But he sure pulled a good one by turning right around and taking Mary Harder away from your boy Lafe. And I hear you threw Mary right out of church, too!"

Hannah bit her lip sharply. "But that's what happens when Christians don't live separate."

"Well, now, I'd say your boy Lafe isn't living so separate himself. Wouldn't you? Because he's the deacon's son he can do what he pleases."

She swung around without a word and hurried back toward her car, her ears burning with shame. *Oh, how could life be so confusing—so unfair? Lafe—bitter and resentful—was turning into a carbon copy of Dan Smith and he knew it.* She cringed at the thought.

She was almost home when she remembered her resolve to visit with Ann, but her anger at Dan and his infuriating remarks had driven everything else from her mind.

"I'll call Ann tomorrow and explain," she decided as she went out to start with the chores.

But it was Ann who called first—very late that same night.

"It's Lafe, Mom Penner," Ann's husky voice sounded disturbed. "He raced down the Smith driveway and his car rolled over where the bridge is out."

Fear clutched at Hannah's heart and she almost dropped the receiver from her hand. "Is he—"

"He's hurt, and his car is a total wreck. I thought you ought to know. He'd been—drinking."

For a long time Hannah couldn't speak. Then she said weakly, "Thank you, Ann. We'll be over right away."

26

Wayne Penner sat on the corral gate and watched the horses stamp impatiently in the barnyard. Hannah stood behind him in the dusk of early evening.

Already the sun teetered on the edge of purple mist that hung over the horizon. In a few minutes it would dip behind the world, carrying its flaming torch as it went to meet the darkness.

Cicadas shrilled in the cottonwoods and frogs croaked lustily in the pond. To Hannah it had always sounded as though they shouted:

"Come here! Come here! Come where? Here!"

Wayne laughed heartily when she told him about it, his bare toes wriggling on the unpainted bars of the gate.

"I never knowed frogs talked. Wonder if they can talk to the fishes in the pond, Gran'ma?"

She leaned her head wearily against the sturdy little body on the gate. "I wouldn't be surprised! That's one thing we can't understand."

"Like I can't talk German," he said huskily. "It sounds so rattly-fast when you and Gran'pa jabber!"

This time it was Hannah's turn to laugh. She traced a half-healed scratch on the boy's leg with her forefinger.

"Someday," she said quietly, "someday maybe you can go to school and learn the German, like I had to go to learn English. Say, where is your grandpa?"

"Oh, he's saddling up George for me to ride. Only—" the boy hesitated.

"Only what?" Hannah prompted.

"Well, I wish you'd have a horse that was closer to the—the ground. Like Balzers'. They got a little one."

"A pony?"

"Yes. That's what it is!"

A smile touched Hannah's lips and her eyes misted as she watched the sky change to pale opal.

Lafe came out of the barn, leading the high-stepping bay. The horse followed him toward the gate and together they paused in front of Hannah and the boy.

"Ready to go humpety-hump, bumpety-bump?" Lafe teased, riffling Wayne's dark blond hair with his free hand.

The boy's blue eyes narrowed. "You—you won't let George bump me off, will you, Uncle Lafe?"

"Of course not! I'll swing you up into the saddle—just like—this!" And he lifted Wayne onto the high back and jumped into the saddle behind him and held him fast.

Hannah's eyes searched the barn door anxiously. "Where is your father, Lafe? I thought he was bringing the horse around."

"Dad said he felt kind of tired," Lafe called as he clucked to the bay and they moved away from the gate. "He hated to disappoint Wayne. So I said I'd give him the ride."

The horse trotted away and down toward the sunset in the pasture. As Hannah watched them go, her thoughts turned to John.

How like him! John, who'd always seemed so tireless —so timeless! He hated to back down on anything. But lately he'd wearied so easily, and his energies lagged. Age was creeping up on them with creaky joints, and Hannah sighed.

"Am I really sixty already?" she asked herself incredibly. No wonder her face muscles sagged and her once-dark brown hair was frosted with white. It was hard to believe she and John had been married forty-two years.

And Lafe. The accident that night on the Smith driveway had sobered him. He'd been so contrite, so penitent.

"To think I might've been killed!" he sobbed the night Hannah and John had brought him, bruised and shaken, home with them.

He confessed more. "I danced and played cards— gambled, really. And went to shows—" All of which was against the rules of the church. "Oh, I acted terrible! And all because of a silly girl. . . ."

John had been adamant. "Lafe, you know you've got to make it right. Ask the church for forgiveness.

Mennonites must live separate, and you've sinned against God and the church!"

It hadn't taken any heavy persuasion for Lafe to agree. "I know. And I'll do it, Dad."

Hannah thought she'd never forget that Sunday afternoon while they were having "brotherhood meeting."

"Lafe Penner," Pastor John Reimer had said gravely, "has something to confess."

Lafe's complete honesty, his frank humility, had won the hearts of the whole congregation. With a vote by the members and a handshake from the pastor, Lafe was restored to fellowship.

He had long ceased to mourn Mary's faithlessness and worked harder than ever on the farm. If it hadn't been for Lafe, Hannah thought, she didn't see how they could have managed. The REA had brought electricity to the community now, and with electrical appliances things were made easier. Even the arc-swinging kerosene lantern was now outmoded. A tall, bright yard light beamed with light and flooded the yard with a flick of a switch.

Now as the western skyline writhed with orange and red, mauve dusk stole softly over the fields. Hannah felt a peace and gratitude well up in her heart. *Life was so good—so good—*

"Come here . . . come here . . ." the frogs were still croaking from the mossy rocks of the pond. Anguished croaking.

Or was it a human voice calling?

Hannah paused to listen. Then an unmistakable scream tore through the night and she hurried toward the barn. Flinging aside the Dutch doors to dispel the murky darkness she paused in the doorway. Then she pushed the button and the barn was flooded with light.

John, lying strangely, grotesquely on the hay-littered floor, was very, very still. And over him cowered Wayne's sobbing figure.

"Gran'pa—he falled down—all by hisself!" the little fellow blubbered. "He—Gran'ma, *he groaned awful....*"

Woodenly, Hannah propelled herself forward and bent over John's still form. Trembling, she picked up his hand. It dropped limply to his side like the arm of a rag doll. She threw her head against his chest and listened intently for his heart. *There was no throbbing....*

"Lafe—" the word hung in her throat. "Lafe? Where are you?" she went on painfully, querulously.

Lafe appeared in the brightly lit corridor of the barn, carrying George's saddle.

"Did you call, Mom?"

Don't faint, Hannah.... Be strong ... this isn't real ... it's just a silly dream....

But it wasn't. John— Good, easygoing, dependable John was gone. And with him, Hannah's reason for living.

"He went so quick."—"Why, just yesterday he brought along my cream can from town"—"Remember how he prayed last Sunday when he made the opening prayer: 'Lord, we are in Thy hands. Be Thou nearby.' Did he know?" Voices. Voices. Faraway, murmuring voices clamored somewhere around her in the hours

223

that followed. Hannah couldn't cry. The ache was there
—terrible, excruciating, constant. Like something she
must drag with her forever. She tried to push it away,
but it remained, pressing onto her, choking her.

In the darkness there was only the high, shrill
sound of cicadas, the croaking of frogs—"Come here!
Where? Here!"

*Here, John. . . . Come here! Where? Come, come.
God's voice.*

Where are you, John? Here? Her hands went out
before her, seeking him—the dank, murky waters of
the pond shrilling with a thousand voices— *Here . . .
here . . . where? Where? Come. . . . The emmer's
in the cistern*—Emma? *I still say that Emma Peters
liked your Johann Penner—Mahm's voice.*

But Emma didn't marry John. I did. Hannah fought
for self-control. *I mustn't yield. John is with the Lord.
Oh, John—why didn't I ever tell you I loved you?*
There! There it was. Out in the open. The pain that
had tortured her. John had never been quite certain of
her feelings. *And I never told him. I never told
him. . . .*

She only existed through the hot, torturous days that
followed, numb and unable to cry, the ache inside of
her like a cancer, eating away her heart.

Forty-two years. Forty-two years she and John had
shared their life together. She and John. Not Dan. Not
Emma. And it had held. Because she had loved John—
and he—whom had he loved?

John's will. It was an enigma. "I bequeath all my
possessions to the one I love. . . ." Whom had he
loved? Hannah? Emma?

Emma had come to the funeral, tall and brown and stylish, her streaked auburn hair cut and curled with a beauty shop set. Emma, once stooped and fat. Hannah remembered Mahm's words: "Emma is always so awkward—so *schlunsig*. . . ." But Emma walked like a queen, as she came toward Hannah.

"Hannah—" she'd pressed the cold, clammy hand. "I know how you feel. If I'd only listened when J—" she'd swallowed hard, "when the man I loved begged me to marry him. . . ."

Hannah's thoughts whirled crazily, wildly. If she could only cry—

Grace moved toward her like an unsure spirit, her face taut and grim, her birthmark a livid brown.

"Mom—" her slow, husky voice pulsed with concern. "Mom, you still have us—Lafe and me, and the others. Don't—don't go so far away—"

But I'm not far away. I'm here—over here. But she wasn't really.

It was when Lafe asked if he could bring Amanda Ediger home for Sunday dinner that Hannah's mind began to function again.

"Amanda? You want to bring her here?"

Lafe shrugged. "Well—yes, Mom. I—thought we might as well get married next summer. That is, if it's all right with you."

As simple as that. Lafe, who'd suffered a broken heart once, could look into the future without pain.

Without pain. Dear Lord, help me to accept what I cannot change!

Then the tears fell—cleansing, purifying—tears of resignation. Floodgates opened, and for the first time

225

in weeks Hannah could smile at her children.

"Let's make it a family reunion, shall we? Let's invite Alice and Harve, and Hank and Ann and their families. And maybe Ruby and Ty, too, if they can come. It's about time we planned for the future."

Amanda and Lafe— Another link in her close-knit family. *Yes, Lord. Not my will, but Thine. . . .*

27

December 1941 rushed upon Hannah. This year she must shoulder the burden of Christmas gift-buying all alone, and she missed John's keen interest in selecting presents for the grandchildren.

"That dump truck's just right for Wayne," he'd insisted last year.

Hannah had turned over the price tag. "John, this is more than we should pay!" she'd exclaimed. "We have three more grandchildren, you know."

Still, when John made up his mind about something it was hard to change.

Hannah sighed that Sunday afternoon as she flipped through the pages of the mail-order catalog.

"This year I won't tramp the stores to buy presents. I can do it easier by ordering from the catalog."

Grace, her blond hair curling slightly around her

pensive face, leaned over and turned on the radio.

"Well, Mom, I guess I could help you shop, if you'd want to go to Wichita. We could take a day off—"

Her words were interrupted by the announcer's grim words. "Pearl Harbor . . . bombed by the Japanese . . . war. . . ."

Only words penetrated Hannah's thoughts. The United States wouldn't be foolish enough to go to war, would it? Wasn't it Europe's war? And where was Pearl Harbor that it should affect the Mennonites of Kansas?

Both Lafe and Grace were excited. "Mom, you don't know what this can mean!" Lafe said stoutly. "Boys have been drafted before this. What if I have to go?"

Draft! Languishing in a flea-bitten camp like her brother Albert years before? Influenza— If only Lafe could stay out.

The news on Monday confirmed Hannah's fears. "U.S. ENTERS WAR!" the headlines screamed.

Christmas. Where was the "peace on earth" the angels had sung about nearly two thousand years before? I don't feel like buying a single present, she thought dully. And yet Hank's little Wayne and Lucy, Alice's Marlene and Louise would expect something from Grandma as usual.

As the days dragged by, Christmas came and went. There was talk of farm deferments from the draft, if the farmer had enough "points." Lafe sat up for hours, figuring and counting to see if he qualified for a deferment.

Hannah lay awake at night worrying about it. How she needed John and his wisdom! He would know exactly what to do. What of Lafe? He wasn't married. She couldn't farm the land by herself. . . . She peered wearily around her darkened bedroom, the furniture knee-deep in night.

Suddenly the solution projected itself squarely into her mind. Yes, that was it! She would have a farm sale, and she and Grace would move to town. Then Lafe and Amanda could marry and farm the homeplace. That's the way it had to be.

She turned over and slept peacefully the rest of the night.

In the morning, when day rushed in through the frosty palm-feathered windows, Hannah dressed herself with trembling fingers and moved heavily into the kitchen.

As she stoked the dead ashes in the range, her mind was busy. Today they would go to town and look for a house. And then they'd make plans to sell everything they didn't need.

Lafe, who had been to see Amanda the night before, was full of talk at the breakfast table.

"They say Ernie Enns enlisted in the army last Friday. I always thought he'd go as a CO," he said, buttering his second biscuit. "I guess I'll go as a CO. . . ."

"You, Lafe?" Hannah echoed. "But I need you on the farm! Any anyhow, if you get married and live on this place—"

"I don't want to drive you off, Mom. And if Hank would farm your land—"

Hannah shook her gray head staunchly. "No, Lafe. You're going to live here, and Grace and I are moving into town."

She never quite knew how she survived the long hours of sorting and listing, of planning and considering, for the ensuing sale and the move to town. The cars and trucks that lined up, row on row, in the pasture and the crowds that milled on the yard on that blustery March day with the auctioneer crying, "How much am I offered? *Hut*-dollar-dollar-dollar—"

Maggie, her expressionless face almost grim, grabbed the sleeve of Hannah's blue sweater.

"I'll miss you, Hannah," she said in her flat monotone. "Plainfeld won't be the same without you."

"But I'll come to church every Sunday, as long as Grace is home and we can drive. And I'll still have a phone so you can call me up," Hannah told her almost irritably. She wondered how the Ladies' Aid was holding out with the hot soup they were selling in the granary.

Maggie sighed. "But it's not like having you here. I could even walk over. Now I'll never get to see you!"

Hannah moved toward the door of the almost-empty house. They were selling the oldest pieces of furniture, for she was buying some new things for the house in town. Maggie trotted close on her heels like a faithful puppy.

"That's what they say. The drink-making still—" Lehn Thiessen was chattering in Low German to Mrs. Unruh near the door. "Abe Harder stealing! If Ed Leppke hadn't seen Harder himself sneak away from the storm cellar with that big ham—"

Maggie, her drab face tinged with color, tried to lead Hannah aside.

Hannah pushed her away. "What's going on, Maggie?

230

Do you know?"

Maggie nodded, her wispy gray strands falling into her face. "Yes, Hannah. It's—it's too bad. But we've known it for some time now. For years the Harders have been stealing hams around here. People used to blame us, you remember. But it was always the Harders. And that's not all."

Hannah leaned weakly against the doorjamb. Abe Harder? But Abe was church janitor. Had been for years. He was looked up to. . . .

"Then there's the—the still," Maggie went on in her sonorous voice. "In our woodlot. Dan—Dan has gotten his liquor there for years. That's also where Lafe got his drinks after Mary threw him over, you remember. Abe—Abe has been making whiskey for a long time. He—he got caught yesterday."

Trembling, Hannah groped for a chair. The old walnut rocker stood silently in front of the south bay window, and she sank into it limply, gratefully. She recalled Maggie's grim words years earlier. "Mary's folks aren't much better." But what the Smiths had known she had not.

"If—if Dan knew—about the—still," she ventured hesitantly, "why didn't he say something?"

Maggie shrugged her thin, stooped shoulders. "Why should he? His place to get liquor, you know! And there's another reason why he despises the Mennonites. He says they talk about living 'separated' and then they do that. He says they're inconsistent."

Now Hannah knew what Dan's and Maggie's insidious remarks about the Harders had meant. Knew, and recoiled.

231

28

The little white bungalow on Hilton's main street sat back sedately on its tiny patch of green lawn like a timid maiden at a party, with early daffodils pushing through the sun-warm earth beside the walk. Mahm had been laid to rest the week before, and the busyness that followed had kept Hannah from her riotous petunia bed.

Grace reclined on the porch swing from her vantage point on the front porch, a magazine fluttering in her hands. She paged through it as Hannah bent over the flower bed, pulling up a stray but stubborn dandelion.

"Wow!" Grace's liquid voice reached her from the porch. "That's the kind of house I'd like to live in!"

Hannah glanced idly at the pictorial blur of masonry and stone that Grace held aloft, then resumed her weeding.

"Places like that are only for the rich, Grace."

Grace laughed nervously. "Oh, I know, Mom! That's why I think Arch—say, he's that tall guy who's got the fabulous farm up there in Nebraska and that perfectly gorgeous house. If he asks me to marry him, I'm going to say yes."

Hannah looked up quickly. "You mean you would marry Archie for his money?"

"Oh, Mom!" Grace gave a delicate snort. "Don't say that! Archie Wiens is a great guy. He's all Mennonite, and knows how to farm. More than that, he's a choir leader in the church. Mom, what more could I want in a husband?"

"Don't you want to finish college first and teach school, like your sister Ruby?" Hannah parried.

"And miss a marvelous catch like Arch? Mom, don't be ridiculous!" Grace went on shamelessly. "Ruby's still teaching to help Ty improve that wheat farm of his. Doesn't settle down to raise a family. Me—I want a husband *and* babies! Arch likes me a lot. I don't think he'll be back in school, either. He'll have to stay on the farm if he wants to stay out of the draft."

"I see."

Hannah pulled herself up the steps by the gray-painted railing and seated herself on the porch chair nearby. "But don't marry in too big of a hurry, Grace."

The blond girl laughed restlessly and threw down her magazine. "Arch hasn't asked me yet. But he will. I'm quite sure he will."

Later, in the tiny kitchen where Hannah prepared lunch, she pondered over Grace and her romance. Was Grace more interested in Archie's money than in

Archie? She fervently hoped not. But with the moody Grace she could never be quite sure.

It was only a week later, when Grace danced into the house wearing an enormously cut diamond ring on her left hand, that Hannah asked her about it again.

"You didn't hint about wanting to get married, did you, Grace?"

"Oh, no, Mom!" Grace cried out aghast. "Arch loves me. He really does! And we decided he needs a wife to cook for him during harvest."

"Being a farmer's wife isn't easy, you know. Long, hard hours—"

Grace laughed nervously. "Arch can afford to hire help for me, if he needs to. Don't you worry for a minute about me, Mom."

When the grim news came that Ernie Enns had been killed in action, people responded with mixed emotions.

"That's what happens when you carry a gun instead of going as a CO, like the Bible says," storekeeper Fred Siemens said tersely when Hannah went to pick up her weekly supply of groceries. She still couldn't get used to the idea that when one ran out of food during the week, the stores were nearby.

She picked up a package of prunes for *pluma moos* and laid it on the counter. "But how about my brother Albert? He didn't take a gun, and he died. He—"

"But that's different from getting shot down and rotting in the sun!" the storekeeper said cynically.

"Which is all you Mennonites think of!" a low, sneering voice grated harshly in Hannah's ear behind her. "How can you escape the horror of war by hiding behind your religious skirts?"

Hannah turned slowly. Dan Smith, his dark, handsome face covered with its usual gray stubble, leered down at her.

She clutched her purse tightly. "But you don't understand! War is wrong. It—"

"You're right. I don't understand. You Mennonites say one thing and do another. You claim war is wrong. That you're supposed to be kind to the enemy. But what do you do? When my parents died, they were refused burial from your church? Where is all that holy love you claim to have? Please tell me that!"

Hannah shrank back. *Was Dan right? Was there something to his usual sick reasoning?*

Silently she paid for her groceries and followed the delivery boy out of the store.

There was much work to be done for Grace and Archie's wedding. Grace darted about like a flighty wren. "Things have to be done just right, Mom. The Wienses are rich. Like the wedding cake—couldn't we have it baked in Wichita?"

"Mrs. Hiebert has baked lots of wedding cakes, Grace," Hannah remarked tartly, "and she's baking it good enough for the Wienses!"

With a resigned sigh Grace picked up her list of attendants. It was a shame, she muttered, that the church wouldn't allow more than two bridesmaids.

"I'll be a nervous wreck by the time my wedding's over," she lamented. "Luckily we'll be going on a nice, long restful honeymoon."

In spite of her apparent happiness, Grace grew more

tense and depressed, and Hannah was apprehensive. Something was wrong. Something she couldn't put her finger on.

29

Loneliness enveloped Hannah when the hectic June days of Grace's wedding were over and the couple had departed on a gala honeymoon.

Mechanically she picked up an invisible thread from the new divan in the "front room" and flicked at dust on the lamp table that wasn't there.

I'm as restless as Grace, she thought. She wished John could've been at the wedding. He'd have enjoyed Archie's pleasant, pompous father, Ed Wiens, and his chatter of corn and hogs.

"*Yah,*" he'd ranted on and on, "corn has a mighty good price this year. My boys are all good farmers, all three of them. We'll do extra good."

The Wienses had built a new brick cottage on the far end of the yard for Archie and Grace.

Hannah tried to picture her youngest, flitting about

the spotless, tiled kitchen, frying eggs and baking biscuits.

"Just so Grace is happy," she told herself again and again. "Archie is a good Mennonite boy, and thrifty. I guess that's what John would want."

Grace's letters were long and full of news of the fine farm.

"We got us a beautiful new bedroom set yesterday," she wrote gaily, "for more than we'd planned to pay. But everything's so picked out at the stores, and the factories are all converting to war materials, you know; so we had to take what we could get. But Arch says what's money for, if not to enjoy? And you ought to see the latest pig litter—it's absolutely fabulous!"

Grace's next letter disturbed Hannah vaguely. "The draft board's reclassifying around here. Arch's dad has two other boys, you know, and they can't all stay on the farm. Lynn is already married. . . ."

Two weeks passed, then three, without a word from Grace. Maybe the corn-picking season had begun, or silo-filling, and Grace was busy.

Then it came—the bombshell Hannah half expected. Archie had been drafted, in spite of being a farmer. Grace sounded hysterical over the phone when she called to tell Hannah about it.

"Oh, Mom, I just don't know what to do. All alone here—"

"But Archie's folks are there, aren't they?" Hannah said gently, trying to probe under the surface of Grace's disturbance. "Other women's husbands have to go into service. He'll go as a CO anyhow, won't he? Maybe you can go with him."

A long silence at the other end of the wire answered her question.

"No. Arch—Arch is going into noncombatant service. Ambulance, maybe. He—he feels he should. . . ."

"Well—you'll be all right, child," Hannah tried to hide her disappointment. The Mennonite way was the way of love, not the sword. Arch was not all-Mennonite after all.

"But that's just it, Mom. Arch is going away! Don't you understand?" her voice rose into a shattering shriek in Hannah's ears. Then suddenly the receiver clicked and Grace was gone.

Archie left for basic training two weeks later. Then, after six more weeks the word came that he'd been sent overseas. Grace's letters, short and cryptic now, mystified Hannah.

"Arch is going to die," Grace wrote with a melancholy air, "I just know he is. And it'll be my fault, for marrying him for his money. Just like it was my fault that Jenny died. I went into her room, and all at once —she was dead. Everything's my fault. . . ."

Hannah groaned at Grace's strange words. The girl, always moody and depressed, was apparently succumbing to a mental collapse.

"I must go to her," Hannah decided quickly. "She needs me. I'll stay until she gets better."

Frantically she packed the battered old brown suitcase, called to the depot to verify train schedules, and after talking Lafe into taking her to the station, she was on the train as soon as it pulled in.

As it rumbled rhythmically down the tracks, Hannah stared unseeing at the panorama that glided past.

Autumn, like a gypsy princess, had donned her gold and scarlet mantle, edged with bands of brown fur and hung with bronze jewels.

To Hannah it seemed incompatible that the season could be so vital, so alive, when Grace was sick in spirit.

When at last the train pulled into the little Nebraska station and she hopped wearily onto the bricked walk beside it, she trembled.

"Phone," she mumbled to herself. "I must find a phone and call Archie's father to come after me."

The short ride to the farm disturbed Hannah. The Wienses seemed unconcerned about their daughter-in-law.

"She's just been upset because Archie had to go to the army," Ed shrugged. "There she sits all day, in her fine new house, not bothering about the hogs or chickens. She doesn't even pick them late tomatoes but lets them rot on the vines. We can't figure out what ails her. If we didn't all the time check on her garden and her livestock—"

"But Grace is sick!" Hannah cried out vehemently.

"Then why doesn't she go to bed, instead of mooning around all day long in Archie's rocking chair?"

They don't understand, Hannah thought wildly. *They can't see that she's emotionally ill.*

As soon as the car had rolled into the shrubberied drive Hannah ran up the red-tiled patio of the little brick cottage and knocked hesitantly on the front door.

"Grace?" she called out anxiously. "It's me—your ma. . . ."

When there was no reply, Hannah gently turned the knob and walked in.

240

Grace sat in the large reclining rocker in the softly carpeted living room, her face drawn and white, her hair disheveled, and her eyes blank and staring. And the brown birthmark livid and puffed out.

She stifled the impulse to rush forward and smother Grace in her ample arms. Instead, she remained in the doorway and spoke in a firm voice.

"Grace Wiens, you have a visitor—all the way from Kansas! Aren't you inviting me in?"

Grace turned slightly and said in a lifeless tone, "You shouldn't have come!"

"But Grace—"

"No," the distraught young wife shook her head dully, "I just want to be alone. There's nothing left—without Arch. . . ."

"But Archie wouldn't want you to mope around. He'd want you to go ahead and live and work—" Hannah tried to reason with her daughter.

"Arch will die," Grace said in the same dull monotone. "And it will be my fault."

Hannah's heart sank. *Dear Lord, what can I do for my baby? How can I help her?*

She seated herself beside the rocking chair and looked about the light, airy paneled room.

"My, you do have a nice house, Grace," she said with an attempt at gaiety. "Everything is so fresh and bright and clean."

"Arch will die," Grace repeated in a deathlike voice, "and it will be my fault."

"But why, Grace? Why is it your fault? You—"

"I loved Arch's money. And now he will die. . . ."

Hannah shook her head. "No, Grace. You mustn't

say that. You love him, don't you?''

The merest sigh escaped Grace's pale lips. "I love Arch—very much. But I love his money, too. God is punishing me. He is taking everything from me. . . ."

"But He isn't!" Hannah said fiercely. "God loves you. He gave you a fine Christian man, who happened to have such a nice farm. Archie is doing his duty for our country. He—"

"He went into the army. People who go to the army die. Uncle Albert did, and Ernie Enns. They don't love their enemies. God punishes people who love the wrong things. They—"

"Stop it!" Hannah cried out in alarm. "You don't know what you're saying, Grace. It isn't that way at all. God loves everyone, and He stands ready to forgive. He says, 'Blessed is he whose transgression is forgiven, whose sin is covered.' And He doesn't punish us that way. He isn't that kind of God."

Grace stared blankly at her lap, as though she hadn't perceived a thing Hannah had tried to tell her. She repeated dully,

"Arch is going to die, and it's my fault. . . ."

Anguished, Hannah gave up. She couldn't reach Grace, couldn't pierce through Grace's feeling of guilt. She got up wearily and went into the kitchen. What had once been a spotless, tiled kitchen was a shambles. Coffee stains and crumbs littered the chrome dinette table; grease crusted the white enameled electric range; dishes filled with untouched food stood forlornly on the cabinet and flies buzzed around the sticky plates.

Hannah hunted for clean cups in the steel cupboards and set the coffeepot on the stove. As she scraped plates and wiped up crumbs, the odor of boiling coffee soon permeated the cozy kitchen. Presently she returned to the living room with the two cups and held one out to Grace.

"Here, child, drink a cup of hot coffee. You'll feel better."

For a moment Grace stirred, then swung her hand sharply against the cup so that its scalding contents splashed over Hannah's hand, then crashed to a shattered heap on the floor.

"There! That's what drinking does to a person," Grace said harshly. "Like what it did to Lafe! He loved Mary and she went off and married crazy Eric. And look what it's done to Dan Smith. Why, if he hadn't pushed Lafe into drinking—"

"What—do you mean, Grace? Dan Smith—gave Lafe —the drink?" Hannah gasped.

Grace nodded bleakly, like a child who had revealed a sworn secret. "He always—hated us all. So he tried —to kill us. Dared Lafe to drive through that ravine. . . . We used to taunt Dan at threshing time— Lafe and I. Remember the temperance song we learned in school?

'From alcohol and poison free,
My drink shall pure cold water be;
The crystal stream that floweth by
Shall quench my thirst when I am dry.'

It made him furious when we'd sing it to him. Promised us he'd get even with us. Said if we wanted the pure cold water he'd dunk us in the tank and keep us there, like he did Hank once. He said he'd do anything to get even with you, Mom, for not marrying

243

him. But you never believed him. He'll do it, too. I was always scared of Dan— But I married Arch and got away—clear away from him." She lapsed into depression again.

"Grace—" Hannah whispered. *Grace is deeply disturbed and she doesn't know what she is saying.*

As Hannah swept up the shattered cup and carried it into the kitchen, her mind was in a daze.

Something—something far back had caused Grace to be moody, depressed. Some kind of bleak emotion. She'd always lacked Jenny's ability to be completely, spontaneously happy. Was her problem entwined with Dan Smith and his brutal actions? It was hard to believe.

After Hannah had bathed her hand and tidied up the kitchen she decided to start supper. Grace might enjoy a nice thick *borscht*. She had seen a jar of beef broth in the refrigerator. Maybe Grace would respond more normally if she ate a good meal.

"I'd better see if she has *peta-selg*—parsley," she decided suddenly. "*Borscht* isn't flavored right unless it has *peta-selg*."

"Grace?" Hannah called, stepping toward the dining room. The reclining chair was empty. Probably she had gone to the bedroom to lie down on the bed which had "cost more than they'd wanted to pay."

After a quick survey of the brick cottage Hannah returned to the kitchen, puzzled. A nameless dread gripped her. Where was Grace?

30

"She probably ran over to Archie's folks," Hannah reminded herself dutifully. "Or is out with the chickens."

And yet, hadn't Ed Wiens maintained Grace cared nothing about her place?

Deciding to wait, Hannah got out the potatoes and a head of cabbage and began to prepare the soup. The broth was bubbling in the kettle now, and she added more water.

Onions. The best *borscht* always had onions. With the savory smell of cabbage and potatoes in the broth, and the tang of strained tomatoes, Grace would perk up.

The fact that Grace's moody personality had stemmed from an unstable childhood disturbed Hannah. The taunts to Dan about his drinking, for one thing, and his promise to "get even" by intimidating and jeering. And it was common knowledge in the family circle that Dan

Smith had once held Hank in the stock tank that busy threshing day when Jenny was born.

Although John had always cautioned the children never to repeat this unlikely story to anyone else, Hannah had never said a word about it because she hadn't wanted to believe Dan would be so cruel. But her silence had lent doubts to the already emotional Grace, and in all probability this had taken root in a deep-seated fear.

"Fear of what?" Hannah asked herself grimly. "Fear of losing her love—her being safe?"

The savory smell of *borscht* cooking wafted through the half-open window. Hannah glanced at the electric clock atop the gleaming steel cabinets with the plaque of luscious cherries tilting over the rim. Nearly an hour had passed, and Grace hadn't returned.

Mechanically Hannah reached for the telephone and rang the main house. Had Grace been there? No, Grace rarely went outside since Archie had gone. But where was she? Where? No one seemed to know.

Hannah's heart began to pound with fear, remembering Grace's distraught actions. Her guilt complex, her fears—

I must find Grace quickly, she told herself fiercely. The late afternoon was warm and she hurried outside without a wrap. Where to look first. She didn't know the huge farm. The henhouse under the fringe of mulberry trees.

Panting with trepidation Hannah pushed aside the door to the nest room. The stale odor of damp straw and wet mash greeted her. No Grace. Perhaps she'd gone to the hogpen to feed the new litter. Only the lazy grunting of the old boar and the squeal of black-and-white piglets met her anxious gaze.

Swiftly she strode to the barns—the cowsheds—the machine sheds, calling out hoarsely as she stumbled among the unfamiliar buildings.

"Grace—Grace—where are you?"

No answer. Only the distant cackling of hens and the patient lowing of hungry cattle echoed through the late afternoon shadows.

Her heart constricting with fear, Hannah pushed her way through the barbed-wire fence and crept toward the sheep shed, her blue dress ripping as she crawled under.

"Grace—"

Dear Lord, where is she? Tears stung her eyes as she returned defeatedly to the house. Perhaps Grace had come back and was sitting in Archie's reclining rocker.

Only the vigorous bubbling of savory cabbage soup broke the silence of the house. Lethargically she turned off the burner and sat down at the table. *What next? Oh, dear God in heaven, what next?*

Help. I must have help. She rang frantically for Archie's parents. Two longs—one short. *What was taking so long?*

"Hello?"

"It's Hannah Penner again," she gulped. "I—can't find—can't find Grace! Where—where would she be?"

The voice at the other end took unmercifully long to formulate a reply. "But she almost never goes outside! She can't have gone far. In the barn, maybe?"

"I've searched every place!" Hannah cried out in

247

anguish. "She just isn't anywhere!"

The slow voice grew suddenly alert. "Well, I'll send Dick to look in the cornfields with the truck. Pa can go down the road in the car, and I'll look in the orchard."

"Is there any other place?" Hannah pleaded desperately. "We must find her."

"Well—" the voice grew thoughtful. "No place—except—except the old well down by the west pasture. But Grace wouldn't—"

Hannah didn't wait for the voice to finish. She grabbed a sweater and made her way out of the house and across the yard in frenzied haste. Slipping through the gate she headed instinctively toward the pasture that lay like a tapestried mauve-and-brown cover to the west of the farm. Already long shadows of early evening bent across the land, blotting out the late October brilliance that reflected the western sky. It was like a dark wash of water color over a landscape painting that deepened slowly into purple.

For years now, her legs had lost their coltish alacrity, and now they ached every time she thrust them forward. The fence that ran along the road seemed to mock her with its strong marching posts, its vicious barbs. Hannah clenched her fists at their mock surety.

Grace . . . Grace . . . Grace . . . her tired footsteps echoed slowly through the growing dusk. *Let me find Grace, dear Lord. . . .* Hannah prayed incoherently, weariness and anxiety constricting her throat. *Let me find Grace—find grace . . .* grace to help her face her fears. . . .

The long, lonely tower of the windmill rose abruptly,

suddenly, before her, and gave impetus to her tired footsteps.

With almost superhuman burst of strength Hannah propelled herself forward. Then at the sight that met her eyes she drew back, afraid.

For seated on the well stoop, her back toward Hannah, her feet dangling over the edge, drooped Grace's forlorn figure. . . .

31

Hannah wanted to cry out, to scream, to run forward and snatch Grace to safety. Instead, she stood paralyzed. She knew she must not frighten the distraught girl, whatever she did. *Be calm, Hannah. Grace wants to die because she is all mixed up. But she mustn't die—this way—she must live. . . .*

Mustering together her strength and courage, Hannah walked slowly around the peripheral area of the windmill and stopped several feet away.

"Grace?" she said softly.

The drooping figure sat motionless, and there wasn't even the merest flicker of an eyelash that Hannah could see. The face was a whitish blur, marred only by the thick brown nevus on her forehead.

Hannah inched forward cautiously.

"Don't come any closer, Mom," the gray, defeated voice spoke dully.

Hannah's heart pounded violently and she trembled. "Grace—please, Grace, won't you come away from that well? Let me help you."

"I warn you, Mom, I mean it. If you come any closer, I'll—I'll jump!"

"Grace—"

"I loved Arch's money. Arch is going to die, and I must die," the lifeless voice went on, the disheveled head bent.

"But not this way, Grace," Hannah pleaded. "Let God decide when you are to die. Life and death are His to give and take—not ours."

"*I deserve it,*" Grace went on brokenly. "I *must* die!"

Scalding tears welled up in Hannah's eyes and pressed hard against her eyeballs.

"Grace—" she stumbled on, heedlessly, "it's dark to die without God! He loves you—we love you—Arch loves you so much. We can't let you go!"

For a moment the tousled head lifted and looked directly at Hannah. "Arch—Arch is going, and so must I. Can't you see that, Mom?" the plea in Grace's voice was pregnant with despair.

Oh, Lord, help me! Hannah wept silently. *Don't let her do it!*

Hannah knelt down and thrust out her hand toward Grace, praying for words, the right words.

"Grace—you're letting us down—your daddy, me, Archie—every one of us, you know. Yes, even Jenny. We were *so sure* you loved us all. But—we were wrong then. You didn't love us. . . ."

Grace turned her head quickly. "Don't say that, Mom! I do love you—I loved Daddy and Jenny and everybody.

And oh, I love Arch—so much . . . even if we should have nothing. . . ." Her voice broke and she began to weep. Blindly she reached out her hand toward Hannah's.

"Oh, Mom, I'm so sorry! I didn't really want—Oh, help me, Mom!"

Crying aloud, Hannah stumbled to her feet and put her arm gently around Grace's quaking shoulders. Then she drew her carefully from the well's edge and held the weeping girl in her arms and let her cry.

Motionless, the two women stood in embrace while the cleansing, healing tears flowed.

Hannah was unaware of the car that had pulled up on the road nearby, until the pleasant, pompous voice of Ed Wiens called out.

"You ladies need a lift? I'm going back to the farm."

Tenderly Hannah led Grace to the barbed-wire fence. In a minute the father-in-law was there, helping both women through.

No one spoke during the half mile ride to the farm. When the car purred into the driveway, Mrs. Wiens ran out to meet them.

"Grace—Grace, child—my daughter . . ." and she lifted the slender young woman almost bodily from the car and led her into the house and into the big, spacious upstairs bedroom.

In the comfortable kitchen Ed faced Hannah. "I guess we just didn't know she was as bad off as that," he said trembling. "She was always a little bit quiet, and we just thought it was because she missed Archie that she didn't go anywhere, after he left. What can we do now?"

Hannah sank ponderously into one of the chrome kitchen chairs and passed a hand over her eyes.

"I—don't know, Ed," she said dejectedly, her legs shaking from the ordeal. "I think Grace needs—psychiatric help for a while. She's quite mixed up. You see, she feels she loved Archie for his—his money, and when he went to the army. . . . Oh, it's more than that. She really loves your son; she has always been moody, and her nerves—just—gave out. But if you can see that she gets the help she needs—"

"Anything. Anything at all!" he said fervently. "We'll take care of everything. We'll see that she gets into the right hospital and we won't fail her again."

Hannah nodded dumbly, gratefully, suddenly too tired to say another word. Archie would want it this way, she was sure.

The phone rang and Ed Wiens rose languidly to answer. Hannah stared moodily out of the window, wondering when the whole ordeal would be over. She felt drained of energy. *If I could only go to sleep*, she thought wearily.

When Ed turned away from the phone his face was grim, yet relief flooded his pompous features.

"That was the veterans' office down at the capital. Archie—Archie's been wounded. He—he is being discharged. For good."

The words penetrated Hannah's ears heavily and she sat in stunned silence.

"Archie—coming home?"

"Yes. As soon as he is able to travel."

Like a shot of adrenalin to her system, Hannah felt sudden strength surge through her body. She threw back her plump shoulders.

"I think I'd better tell Grace. And—and I think she'll get well lots faster now."

With that, she walked resolutely to the door of the guest room and opened it.

PART THREE

32

Hannah Penner sat in the old walnut rocker and peered out of the big window at the blue sky that seemed to shroud the landscape with gray and shut her in. A low wind moaned through the bare elms and blew the ragged leaves down the street.

She laid down the letter from Grace with a faint smile. It was hard to believe Archie and Grace's Adelle, was almost twelve years old. Was it so long ago that Grace had been ill? That Archie had come home with a limp that he would carry all his days? Grace had grown up since the war, that was all too evident.

"And I hope none of my children will ever be as foolish as I was!" she wrote in her firm, round hand.

"If I wasn't so tired," Hannah murmured to herself, "I'd go up and visit them for a week. Grace could use my help with the new baby coming and the expanded farm. But I'm getting on in years now. Time has gone by so fast."

Was it sixty years ago that she'd been a gay, carefree girl, flying on horseback on those long summer evenings which deepened to verdure in the draws? That dark-eyed, handsome Dan Smith had managed to meet her when she rode after the cattle in the pasture?

A faint smile tugged at her lips. Life might have been very different, had she decided to marry Dan instead of John. Dan, with his rough-gentle touch and his lazy ways; his utter disregard for spiritual truths. . . .

"Oh, I'm so thankful Thou hast led me, dear Lord," she whispered with a catch in her voice. "Thou hast—"

A knock sounded at the door, and before she could ease herself out of her rocker the door opened and Wayne burst into the room—Wayne, followed by a petite girl with a narrow face framed in fuzzy blond hair. The open-eyed pert face that was accented by a left-eyed wink.

"Hi, Gran'ma!" Wayne greeted her effusively. "No, don't get up. Just stay put. I wanted you to meet—"

The girl was standing in front of Hannah now, her jaws working furiously on a wad of chewing gum, her wrinkled, none-too-clean figured dress hanging jadedly over her lumpy knees.

Hannah started. The girl looked so achingly familiar. As if she'd met her before. As if—

"I want you to meet Sylvia Lawson, Gran'ma. Syl's going to marry me. Aren't you, honey?" he reached over and squeezed her hand.

The gum popped once or twice. "Sure am, Waynie-boy!"

Taken aback, Hannah suddenly remembered her manners. "Pull up some chairs, Wayne, so you two can sit. I—I'm happy to know your bride. Where do you live, Sylvie?"

The girl laughed a gay, embarrassed little titter. "I'm from Moberly. I understand you knew my folks, Fred Lawsons."

For a moment Hannah pondered. "No-o, I can't say I do. The name is new to me."

Wayne had pulled out two dining room chairs and shoved Sylvia into the nearest one, straddling the second one himself.

"You prob'ly won't know her dad, Gran'ma. But her mom's more or less a native. A relative of the Smiths. Used to be Fidelia Gibbons, in case you remember her."

"Fiddy!" Hannah gasped. "You mean—you are—you are Fidelia's—daughter?"

"Sure, Gran'ma. Isn't that something?" Wayne said with a grin.

Hannah was stunned. Fiddy—wicked, insidious—Fidelia Gibbons. Memories rushed upon her like an opened floodgate.

Fiddy . . . a bad, mean girl. . . . Fidelia hit Ruby with a rock. Deliberately. . . . Words. Words. Bitter, stinging words. . . . And Sylvia was Fiddy's daughter!

"Well, Gran'ma, aren't you going to say anything? Congratulate us?" Wayne went on, mildly amused at her stricken silence.

Hannah caught her breath sharply. "Oh . . . I guess I was so—surprised. I never dreamed—"

258

"No, I guess you didn't," he said briskly, grinning at Sylvia. She winked at him. "You sure wowed my grandmother, Syl. She's flabbergasted, all right. If you hadn't come to visit Dan and Maggie that Sunday afternoon when I went horseback riding— Well, a good thing we were neighbors. I still can't get over how I was riding along and—there you were!"

They both laughed at the memory. Hannah rocked silently, her neck feeling hot and tight, and wishing only that she could wipe out the fact of Wayne's announcement.

Wayne, riding horseback, meeting this—this girl. . . . Hannah, on her horse, meeting Dan Smith. . . . *Oh, it was all so wrong, so wrong!*

After Wayne and the girl had left, she sat back and closed her eyes wearily.

Sylvia, Fiddy's daughter, to marry her favorite grandson, Wayne. Always so friendly and generous and lovable. Like Lafe. And now he would make the same mistake Lafe had almost made.

"He mustn't!" she cried out to the room that mocked her in its silence. "Wayne mustn't get married to Fiddy's daughter. It's all wrong. . . ."

She talked to Hank and Ann about it the next Sunday when they took her out to their farm after church.

"How can you let him?" she said almost belligerently. "That Irene—and that Fiddy . . . a *shlut!* Both of them! And you know it, Hank!"

"Now, now, Mom," Hank said, patting her shoulder placatingly. "We like Sylvia. She's a good girl. Not too well mannered. But a nice girl."

"She's Fiddy's daughter! That speaks for itself."

Hannah said vehemently in Low German. "She's not a Mennonite, for one thing. And is she a Christian?"

Ann shook her head testily. "Not yet, Mother. But she's interested."

"So was Fiddy when she married Eric. But she never did listen to Hen Schroeders seriously."

"Sylvia has a good father," Hank went on. "In spite of Fidelia's lack of self-discipline, Fred Lawson is a quiet, decent man. He keeps his wife under control pretty much. Sylvia is like him in many ways."

Hannah shook her gray head stonily. "It makes no difference. She's still Fiddy's daughter. A—a *shlut!*"

To make matters worse, if Wayne married a non-Christian the church wouldn't even put him out. Not anymore. He could go right ahead being a church member and the others would do no more than shake their heads and offer a weak "tch, tch" behind his back.

Wayne swung jauntily into the room in time to overhear Hannah's torrid remarks. His face purpled. "It doesn't concern you whom I want to marry, Gran'ma!"

"You are my grandson, Wayne Penner!" Hannah said tartly. "It does concern me. You don't know that Smith outfit like I do!"

"I thought you liked Maggie," Ann said anxiously. "Why can't Sylvia become one of us, if we give her a chance? Maybe if we let her, she would—"

Hannah interrupted hoarsely. "A Smith turn into a Mennonite? Don't be ridiculous! Maggie is weak-kneed. She does anything we ask! But not the others!"

I sound like John, she told herself proudly. *He always said that when I tried to defend them. Now I know what he meant.*

"Well, you keep out of this, Gran'ma," Wayne growled. "It's my affair."

Hannah refused Ann's light-textured zwieback for supper, and sipped only her coffee stubbornly. *This— this was terrible.* And it wasn't going to happen, if she could help it!

Maybe—maybe Maggie could talk Sylvia out of it. Maggie knew how Hannah felt. Maggie, drab and brown, but sensible. Yes, that was an idea. The Smith farm lay across the road from Hank and Ann's place.

Impulsively, she got up and went into the bedroom for her coat. It was of black cloth, with a round black collar and shiny carved buttons.

"Going home already, Mom?" Hank asked as she reentered the dining room.

She shook her head. "I want to take a little walk. When I come back you can drive me back to town."

Without another word she opened the door and went out into the early winter afternoon.

A few white clouds pillowed the sky overhead, deepening to dull gray in the southwest. Winter shadows bent across the land, blotting out the pale sunlight that pushed its feeble way past the cloud-piles.

As Hannah panted up the long, rutted drive and paused at the draw, she noticed the bridge planks lying jagged and splintered from the years, and she stepped cautiously through the deep ravine. Ahead the Smith place bore that same hopeless, despairing look as always.

She held on to the rough, unpainted porch pillars as she skirted the two broken boards and knocked timidly.

261

The door opened, and Dan's dissipated, paunchy figure emerged.

"Well, if it isn't Henny Penny," he said in his faintly mocking way. "So you've come out to see me again. How touching!"

Hannah drew herself up proudly. "I came to see Maggie. Is she here?"

"Sorry to disappoint you, Henny my dear, but Maggie's not home," he went on with mock civility. "She's spending a few days with an aunt in Arkansas. Won't you come in anyhow?"

Hannah shook her head staunchly. "No. I'd better not. I—"

"Well, seeing as we're going to be almost relatives, what's the harm? You aren't afraid of me, are you?" he smiled derisively, and she caught his cynical glance.

She leaned wearily against the side of the weather-beaten house. The walk had tired her out more than she had anticipated.

"If I could rest—a few minutes—"

"Of course. Come on in," Dan seemed almost eager to lead her inside.

The stench of manure-encrusted boots and stale tobacco rushed to her nostrils as she stepped inside the dismal kitchen and sank into the nearest chair.

He stood before her, looking down at her silently.

She squirmed. "What you said—about being almost relatives . . . on account of Sylvie and Wayne, you mean?"

"Sure, why not? Why shouldn't Sylvia marry Wayne? I hope you don't object."

"But Dan—you know and I know they are brought

up so different!" she cried. "If Sylvie could just see how different. If you could tell her—"

He shook his head stubbornly. A malicious gleam penciled his black eyes, and he folded his arms across his chest smugly.

"So we're going to catch up at last, Henny Penny. You and I. Your grandson—and my granddaughter. Isn't that nice and cozy?" he laughed.

Shivers raced down Hannah's back at his coarse laughter and she shrank back. "Your—Sylvie is Irene's granddaughter: You and Irene are only cousins. You—"

His fetid gaze bored into hers. "You heard me. Irene and I are cousins, sure. In case you didn't know, Irene has never been married. I'm human, too, Hannah, if you've forgotten! *Fidelia is my daughter!* You refused me, but Irene didn't. And now—"

Hannah's senses reeled. Dan's words hammered against her and she felt faint. She stumbled to her feet. Her hands went out before her, seeking . . . *the dank water, frogs croaking . . . come here. . . .*

"You—you're lying!" she screamed, beating her hands against his thick, filthy chest. "You're lying—lying. . . ."

He laughed again, cruel, shrill laughter that echoed hollowly through the dingy room. Then he pushed her roughly into the chair again. Pain knifed her back. Dan, always cruel, ungentle.

"No, I'm not lying, Hannah," he said soberly. "And you'd better face it. Ironic, isn't it? You, who refused my love these many years ago, are helpless at my own offspring's love toward your grandson.

"And you'd better face another thing. Remember years ago when the first graders struggled through the story of Chicken Little? Well, your sky is falling now, Henny Penny. Your great big beautiful Mennonite sky! First, it was Eric Schroeder, that gay, divorced wolf, who married that flirty Mennonite Mary Harder. Then the Abe Harders, good church members, thieves and distillers. And now Wayne. Where's all your 'separation,' Hannah? Your 'better-than-the-Englishers' creed? Well, let me tell you. Nothing would please me more than to see my granddaughter marry Wayne Penner. To get even at last. And so help me, I'm going to encourage her all I can!"

For a moment Hannah felt drained of emotion. Her head whirled. Life, cruel and harsh, had caught her in its ruthless clutches and was slowly sapping her spirit. She felt numb—dead. . . .

Slowly, and under great stress, she arose and stumbled toward the door. Dan, without a word, held it open and she stepped out into the deepening winter twilight.

33

How she got back to her own little bungalow in Hilton Hannah never quite remembered. Time, dark and endless, stretched before her, and she could not halt its plodding pace.

Her heart felt battered and torn from bitter emotion. Dan had triumphed over her, and she knew it. Long ago she had thought of her full, joyous life as being that of the "fat kine," and Dan's as that of the "lean"; and now at last, at last the lean had devoured the fat. . . .

"I knew it would happen—someday—but it never did," she half whispered to herself. And now at last it had.

Always, always she had been so proud of her family—her Christian strength and faith—her Mennonite heritage. Everything had seemed so stable, so eternal. It could never falter.

Now she sat in the old walnut rocker, staring un-seeing at the bright November sunshine. For so many years she had maneuvered—"managed," as Pa and Mahm had before her, and it had always come out all right. Unconsciously, perhaps, but it had.

As it had when she'd obtained a Christian funeral for Hobart Smith without going to the church about it; working it so that Jenny could die happy, believing Paul loved her; leading Maggie to the Lord without leading her to the church; helping Grace through her ordeal without compromising with the Mennonite po-sition against war. Oh, there were many things that worked for the good of everyone without upsetting her world or shaking her faith. Until now.

Life hadn't always demanded reasons. Until now. This was something she could not "manage"—dared not attempt to change. For it was out of her hands.

"Oh, dear Lord," she cried in anguish, lowering her-self to her arthritic old knees, "Lord, why hast Thou dealt bitterly with me? Haven't I been true? Haven't I served Thee faithfully? Where have I failed?"

She buried her head in her arms and sobbed aloud. The gaily pieced pillow that cushioned the seat of the old walnut rocker grew damp with her tears, but Han-nah was oblivious to it.

Where had she failed? Why had things mushroomed out of control? Thy sky. The firmament, once so secure above her, had fallen, crushing her long life with its weight.

One day Chicken Little was in the woods. A nut fell on her tail.

"Oh, oh! The sky is falling,"

said Chicken Little,
"I must run to tell the king."
So she ran, and she ran.
On the way she met Henny Penny . . .
"Who told you?"

The King. . . . But I've told Him. And the burden is still there. Stop the sky—stop it! Oh, God, stop this awful crushing weight on my heart—*Come here! Come where? Where? . . .*

Dan was right. Handsome, ugly, gentle, cruel, laughing, scornful Dan Smith had said it succinctly. Her sky had fallen—crashed down all around her—her big, beautiful Mennonite sky. . . .

Where was God? Had He crashed with her world? But if God is no longer here— Oh, where art Thou, Lord? *Where?*

Despair washed over Hannah in great, stifling waves that smothered her and choked the soul within her. This was something she could not face—she could not. . . .

Alone . . . alone . . . she was alone, with her overwhelming burden, and she struggled to shake it off. But its weight pinioned her to her knees, and there was no light.

The sky is falling. . . . Who told you? Who? God didn't.

Trembling and broken, Hannah reached out and picked up her well-worn German Bible. Always John had gone to the Scriptures, like Pa, to find the answers. She needed answers now, and strength—faith and strength. . . .

Aimlessly she paged through the brittle pages—the

Psalms—the Prophets—the Gospels. Nothing arrested her. One verse from Psalm 46 leaped at her and soothed her momentarily. It said, "Be still, and know that I am God." *Be still—and know. . . .*

What of the answer, dear Lord? Why? Why? her heart cried out. I have never questioned You since Jenny died. Yet now I *must know!*

Suddenly, she seemed to sense a Presence that filled the dismal room with light. She dared not raise her head to look, lest the Presence vanish. It was a holy Presence, awesome and electric. Then a Voice, a calm, throbbing Voice of love.

"My child, it is not yours to ask why. Just know that I shall never fail you. . . ." And then it was gone.

Hannah looked up slowly. The room was the same as always, with its green-sprigged wallpaper, its comfortable furniture.

She glanced around until her eyes met the sampler on the wall—the sampler she had embroidered so many years before. It had hung above her many times but she had never really read it before.

Befiel dem Herrn deine Wege . . . "Commit thy way unto the Lord. . . ." Commit. That was the secret! She was still paging through the Bible as she got up slowly and seated herself in the rocker. A verse struck her like a bolt of lightning.

"Heaven and earth shall pass away, but my words shall not pass away."

The sky could fall and crush her, but it was only her own lack of faith that told her so. God's Word would stand forever. Of that she was suddenly sure.

Of another thing she was certain. Her Mennonite

heritage, with its ideals and traditions, was very precious. Maybe it didn't always make sense to people who didn't know what it was all about. She didn't always understand it all herself. God had used her people mightily—through the vast amount of relief work in desperate countries overseas, and through the Mennonites' aid to others in distress, in times of disasters, floods, and storms. And through the ministry of reconciliation. And God would continue to use the Mennonite witness—somehow.

She smiled wanly through her tears. "So that's the way it's going to be, dear Lord. It won't be easy, but if You say so, I'll make the best of it. I'll do it. I'll give Wayne and Sylvie my blessing!"

34

Hannah raked the last of the scattered, ragged leaves onto a gigantic pile in the alley and lit a match. The fire reached hungrily for the dry leaves and crackled with the acrid odor of dead autumn. The pile blazed into an intense bonfire, its lazy smoke drifting languidly over the yard.

She sighed as she surveyed the freshly raked yard. *My legs,* she winced as she struggled to stamp out the last wisp of fire, *are showing my age!* And my garden needs a younger hand—

Was that the phone shrilling from the house?

"Coming! I'm coming," she panted as she eased herself up the steps. *Let it ring seven times. . . .* These new dial phones were nice that way. They kept right on ringing and ringing until the other party grew tired of waiting.

She let the screen door slam behind her and padded to the phone. It was Maggie.

"Hannah, could you come out right away?" she said, her flat voice urgent. "It's Dan. He—he's dying, and he wants—you to come. Please?"

Dan—dying? Hannah's hands grew moist with trepidation.

"As soon as I can get there," she said thickly. "How about the doctor? Have you called—"

"No. Dan refuses. He just wants you to come quick!" Maggie's colorless voice rose. "Please hurry. . . ."

Hannah turned away slowly. She hadn't driven the car for years now, but there it stood in the garage. Lizzie Graham next door was her chauffeur. All she needed to do was ask Lizzie.

"Sure, I'll take you. If I can sit in the car and work on my knitting," was Lizzie's standard reply.

"Hurry?" Hannah mumbled to herself. "I can't hurry anymore. But I must put on a clean dress and comb my hair."

So Dan had at last reached the end of the road. She had noticed his sallow complexion and the deep lines etched on his flabby jowls. He had long lost his swagger, and his once-firm legs sagged when he trundled heavily across a room. At Wayne and Sylvia's wedding last winter he had looked pathetic in his restlessness.

Lizzie drove carefully and with utmost precision, and she was never accused of speeding. Hannah had always appreciated that. Today she almost wished Lizzie would abandon her caution and drive a bit faster.

271

"How come you're going way out there, Hannah?" Lizzie asked in her careful English, as she eased the car onto the last mile of gravel. "Relation?"

Hannah shook her head. "They were always our neighbors. We had lots to do together."

Lizzie laughed shortly. "That's funny. I thought you told me once your parents didn't allow you to associate much with non-Mennonites."

"Well, that was a long time ago," Hannah said. "Things are changing. But Maggie and I—we always were good friends."

The car turned into the long rutted drive now, carefully dipping into the deep ravine where the plank bridge once was, and then puttered onto the weed-choked yard.

The same bleak lifelessness hung over the decadent buildings that Hannah remembered, and she shuddered as she hopped over the broken porch timbers to the door.

At her feeble knock, Maggie's careworn face appeared at the grimy glass and motioned her inside.

The familiar stench permeated the somber kitchen. Maggie, her plain face gray and distraught, hobbled ahead of her into the sickroom.

Dan lay on the pillow, the once-handsome face covered with a shaggy gray beard. His eyes stared dully at the cracked ceiling.

"It's his liver," Maggie murmured as the two women walked toward the bed. "Cirrhosis. His drinking, you know. Hasn't been well for some time now, and lately he's begun to swell. His legs are puffy and he hasn't eaten anything for days. All he wants now is to lie here and have someone to talk to. He—I think he's afraid, Hannah!"

Scornful, fearless Dan—afraid? Of course! Of meeting death.

"Dan?" Hannah said softly, touching the hot, feverish hand on the ragged cover.

He turned his hollow, sunken eyes on her. "Henny Penny? So you did come. I wanted—you here. . . ." He fumbled for her hand and held it weakly.

Hannah's heart twisted with compassion at the pitiful suffering of this once virile man.

"Dan—you're very sick, Maggie says," she said, knowing she had to say something. "And—and if you'd only—"

"No, Hannah, I don't want to hear it," he interrupted shortly. "I want to talk—now. I've loved you for a long time. Never will I forget the slim, tall girl riding her horse over the prairies, her braids flying. When you threw me over for—for John Penner, I became very bitter. I realized later—it wouldn't have ever worked—you and I. We're—different, Hannah. Still, I kept on trying to hurt you, because you'd hurt me so. You kept right on living. . . ." His voice faltered for a moment.

Then he took a deep breath and continued. "My share of the farm—the—the buildings and forty acres —are to go to Syl. Maggie has the rest. Syl—Syl doesn't know I'm her grandfather. Somehow, I couldn't tell her that. I wanted to spare her the dignity of believing that her grandmother Irene— Well, she thinks of me as 'Uncle Dan'—as her grandmother's cousin, you know. The farm's awfully run-down and not worth fixing up. So don't allow any of your 'disaster units' on the place! But I just had word that an oil company is interested in leasing it for drilling. The possibility of oil does exist. Help her to understand that I—wanted to do something—for her. Maybe in a sense—I'm trying to do something—to make up to you—what anguish I c-caused. . . . Be good to her, will you?"

"Dan—"

"No, let me finish," he said thickly. "Also, I must tell you about—about John and—and Emma—"

Hannah caught her breath sharply. She wanted to cry out, to protest that she didn't want to hear.

But all she could do was utter in a stricken voice, "Go on, Dan."

His voice faded to a whisper, and she bent over to catch what he was painfully trying to confess.

"One—day when I was in the woodlot—near the road, I s-saw John slow down with his c-car and stop. Then I saw Emma. She had a flat tire on her Ford. John—changed it for her. Then she told him in English, 'Thank you, John. You were always a good man. I hope Hannah appreciates you.' And John said in a heavy voice, 'I love Hannah, Emma. She's the most wonderful wife in the world. But she's never told me how she feels—' And Emma's voice caught in her throat as though she was crying. She said, 'Oh, John, she loves you, too!' I almost came right out then and told John, 'No, she doesn't love you. She's always belonged to me!' But something held me back. I couldn't say it.

"Ugly Emma lives in her fine house now, and wears stylish clothes. Still, I don't think—she's very happy.

She hoped—no one would ever know that she loved—Jake Thiessen, Lena Toews' husband. Emma refused him at first, years ago. And when he married Lena, Emma was through with love. But with me, it didn't work. I love you still!''

Jake Thiessen! Hannah couldn't speak. Oh, John had loved her. And to think she'd never been sure!

Dan began to cough, and for a moment Hannah was afraid the phlegm would choke him. Maggie appeared mysteriously with a bit of cotton and wiped out the inside of his mouth.

He looked about wildly, and Hannah pressed his hand reassuringly. He turned his burning eyes on her again and his crooked lips trembled.

"Hannah—for years I've dreamed—of your kisses—upon my lips. And when I couldn't have you I wanted so desperately to hurt you. I think you—guessed it—John—at your chivaree—and when Hank was small . . . through Lafe—and Syl—you were always a bit less ready to believe the worst of me. If only I hadn't loved you so. . . . If I could've done like Emma. . . . Now my time—has run out. Can you—ever forgive me, my d-darling?''

The words were wrenched from him with a struggle now. Hannah's eyes flooded with tears and she wept silently.

Suddenly she stooped over and brushed his lips with hers. The stubbled beard crushed her mouth.

"Yes, Dan. I do forgive you.''

He gasped. "Th-thanks—for that, Henny Penny. It's enough—now. . . .''

"Dan,'' she cried out, alarmed. "You're—dying. What

275

about the Lord? You'll have to face Him. . . . He—
He wants to forgive you, too. Why don't you just ask—"

Fury darkened his face and he pushed her hand
away from him.

"I want—nothing from the God of the Mennonites!"
he flung out bitterly. "I've never been—good enough
—for any—of you! That's why I was so glad—so glad
that Sylvia was good enough for your—grandson. But
as for God—"

He began to curse, and Hannah clapped her hands
over her ears so that she didn't need to listen.

Maggie, beside her, stared in horror at the ashen
face of her brother.

"Dan!" she screamed. But his face was etched in
stark horror and the vile lips ceased their contorting.

Maggie began to weep uncontrollably.

A great sense of emptiness swept over Hannah at
the awfulness of death and she trembled violently. The
curses burned into her heart and she felt faint.

The dark, writhing face was suddenly still. A shadow
seemed to fall across the room, and she grew cold in
its awful desolation.

Suddenly Hannah remembered the words again.
"Heaven and earth shall pass away, but my words
shall not pass away." *I will never leave thee, nor
forsake thee. . . .*

Strength flowed into her and she rose resolutely and
placed her arms around Maggie's thin, quaking
shoulders.

After Maggie's storm had spent iself, Hannah murmured in a low voice,

"Dan is—gone, Maggie. It's all over. Now we must

think about you. Life must go on. For you we will make a place—somehow!"

35

"Gran'ma," Wayne, perched on the railing of Hannah's front porch, riffled his fingers through his dark blond hair. "I'm gonna miss you when I'm gone. But Syl's going to need looking after, and I wondered if you could suggest—" his voice trailed off lamely.

Hannah peered over her bifocals and she laid her knitting into her lap. "I'm glad you're going into I-W service."

"Voluntary service, you mean! Well, haven't I been active in MDS for the past three years? When that tornado hit in Oklahoma last fall we Mennonite Disaster men weren't exactly lazy! And now I'll be doing Pax work—or whatever other assignment I'll be given at Mennonite Central Committee headquarters. I can't take Syl with me yet, you know. And I'm fulfilling my government obligations, of course. Sometimes this demands sacrifices even as conscientious objectors."

"I understand, Wayne, and I'm proud of you. But what does Sylvie say about it? Does she know what it all means?"

Wayne smiled wistfully. "Syl loves me, Gran'ma. She's ready to agree with me. Whatever I do is OK with her. But somehow she's never taken the complete step—hasn't ever given her heart wholly to the Lord. That's why I say she needs looking after."

Hannah nodded. "I see. Too bad you'll be away when the baby comes."

"Yes," Wayne sighed as he rocked himself back and forth on the railing. "That's what is going to make it so tough for her. And the baby only weeks away. But she's real game. I wish she could stay with Mom and Dad, only Mom isn't well. And Syl's mother—well, I'd rather—"

"I know what you mean, Wayne," Hannah said wryly, remembering Fiddy as she had looked at Wayne and Sylvia's wedding in the Lawson cottage—her face raddled and gray under the garishly colored, over-curled hair, and the coarse laughter. Sylvia was so unlike her mother.

Wayne rose wearily and thrust his big hands into his pockets. "Well, I guess I'd better be getting on then. I'll come around and say good-bye before I leave."

"Wayne—" Hannah startled herself by saying, "would—would you care if Sylvie came here and stayed with me while you're gone? I mean, my house is old-time-ish, and I'm a cranky old lady sometimes. But if I can help her—"

"Gran'ma!" he shouted like a schoolboy. "Would you?

279

Would you really? Oh, boy, wait 'til I tell her!"

Syl was no less pleased than Wayne himself. She wore her thick blond hair tied back with a short piece of blue ribbon which made her look almost like a little girl. Except that her maternity smock billowed out like a tent in front of her.

In less than a week after Wayne had left she was settled in Hannah's spare room.

"This is real cool of you, Gram," she said excitedly, her left eye closing in its familiar wink. "Wayne thinks you're the greatest. That's the reason it must be true. And I kinda like your funny little kitchen with that old-timey clock, and that ancient creaky rocker there by your window. It must be an antique! Looks so cozy-like, though."

"We'll get along, Sylvie," Hannah said stoutly, "if you'll drive me wherever I want to go!"

"Be glad to. All the way to Plainfeld church sewing circle," she giggled, popping her gum in her droll way. "It was swell of the Plainfeld church ladies to give me that big baby shower, wasn't it? Imagine me, Syl Lawson, going to sewing circle. I think my mom'd have a fit if she knew. Although the way you Mennonites cleaned all that muck and slime outa folks' houses after the flood last July—well, I think she's gettin' real sold on all of you."

"Your Aunt Maggie would be pleased, too," Hannah reminded her. "We'll drive over and see her sometime. She seems to like it at the old folks' home."

Syl winked her left eye. "I'm sure glad she's off that rotten farm. I don't see how she stood it there so long. But I guess she had no other place to go."

"That farm is yours, Sylvie," Hannah said, putting the prunes and raisins on to cook for *pluma moos.* "Maybe someday you and Wayne want to live on it."

Sylvia seated herself heavily at the tiny kitchen table and thrust out her shapely legs. "Call that a farm? I think it's a junk pile. After Wayne gets back we're gonna lean against every building on the place until they fall down! Then we'll build a bonfire and have a weenie roast. Or maybe we can smoke some *shinky-flaesh.*"

Hannah laughed until she shook. "You mean— *shinka-flaesh?* Smoke the hams, Sylvie? You're already starting to talk like a Mennonite!"

"Do I?" Syl said eagerly. "I sure hope so. Tell me what Mennonites really are, Gram. Mom thinks they're kinda stuffy, and I know Uncle Dan practically hated them. But what's a Mennonite, really?"

Hannah turned the fire down under the kettle and seated herself across the kitchen table from the young woman. A palliative sigh escaped her.

"I hardly know where to start, Sylvie. It goes back so many years. My father told it to us many times. It seems that believers broke away from formalistic churches and organized churches of their own. They believed in being converted, in baptizing after they knew what it was all about, and in living separate from the world. Also, in loving one's enemies and not bearing arms because the Bible says to 'do good to them that hate you.' Also, in helping others. Only, sometimes we've lived so separate that we have shut our doors to those who weren't born of Mennonite background!"

281

"Like me," Syl murmured quietly.

"Well—" Hannah hesitated. "Yes, I guess that's right. But we've been wrong in that. We've always felt we were so good, and most of the time we were. But it wasn't always true."

"I see. But Mennonites are such dear people, Gram. I like the way you are so openly friendly, so—sorta brotherly, I might say. There's somethin' special about the way you feel toward each other, and I like that. I don't exactly understand it, but I keep wishin' I could—well, like the way the church ladies had that shower for me, you know. What's being converted mean, Gram? I'm not quite sure."

The sudden question startled Hannah. The bubbling fruit in the kettle made a soft purring sound, and she got up and stirred in the sugar-flour-cream mixture until the fruit thickened. Then she turned off the fire and returned to her chair.

"Sylvie, the Bible says we're all sinners—Mennonites as well as anyone else. It says that no one can get to heaven unless they ask the Lord to forgive their sins and come dwell in their hearts. Christ says He has 'come to seek and to save that which was lost,' and 'him that cometh to me I will in no wise cast out.' When we come to Him, we turn away from the life of sin and live for the Lord. I guess that's about it."

"And that's what makes people Christians?"

"Yes, Sylvie."

Without a word, Syl threw her head on her arms on the table and began to pray.

"God, You know I'm a Smith and my background's kinda shoddy, and I'm not really good enough to be a

Mennonite. But if You'll clean me all up inside and help me to be worthy of folks like Wayne—and Gram here—" she lifted her head and looked imploringly at Hannah. "Am I doin' OK? Is that what I should tell Him?"

Hannah's eyes swam with tears. "Tell Him whatever's on your heart, child!"

When Syl lifted her face again it was radiant. Hannah grew limp with the glory of it.

Then the girl got clumsily to her feet. "Now I want to go all the way—be a good girl for you, Gram. There's so much I need to change—to learn. Gram, will you teach me?"

Syl's pathetic eagerness and direct honesty moved Hannah to a fresh flood of tears.

"You mean, you want to learn how to make *pluma moos*? And *borscht?*"

"Yes. And those two-story biscuits you bake every Saturday for Sunday supper!" she added breathlessly. "Do—do you really think I can?"

"Zwieback for *faspa?* Oh, but if you're going to be a Mennonite, you had better learn!" Hannah replied whimsically.

Syl lumbered to the wastebasket and spit out her gum. "Well, that's another thing I'm gonna quit. Guess I'm gettin' too big for poppin' my gum, ain't I? Wayne and I, we're gonna raise our family like Mennonites. That is, if they'll have me."

"They?"

Syl sighed gently. "The church. After all, I'm an Englisher and—"

"You are a Christian and that's what counts!" Han-

283

nah said staunchly.

A spasm crossed Syl's face. "Oh, Gram, no! Don't tell me it's coming. The baby, I mean."

Hannah leaned forward anxiously. "You think so? How does it feel?"

Before Syl could answer, another flicker of pain marked her face.

There was no time to lose. Hannah struggled to her feet and began to scurry around.

"I'll get your bag ready while you get dressed. Lizzie will drive us to the hospital as soon as we're ready."

"Us? You mean you're comin' with me? You don't have to, you know."

Hannah clucked. "I can't let my family down, Sylvie. Remember, we're in this together!"

Syl laughed lightly. "You're precious, Gram. But I know I—I won't be scared if you—if you stay with me until it has arrived," she said wistfully.

Hannah was sitting calmly in the hospital waiting room a few minutes later, waiting for the ordeal to pass. The late October afternoon lay in a breathless panorama through the window. The tree-shaded lawns of the hospital grounds already had turned to a deep onyx-green; the elms had doffed their vibrant summer green for mantillas of gold; the maples blazed with red like the sunset sky that simmered toward twilight. Slowly the afterglow softened to purple, wreathed round by gray cloud folds, melting·into exquisite pink like an echo of daylight glory.

Hannah, stirring in the comfortable chair, remembered that long-ago summer day. The ominous clanking of the mover wagon as it creaked on the rutted road behind

284

the hedge. The beginning of the drama which was being enacted through her life. Birth and death were nothing new to her, after these many years. Happy years. Rich, full years, in spite of trials and tribulations.

Eric and Mary Schroeder had come back to the Lord. Both were now active in church, for the church had forgiven their transgressions even as God had. Sylvia would be baptized into Plainfeld Mennonite Church in the spring after the weather warmed up and the creeks were full, and so would Maggie. The doors had opened at last.

"Thou hast done it again, dear Lord," she prayed quietly in German. "Life. Eternal life—physical life. *Alles in deine haende* . . . 'All in Thy hands. . . .'"

She seemed to sense John beside her as he was when Alice was born, and he'd clasped her hand tightly in his. Again—and again. . . .

"You loved me, John," she murmured softly. "I should have guessed. We shared so much of life—and death—and hopes and dreams of the future. I only hope you knew—in the end—how much I loved you!"

I'm going to give Sylvie the opalescent hen bowl that Maggie gave us for our wedding. It shall always stay in the family—both our families.

For Sylvie Smith Lawson was a part of her family now—and of God's. How marvelously He led! *Heaven and earth shall pass away.* . . . Though skies wavered and bombs fell, He would never forsake.

A nurse rustled into the doorway. "Mrs. Penner, come and see your little great-granddaughter. She's all of seven pounds and four ounces."

Hannah stumbled to her feet and followed the white-capped figure into Syl's gay hospital room. Haltingly she moved toward the bed.

Syl beamed at her from the pillow. "Come here, Gram. I did it! A girl. And her name's Hannah. Dr. Hoyle tells me that means grace. Ain't—isn't that somethin'?"

Hannah steadied herself on the foot end of the bed. "Did you say—Hannah?" she faltered, feeling suddenly very unworthy of her trusting child.

"Sure. It means 'grace.' Did you know that? And isn't it cute?"

Hannah—grace. God's grace . . . eternal, sufficient, forevermore.

Life would go on for Wayne and Sylvia and their children . . . rich years full of faith and trust . . . in spite of trials—through God's grace. As it had done for her.

Tears welled up in her faded blue eyes and she took off her bifocals and let them fall unabashed. Then she reached out and patted Syl's thin shoulder.

"It's fine, Sylvie!" she whispered tremulously. "Just fine!"

THE END